Ten for Every One

SOUTHWARK PRESS

Acknowledgements

To Mom, Dad, and Jen – thank you for supporting me in the exploration of my interests, and for creating a home that values and appreciates storytelling. I love you.

To Katie Craig, Katherine Rogg, Amelia Kaywood, Nick Flinn, Alli Slaughter, and Bailey Rogg – thank you all for responding to late-night text messages, for reading and critiquing early drafts, and for encouraging me to make this story a reality.

And to Jackie Protos Smith and Lisa Ladd Myers – thank you for your passion for English education, for teaching me the beauty of literature, and for putting up with my shenanigans in class.

Ten for Every One

William Ferrand

"You can kill ten of my men for every one I kill of yours. But even at those odds, you will lose and I will win."

—

Ho Chi Minh

Prologue

"Twenty-five condolence letters in one morning, Parker? Damn it to hell."

It was the last thing Staff Sergeant Miles Parker heard from his commanding officer that morning after reporting they'd lost contact with the twenty-five soldiers undertaking a special reconnaissance mission codenamed "Jungle Moon."

The objective—a raid on a Viet Cong outpost for intelligence on enemy troop movements—was simple in design: two platoons (plus an intelligence officer to identify priority documents) would hike for two days into the jungle near Pele Ketan, raid the enemy camp before dawn, and make the journey home. It was the kind of mission the US Army 10th Special Forces Group was built for, and with aerial surveillance in the days prior to the mission confirming only a small contingent of opposition forces, it was one nobody had expected would turn out so badly.

Parker had only recently transferred back to the platoon following a short stint in a field hospital, and was assigned to stay up and report back all updates to his superiors the night the raid was scheduled to occur.

"What'd you do to draw the short straw on a graveyard shift like this, sir?" asked Private First Class Wilkes.

"I think they resent me for getting to rest in the cozy medical tent for a few days," said Parker. "Of course, they always seem to forget I had to catch shrapnel in the arm to get the time off, but what's a little flesh wound when you're an Army operator?"

"Not a ticket home these days unfortunately," replied Wilkes with a laugh. "In any case, I just put on a pot of fresh coffee if you'd like to grab yourself some, Sarge. I expect we'll be getting the first of the radio transmissions shortly."

The night should have proceeded without issue. Sergeant Parker was expecting three radio comms that night: the first once the troops arrived in the improvised base camp; the second for final mission "go/no go"; and the third once the mission had been completed. After the third transmission (and the confirmation that all enemy troops had been neutralized), Parker would receive the okay from mission command to send in Hueys to fly the troops home. It was a small reward for the soldiers who'd completed the grueling hike to ensure important documents would not be removed or destroyed by the enemy prior to the surprise raid.

Parker, with strong coffee in hand, took his seat next to Private Wilkes just as the first radio transmissions started through the receiver. "Mission Control, this is Captain Craig. We've arrived at Checkpoint Alpha. Over."

Wilkes grabbed his headset and pressed the switch on his microphone. "Captain Craig, this is Mission Control. Your location is noted. What is your status? Over."

"We had some surprise company last night and had to lay low a bit longer than planned, but we didn't need to engage. All troops are accounted for and are in good condition. We're making final preparations and will report back when ready. Over and out."

"Well, that's part one," said Parker. "I'll go wake up Captain Rogg and Major Kaywood to let them know we're almost ready to engage. You stay here in case they need anything."

"Yes, sir."

Thirty minutes had passed when the second radio transmission came through, with Captain Rogg and Major Kaywood now sitting in the tent with Sergeant Parker and Private Wilkes. "Mission Control, this is Captain Craig. Captain Flinn has just briefed the troops on final mission objectives and priority intelligence targets. We are awaiting go/no go. Over."

"Craig, this is Major Kaywood. You may proceed. Over."

"Confirmed. Over and out."

At this point Captain Rogg looked at his watch—based on the enemy troop numbers, the mission was estimated to take no more than fifteen minutes to complete.

"Set your watch, Parker," he yawned.

Despite the importance of the documents to be recovered, the captain's nonchalance was reflective of the mood of the entire room. Captain Craig was one of the finest officers the Special Forces had brought to Vietnam, and his perfect track record of complete mission success spoke for itself. Nobody at headquarters doubted this mission would be any different, particularly Rogg, who had gone through officer training with both Craig and Flinn.

When static crackled through the radio's speakers seven minutes after the start of the mission, Rogg turned to Parker and joked, "Maybe Craig is even better than we thought—he finished the job eight minutes early!"

The static continued, but no voices came through.

"Wilkes, is it?" Rogg continued. "What's going on with the radio? The major and I need audible confirmation from Captain Craig that the mission is complete before we can go back to sleep."

"I'm not sure, sir," said an increasingly anxious Private Wilkes. He proceeded to adjust some of the radio's settings, but the static only got louder.

Sensing Captain Rogg's growing frustration at the young radio engineer, Parker spoke up. "I've heard the rain in the mountains has been messing with some of the radio transmissions lately. Is that true, Wilkes?"

Wilkes nodded his head as he agreed nervously. "Ye...yes. That's been happening a lot."

"In that case, let's just give these guys a bit more time to radio in. I'm sure Captain Craig is already on top of it."

With tensions cooling down in the room a bit, Parker waited as the static filled the air between the men. After a few minutes, however, the sound from the radio receiver stopped completely.

Everyone in the room looked around, puzzled. Wilkes fiddled with settings on the radio, but before Rogg could make another snide comment, they all heard a bone-chilling cry through the speaker.

"OH MY GOD! This is Sergeant Alli! If anyone can hear me, please send help! We're getting slaughtered out here!"

Sergeant Parker quickly grabbed the radio's microphone without waiting for the Major's order. "Alli, give us a sitrep. Over."

Parker thought he heard lightning striking through the radio's speaker, but the strikes occurred so quickly they sounded more like machine gun fire. And after each burst, more screams.

What is that?

After twenty seconds, the odd sounds and screams stopped and the radio's deafening static once more filled the tent.

"I repeat—Alli, this is Parker. Check in! Over."

"Did we lose them, Wilkes?" asked Major Kaywood.

"No sir," he replied shakily. "We're receiving them fine, but they aren't responding now."

Major Kaywood shook his head for a moment before standing up.

"Parker, stay on this. Rogg, you're with me. I need to speak to some people."

◇◇◇◇◇

Though a few hours had passed, Sergeant Alli's terrified scream was still echoing in Parker's head as he flew the Cobra helicopter to the last known position of the raid party. Following the disastrous radio call, Major Kaywood had immediately ordered a platoon of troops on loan from the 1st Aviation Brigade to take the armed Cobras and pick up however many survivors might be left. Due to Parker's proximity to the mission, he'd been ordered to accompany them. In between the fog of exhaustion and jungle heat, though, he struggled to piece together all the events that had unfolded earlier that morning. The repetition in his brain of Alli's shrieks of unbridled terror made it much more difficult to focus.

No point in trying to surprise the enemy now, Parker thought under the whir of the helicopter's rotors. He glanced over and saw a young soldier, beads of sweat forming on his forehead, struggling with rounds of ammunition for one of the helicopter's mounted machine guns.

Might as well bring the big guns.

What he couldn't make sense of were the strange noises they'd heard accompanying the sergeant's plea for help over the radio. Parker was all too familiar with the sounds of the enemy's weapons, but none made the same live-wire type of crackling he'd heard amidst the screams. Wilkes had assured him it was not the radio itself but rather a sound coming through the radio.

While Parker had always been an optimistic man, he knew, in all likelihood, he was flying into the aftermath of a massacre. After years of war, he was no longer squeamish, but having trained with many of the men on the mission, he knew his trip would not be a pleasant one. And to add insult to injury, the enemy intelligence the raiding party was after was sure to be gone following the skirmish. The enemy's first action would have been to destroy all documents they couldn't take with them. These men essentially died for nothing.

"FUBAR!" he shouted out of the open helicopter door into the damp late-morning air.

As the Cobra inched closer to the ground at the coordinates of the impromptu base camp Captain Craig had established, Sergeant Parker grabbed his rifle, slid off the helicopter's deck, and carefully walked toward the large clearing which aerial reconnaissance had painted as the Viet Cong outpost. He heard no gunfire, indicating that the engagement with the enemy was over. Cautiously, he continued onward with the squad who had flown with him on the Cobra until one of the soldiers quietly signaled to take cover. His hand gestures were clear: *three individuals ahead.*

Parker, after crouching close to the entrance of the clearing, took out his binoculars to surveil the scene.

As he panned from left to right, he saw the bodies of both US and Viet Cong troops spread over the clearing. Despite the horrific images he viewed through the magnified lenses, he was puzzled by how many more Viet Cong than Green Berets lay on the ground.

Not only that...the wounds on the bodies don't seem to match any VC weapons.

It was at this moment he saw three US soldiers at the edge of the clearing sitting near a massive cache of documents.

"We've got three Americans alive!" Parker shouted to the soldiers flanking him on his left and right.

Parker walked directly towards where the Americans sat quietly. It was only then that he fully appreciated both the gore of the scene and the shell-shocked faces of the three survivors. As Parker's soldiers began offering medical aid to the three Americans, the experience of the past twelve hours had finally caught up to him. He slung his rifle over his shoulder, surveyed the terrifying scene again, and mumbled, "What the hell happened here?"

Chapter 1

"I really don't see why I can't come on the trip!" exclaimed Emily Lewis. "The timing of it couldn't be more perfect!"

"Emily, this isn't just some vacation, it's an official State Department visit. There are ceremonial events I have to attend," said James.

"Okay sure, but you and Mom are also going around Vietnam for a few weeks after your 'official State business.' Plus, you're going with the Tillmans and Mrs. Santos. That sounds like a vacation to me."

"Yes, they're coming with me and Mom," James said, "and yes, we'll spend some time at a resort. But, at its core, we're using the time abroad to visit some of the battlefields where Ada and I lost friends in the war. The trip is going to have some pretty solemn moments. And in any case, do you know how hot it gets this time of year in Vietnam? You'd be sweating the minute you got off the plane."

"Dad, we live in a swamp. I'm sweating here, right now. Might as well be sweating at a resort."

James smiled slightly. Emily had grown more sarcastic in her teenage years, but he seemed to really appreciate the humor that it brought to the house. He'd said the same thing to her about the days when walking around Washington, D.C. in the summer reminded him of his time overseas. Luckily his job mostly kept him in air-conditioned buildings, cars, and event spaces.

"I bet Sergio and Charlie are allowed to go," Emily continued.

"They are most definitely not going. Ada is basically under the same restrictions I am, and Maria wants Sergio here this summer volunteering before you all go off to college," James replied.

Emily looked incredulous.

"Look..." he continued, "I know it's disappointing, but you know how it is with Ada and me on trips like this. Especially when Vietnam is involved. It's still...emotional, for us to go back there." He paused, thinking over his next words. "That doesn't sound like the kind of fun vacation a new high school graduate would want to go on, does it?"

"I mean, I've never been to that part of the world, and it's only a *major* part of your life," she said. "But I suppose I can respectfully bow out. And of course, I'll just throw some wild parties with Sergio and Charlie while you all are out of town."

James smiled fully this time. "I wouldn't imagine it any other way. And of course, we're still going to do our big family vacation later this summer before you head off to college. Just you, your mom, and me. You're still dying to visit Estonia, right? I'm *Tallinn* you the truth, we'll go."

"Yeah, yeah, yeah!" Emily said, a smile cracking across her face. Through some extensive genealogical work at the National Archives for a class project, Emily had recently discovered that half of James's family had immigrated to the US from the Baltics, not Portugal, as James had thought growing up. Like him, she was eager to learn as much about her new heritage as possible.

"We'll make it happen," James said as he got up from his seat on the corner of Emily's bed and made his way to the door. "*Aitäh* for understanding."

"You're welcome. And thank you for your use of Estonian! I told you that phrase book would come in handy," she said as he tapped her doorframe with his hand and walked out of the room. As the sound of his footsteps grew fainter, Emily's thoughts turned to her dad and his Vietnam experience.

Living up to your parents' reputation was always a challenge for any kid, but Emily knew that for her and her friends Charlie and Sergio, the task was almost impossible. Everyone in the US had heard of the famous raid in Vietnam by "the Miraculous Three." After a team of twenty-four Green Berets were sent into the jungle to raid a Viet Cong outpost for intel, the group found themselves outnumbered in a battle ten-to-one. Calls for backup were radioed in before communications from the field were cut short. Reinforcements were sent in to rescue the bogged-down soldiers, but there was little hope at HQ that any of the troops would survive the morning.

When the reinforcements arrived, they found three soldiers—worn down and a bit shocked, but other than a few scrapes and bruises, unscathed—sitting with vital information from an outpost which was now littered with the bodies of the enemy. Everyone agreed it was nothing short of a miracle these soldiers had survived, though what was unclear was how exactly they'd managed it.

Emily's dad, James Lewis, was one of the three survivors. Ada Tillman, Charlie Tillman's mom, was also there. She served as an intelligence officer during the Vietnam War and was on a rare assignment with the famous raid party to help with the collection and collation of enemy documents. The brass had considered the intel critical enough that she join the team directly, and Ada jumped at the opportunity.

The last of the three, José Luis Santos, was a medic. He was well regarded in his platoon for his brilliance in providing both medical care and tactical support under even the most severe duress. Even in the face of the raid's outcome, Ada and James confirmed his reputation in their after-action reports, noting his heroism in particular despite the raid's failure. Following the war, he attended the London School of Hygiene and Tropical Medicine, which ultimately led him to a career at the World Health Organization studying diseases prevalent in jungle environments. He married the love of his life, Maria, shortly after graduating med school, and soon after that, they welcomed Sergio Santos into the world.

When questioned on what happened during the war, James, Ada, and José all shared the same story: "We were just lucky to survive, and couldn't have done it without the bravery of our fellow troops."

Army upper command accepted their humility without question and the story of their heroic mission spread throughout the ranks. Awards and acclaim for their bravery and service immediately followed, including a Congressional Medal of Honor for each of the three heroes. The accolades led to promising careers as well. James Lewis was later appointed Secretary of State, and in the same year, Ada Tillman was tapped as the Director of the CIA. Sergio's dad, José, eschewing offers of high government offices such as Surgeon General, was content serving as a department head at the WHO.

While the Miraculous Three obtained great notoriety, José (or Dr. Santos as he was more commonly addressed) was especially honored. His eventual disappearance in the jungles of

Vietnam on a mission to study the effects of Agent Orange on local villagers gave him an almost saintlike status. As a body was never recovered, Dr. Santos was presumed dead shortly after his disappearance. Officials concluded that he suffered some kind of accident in the harsh conditions in which he insisted on travelling solo.

"Another testament to his bravery and service" was what his former commanding officer, Major Kaywood, said at his memorial service in 1993 on a cold day near the Tomb of the Unknown Solider in Arlington.

Of course, Emily had heard the stories about the famous battle over and over again her whole life, especially growing up practically as siblings with Sergio and Charlie. The achievements heralded in the stories were the benchmarks against which she and her friends felt like they had to measure their lives.

No, not to measure against—to move beyond. Be better than.

Had the lifelong pressure been worth it so far? Maybe.

I did enjoy the extracurriculars and volunteer opportunities I was compelled to partake in...

Either way, Emily had always felt a sense of control over her own destiny and liked the person she was becoming. She tried her best not to view her life as nothing more than a derivative of some greater story.

But whenever she did think about the battle that had changed her family's destiny so many years ago, there was a nagging feeling inside that told her more had gone down that day in Vietnam than the official record suggested.

She'd often press her dad for details, but would never get more than vague responses like, "We definitely had help. Some of the local people came out and helped tend to our wounds," or, "I can't remember how it all started...before we even realized it, we were looking annihilation in the face." Not satiated with his responses, she'd often try getting Aunt Ada to provide more details.

"The enemy was more heavily armed than we originally thought. While my reconnaissance before the mission told me this Viet Cong cell was specialized in advanced tactics, they still had access to weapons we'd never seen before...But, if I tell you any more, I'd have to kill you," she finished with a wink.

Sergio and Charlie had often tried the same approach, but got effectively the same answers each time. At one point, desperate for additional information, the three teenagers used the new computer at their high school in Georgetown to read an article on the conspiracy theory internet blog *Truth $eeker$ Only*. The blog's theories about the mission were, unsurprisingly, more ridiculous and convoluted than anything they'd heard at home. But like Charlie and Sergio, at the end of the day, Emily believed their parents had survived an insane ordeal, and despite wanting to know more, the trio didn't feel right pressing the adults on what were surely traumatizing events. This was especially true after Sergio's dad went missing.

They were all young when it happened, Sergio even more so, as he had skipped a grade and moved up to Emily and Charlie's class early on in their academic careers. Emily remembered the memorial service: the tears rolling down Sergio's face, the cold rainy weather, the stoic looks of her parents and Charlie's parents as they handed Sergio's mom a folded American flag. A flag which, without a body or casket, stood in for Dr. Santos that day in Arlington.

Maybe it was because of how old he was when it happened, or the strength of his conviction, but Sergio never let the loss of his father slow him down. Over the ensuing years he always excelled in school, in both academics and extracurriculars, and as far as Emily and Charlie were concerned, Sergio was the leader of their friend group. It was therefore no shock to her or anyone else when Sergio was named valedictorian of their graduating class. Emily and Charlie made a respectable showing in the top ten, and were excited that they got to sit next to their best friend on stage.

Charlie had been a great help to Sergio in that time, too. Charlie was more reserved than Sergio or Emily, often more interested in puzzles, technology, and reading historical accounts of battles, all passions he picked up from his mother. However, he cared deeply about his friends. He'd always invite Sergio and Emily over to help him complete some elaborate crossword, and would insist Sergio come along with Charlie's family when they went to one of the many museums D.C. had to offer. He seemed to always know when his friends needed company or someone to talk to.

All these thoughts danced through Emily's head as she turned on the small television on her dresser and flipped on BBC News. An anchor from the Paris desk reported on the "much anticipated" return to Vietnam her dad and Aunt Ada would be making in just a few days' time to commemorate the thirtieth anniversary of the end of the Vietnam war.

Lazily turning her head from the TV to the windows in her room, Emily saw boats going up and down the Potomac River. The warmer weather seemed to have drawn everyone in the District outside. She sighed.

Oh well. There goes my hopes of lying on a boat in Halong Bay this summer.

Chapter 2

A knock came at the door at exactly 5:15 p.m. Without looking through the small peephole in her solid oak door, Ada knew it was James—he had been punctual to a fault for as long as she'd known him.

"You're a few minutes late," she said.

"What?" he replied, checking his watch. "No, that's not possible, I left my house exactly twenty-three minutes ago."

Ada smirked, and catching her sarcasm, James chuckled.

"Come on in," she said.

"How are Charlie and Bill? Are they here?" James asked as Ada shut the door behind him.

"They're both good. Bill took Charlie out for some ice cream as a reward for dragging him along to shop for the trip, so they'll be back in probably thirty minutes."

She'd met Bill at Columbia when she was studying for her master's degree in international affairs and instantly fell for his optimism and passion for others. After he finished law school, the two married and moved to D.C.

"He's still a last-minute packer, I see?" James asked.

"I love the man to death, but if it were up to him, we'd buy all of our clothes and luggage at the airport. Or better yet, once we arrived at our destination." She laughed. "I can't tell you how many jackets with 'X Resort' or 'ABC Tourist Attraction' we have in our hall closet. He always seems to forget to bring one."

"Well, it's a good thing we're going somewhere warm, huh."

"Exactly...exactly. Well, speaking of planning ahead," said Ada, her tone growing more serious, "I want to show you what I've got on José."

She gestured down the long main hallway of her home, past Charlie's room and dozens of family vacation photos, towards her office. As the two walked towards the office, Ada glanced at a photo of three figures in Army dress uniforms shaking the hand of the president. She always loved how happy the three of them looked, knowing it had more to do with making it home safely than receiving the Medal of Honor.

Although the food at the White House was pretty good, too, she thought.

"Have a seat," Ada said, gesturing to an overstuffed armchair in front of a large mahogany-brown desk. She walked to the large closet in the room and opened the door of a skinny metal cabinet-style safe installed inside. She pulled out one of the drawers in the safe and removed an accordion file folder, gently placing it on her desk. James looked down and noted the large tab on the folder: *Dr. José Santos.*

"As you know," she said, "I've been piecing together information from a few local assets in Vietnam, our databases at the Agency, and my own notes and records from our time in country, plus the details Maria shared about what José had been working on prior to his disappearance."

"Right," James said, nodding.

"And up until now, the information has been spotty." Ada grabbed the folder and began to read from a cover page inside.

"'Dr. José Santos: Army Special Forces Veteran and WHO doctor. Departed in February 1993 for a WHO field mission in Vietnam to study the long-term effects of Agent Orange and their correlation to common jungle diseases. Last seen on February 6th. Missing, presumed dead.'"

"Yes."

"Well...I think I've got the piece we've been missing. One of my assets just found a WHO vehicle rotting away in the jungle," Ada said. "And it was off the highway close to Kon Tum."

James looked up from the document he was skimming and stared at Ada. "Where exactly off the highway?"

"Just outside of Pele Ketan."

He stared at her even more intently now, the wheels turning in his head. "Are you saying...?"

"Yes," she nodded. "I think he was looking for something specific near the battlefield. I mean we always suspected he went missing in that area, but we'd never had any definitive proof until now."

James was shocked. "But Ada...you know as well as I do that we're not supposed to make contact with them again. José knew that too."

"I think their intent was more to not talk about the help we received that day, not to necessarily stop one of us three from making contact again. And you know that if José thought there was a chance that they could help him save lives, he would do it. Without hesitation."

James shook his head, trying to process everything Ada just told him.

"James...the more you think about it, the more it makes sense. Can you explain what we saw that night?"

"I've been thinking about it every day for the last thirty years and I still can't," James replied.

"Same here. And if our 'friends' had the type of technology we saw then, it's not a stretch to imagine what other types of knowledge they possess. Especially now, after all this time. The pace of advancement would be exponential."

"Okay...okay. So José went into the jungle to find them. I suppose we always knew that was a possibility. It's what Maria suspected too, though of course she didn't have the full picture," James said slowly, working through the facts in his head. "So let's assume this was his WHO vehicle. Why hasn't he come back?"

Memories of the violence she'd seen the night of the battle flashed uncontrollably through her head. Images and sounds she'd struggled to stop from creeping into her dreams and turning them into nightmares.

"I don't want to assume the worst, but at this stage I think it's safe to say that whatever he was going to ask them about, someone didn't want getting out to the wider public, and that someone took action to make sure that it didn't."

"You think this is a recovery mission then?" James asked.

"I do," Ada replied, somberly.

He looked at her, and from his expression, she knew he felt the exact same way that she did. For years, as Ada worked her Agency connections, James was working his resources at State to help find information about José's disappearance. James had also coordinated several search-and-rescue missions over the years with the help of the Vietnamese government, but without a body, there was little more the State Department could do to keep the search going.

This revelation that their friend was most likely killed in the same area where they had barely survived thirty years prior was bittersweet. She was glad to potentially have some closure about their friend, but confirming his death, especially to Maria and Sergio, would be tough. And of course, the greater mystery of who or what had killed Dr. Santos still nagged at her.

"Right," James said. "Well this trip is coming at a good time then. But if we're going to look where we have to look, there's no way Maria, Bill, and Delia can come with us. I mean, they know what we've told them about that day, but we can't drag them into the middle of this. They can't know about our...friends."

"No, you're right," Ada replied. "What are you thinking as a plan of attack?"

"We're staying in that resort town near the battlefield for a few nights, yeah? One day for an official visit, and another few days in the resort for relaxation?"

"We are."

"Well instead of relaxing, let's tell everyone that you and I have been invited by one of the villages near the battlefield to spend some time memorializing their dead who were killed during the war. That because we fought in the war, it's a special invitation for us only," James said.

"I don't know if they'll go for it. Plus, one day doesn't feel like enough time to do the kind of searching that you and I need to do."

"I admit it's not my most elaborate plan, but look here." He pointed to the map showing the WHO vehicle wreckage. "The wreck site is only about an hour hike from the battlefield. We go back to the battlefield and hike to the wreck site, and then take a few hours to find details. And if we need more time, we can use the satellite phone to call in and say we're staying the night in the village."

Ada pondered the feasibility of his plan. "Do you remember how thick the jungle is near there? There's a reason the Ho Chi

Minh trail cut through it. I still don't think one or two days is enough time to find what we're looking for. It's not like we're going on a lot of information here."

"Hear me out," James continued as she continued to consider the plan. "If what we know from that night is true, as long as we're close, we won't have to really look for anyone. They'll find us." With a smile, James added, "And you can use your talent for subterfuge to come up with a more convincing cover story for our spouses in the next few days."

Despite the serious tone of the conversation, Ada couldn't help but laugh. "Yes...there's a reason you went into public State-craft and I didn't," she joked. "But I suppose this could work. And it's not like convincing anyone to stay in a resort all day while we sweat in the jungle is going to be hard."

As they laughed, they heard the front door down the hall unlock. Instinctively, Ada started to pack up the documents and put them inside the safe.

"I know we've been at this for a long time, but I really think we're really close to the truth. To justice for José," James said.

"Hi Mom! I'm back," Ada heard Charlie shout from down the hallway.

"I think so, too," she told James. As she closed the safe, Charlie walked into her office.

"Hey Mom. And hey Uncle James! Emily said you might be coming over today. How are you?"

"I'm great, Charlie! Was just talking to your mom about the final details of our trip," James replied.

"Where's your father, Charlie?" Ada asked.

"Well after the errands and the ice cream, Dad realized he forgot to pick up his dry cleaning, so he dropped me off and is heading over there now before they close in twenty minutes."

"Classic Bill," James said as Ada smiled at him.

"Sounds good, honey," Ada told Charlie as he went to his room. She turned to James. "I'll walk you out."

The two walked back down the main hallway, and as James got just outside the front door, he told Ada, "I won't mention anything to Delia about our plan until we get to Vietnam."

Ada nodded. "Okay, sounds good. I'll do the same with Bill. Oh, and one last thing, James."

"Yeah?"

"Don't forget to pack your hiking boots and trekking poles— we're not as spry as we were thirty years ago!"

James laughed, heading down the driveway and waving goodbye. Ada closed the front door behind him, and as she did, the implications of their plan finally began to sink in.

Chapter 3

"I've always hated the term *tiger team*. It makes no sense if you think about it," whispered Foster to Walshe.

"I never really thought about it before, but I suppose you're right. Tigers don't really hunt in packs, do they?" replied Walshe.

"They don't. It's just silly. I don't know why they keep using it."

"Well, you can take it up with the boss," joked Walshe as Director Wong walked into the briefing room.

"Ten dollars says he uses it within the first two minutes of the briefing," Foster murmured.

"Good morning, all," started Director Wong. "Let's jump straight in. The office of the Diplomatic Security Service and the office of the Executive Protective Agents within the CIA have assembled this tiger team to coordinate security for the Secretary of State's and CIA Director's upcoming Vietnam trip."

Walshe instinctively looked over at Foster, who rolled his eyes. Walshe laughed in his head as the director continued.

"The start of this trip should be pretty straightforward, but stay with me—they're covering a lot of ground. Secretary Lewis and Director Tillman will be flying to Hanoi from Andrews on Tuesday May 6th at zero nine hundred Romeo. The plane will make a brief refueling stop at Los Angeles Air Force Base at twelve hundred Uniform, and then make the final flight to Hanoi, arriving at Noi Bai International Airport at eleven hundred Golf on May 7th. Secretary Lewis and Director Tillman will be traveling with family and staff, so for those not lucky enough to catch one of the remaining seats on the C-32A, you'll be riding in the secondary support plane.

"Secretary Lewis and Director Tillman have four days of official events scheduled, kicking off with a meeting with Ambassador Larkin at the US embassy. This is where we'll tag up with our in-country officers.

"Day two, Ambassador Larkin, Secretary Lewis, and Director Tillman will meet with the Vietnamese president and prime minister for a small ceremony at the site of the Hỏa Lò Prison, followed by a formal reception and joint remarks at the president's residence. Day three involves a meeting with Vietnam's party general secretary, following which the secretary of state and director will fly to Da Nang. From there they will travel by helicopter to the resort near Pele Ketan.

"Finally, day four involves a tour of the battlefield and portions of the Ho Chi Minh trail with local government officials, the US consul general, and South Vietnamese Army veterans. With this group, the secretary and director will lay ceremonial wreaths commemorating those who died in the war. The vehicle convoy will then take the secretary, the director, and their families back to the resort. You will find details, time-zone breakdowns, and specific assignments in your briefing packets. Any questions so far?"

An officer raised her hand. "Who is on point for security during the ceremonies?"

"Coordination will be driven by the ambassador's office, who will liaise with the Vietnamese government's protocol desk," replied Director Wong. "For the most part, our two agencies will be able to follow the same protocols we typically do when traveling with the secretary and director respectively. As the secretary and director have matching itineraries, other than preparing adequate transportation, you may find we actually have an easier time during this assignment. There will be more officers on the ground to conduct security sweeps at each site than we normally have. What else?"

After waiting ten seconds for a reply and receiving none, Director Wong nodded to his aide who proceeded to pull up a map of Vietnam on the conference room's projector. The map featured color-coded markers indicating the location of each day's events, with additional markers in purple near the battlefield.

"Thank you, Officer Johansson," Director Wong said in his aide's direction. "Now as I mentioned, the first portion of the trip is straightforward. However, the second portion of the trip is where things become more challenging. Secretary Lewis, Director Tillman, and their families will be staying in Vietnam for an additional two weeks following the official ceremonial events as part of a joint family vacation. They will largely be staying in the resort, but may make occasional day trips to different sites around the area."

Another officer raised his hand. "How does this make the assignment more challenging? Not to sound blunt, Director Wong, but it sounds like this is a cupcake assignment. They'll be lying by a pool in a secure five-star resort for two weeks."

"Normally you'd be correct, Laramie. However, the challenge is this: both the secretary and the director have requested security be cut to the bare minimum for this part of the trip. Each has selected an officer from those of you gathered in this room—Officer Foster from State for Secretary Lewis, and Officer Walshe from the CIA for Director Tillman—who will remain with them on the property. They will also be assisted by two of our people in country. The rest of you will be working out of a nearby town or the consular office in Ho Chi Minh City. Following their vacation, we will escort the group back to Da Nang, and then back to Washington."

"How is this even allowed?" Officer Laramie piped up again. "I thought we had to have specific protocols since we can't guarantee their safety in a setup like this. Surely they aren't private citizens simply because they're on vacation?"

"You're not wrong, Laramie," Director Wong said, turning to Officer Foster. "Foster, you raised a similar question to Secretary Lewis. What did he say in reply?"

"He said, 'I roamed this jungle for years when people were actively trying to kill me. You think I can't protect myself at a hotel?' I felt it prudent to end the conversation there."

Wong pointed at Officer Walshe. "And you, Walshe. What did Director Lewis say to you?"

"She quickly reminded me that, 'I wrote the standard for intelligence gathering in Southeast Asia. My in-country assets provide more consistent and reliable information about active threats than I ever got during the war. I'm not worried about someone poisoning my poolside mojito.'"

"Which led to me getting the following message from the president: 'Wong, they're war heroes for a reason. If anyone can manage two weeks on their own in Vietnam, it's those two.'"

Everyone in the room laughed, and even the normally stoic Wong couldn't help but crack a small smile.

"I know it's an odd request, and in fact, I strongly fought against it," noted Wong, "but the president has okayed this. And we will still provide 24/7 support as well. Foster and Walshe will work in rotating shifts with the in-country officers to ensure better coverage, and you all will be a short helicopter flight away at all times. While it may be a vacation for our protectees, it will in no way be a vacation for us."

"And don't worry, everyone," Officer Foster chimed in with a grin. "I don't know how the CIA does it, but I will be sure to bring each of you a mini-bottle of the fancy resort shampoo. It's the least I can do."

"I'd save all the spa supplies for yourself, Foster," said Laramie. "With a face like that, you need all the help you can get."

Foster shot a mischievous smirk in Laramie's direction as the whole group laughed, before bursting into laughter himself.

"Alright, alright, settle down," Wong said. "Continue to review your briefing books, and coordinate with Officer Johansson if you have any questions. Dismissed."

Chapter 4

Sergio was sitting in his room listening to *John Coltrane and the Thelonious Monk Trio at Carnegie Hall* on his old boom box when he heard a metallic creak come from the hallway upstairs. He paused the CD right in the middle of his favorite track, "Bye-Ya," cracked open his door, and listened. The creaking sound continued. His natural curiosity got the better of him, and he decided to make his way into the hall. As he reached the top of the stairs, he saw the ladder to the attic was down.

"Mom? Are you up there?" he shouted, to which he received a faint reply.

"Yup, I'm here!"

Sergio climbed the creaky metal ladder up into the unfinished attic crawl space where he found his mother Maria, flashlight in hand, digging through some dusty cardboard boxes.

"What are you looking for?" he asked.

"Your father gave me a travel blanket for Christmas years ago that I never ended up using, and I know it's up here somewhere. I want it for the plane ride tomorrow." his mother said.

Sergio chuckled. "Mom, you're aware that the plane you're flying on to Vietnam is the same plane the vice president uses, right? I think they're going to be able to find you a blanket if you get cold."

"Nonsense!" she said with a smile. "Might as well be prepared. Now come hold this flashlight for me so I can get a better look."

Sergio walked to the edge of the stack of boxes his mother was actively perusing and grabbed the flashlight. When he looked at the lid of one of the open boxes, he saw the words *Letters from José* scribbled on top. There were at least three large envelopes in the box, with what looked like office supplies and notebooks. He put the flashlight down on another box and grabbed the topmost envelope.

"I think we're going to have to work on your flashlight-holding skills. I'm in the dark here!" his mother joked, turning towards Sergio. Then she noticed the envelope he had begun to peruse. "Ah...Those are all letters from your dad. He'd write me whenever he was abroad on one of his research trips."

"Including when he went to Vietnam?" Sergio asked.

"There are a few from Vietnam, yes," she said tenderly. "You might have been too young to remember, but I always read those to you whenever they arrived at the house."

"I vaguely remember that, but I don't really remember any of the content of the letters."

His mother stood and put her hand on Sergio's shoulder. "I read them again and again after your father went missing, but after a while I just needed to put them away. I figured the attic was as good a place as any for safekeeping."

Sergio opened one of the letters and began to read his father's surprisingly clear handwriting.

July 11ᵗʰ, 1983

> *Maria,*
>
> *Hello from Rio de Janeiro! It's winter down here, but it's only 72 degrees—makes me wish we had this kind of climate in D.C. I've just arrived at the hotel, and the staff at the front desk were nice enough to give me a view of the beach. I can see the waves crashing from the desk where I'm writing you.*
>
> *I'm excited for this conference, as some of the top epidemiologists have flown down to speak. There are some new breakthroughs in blood analysis I'm really excited to learn more about—I'm hoping it will give me some new insights into my own research.*
>
> *I will mostly be inside during this conference, but will try to come back with a tan (and some cachaça for you, of course).*

> *Love,*
> *José*

Sergio put the letter back in its small envelope covered with international postage stamps and moved towards the larger envelope marked *Letters from Vietnam* in his mom's handwriting. He pulled out all of the envelope's contents and grabbed a letter from the top of the pile.

February 3ʳᵈ, 1993

> *Hi Maria and Sergio,*
> *I tried having interesting notes kaptured in a moleskine, but each is no good. Will attempt to create here extra details.*

*With it lucky, learning lots on site each time here. Everyone
makes it nice to have enough jerky, ultimately, not gonna lie.
Easy here outside, provided I not go off the dark field. Really, I
envy nobody doing stuff within inside lab/library. Hope all
very excellent/cool (underscore <u>really</u> excellent).*

> *Love,*
> *José*

Sergio reread the letter three times before putting it down. It
was definitely his dad's handwriting, but the text of the letter was
so strange compared to other notes he'd written to Sergio and
Maria. The typos in his writing were also odd. Sergio grabbed
another letter from the same trip.

February 4th, 1993

> *Dear Maria and Sergio,*
> *Covering lots of soil each try on old learning/discovery
> style in the easy way. I like learning to research yuseful things
> on my agenda. Knowledge evokes critical oasis near therapy
> and credible treatment.*

> *Love,*
> *José*

Well that was no better, Sergio thought as he grabbed the last
letter in the envelope. This one was dated February 6th–the last
day anyone saw his father alive.

February 6th, 1993

> *My dearest Maria and Sergio,*
> *Enough notes, enough medicine. You need excitement and relief. Given I verily embody friendly, relatable, interesting (even nice?) demeanor, seems now ought to echo beliefs outright. Oh keep–the happy excitement you have and visit east to engender creation. Help tomorrow or help each and live.*

> *Love you with all my heart,*
> *José*

Sergio finished the reading the letter, still utterly confused. While it was nice seeing his father's writing again, he couldn't make heads or tails of what it meant. He put the last letter down, then turned towards his mother, who was searching in another box for the travel blanket.

"Mom, why do dad's last letters read like a crazy person sending a telegram? I saw his earlier notes in the box—they were so clear and full of excitement."

She paused, lifting her head. "To be honest, I don't really know. Your dad was pretty exhausted before the trip—he'd been working hard in the lab for months researching a potential cure for some of the diseases he saw in Southeast Asia after the war. Add a twenty-seven-hour travel day to get to Vietnam from here, and you get someone who was pretty sleep deprived. Plus, he had an emotional connection to the country and hadn't been back in a while. I'm sure everything that week was pretty overwhelming."

"I suppose," Sergio said. "Just would be nice to have more information about what he was doing."

"When the last letter came in the mail, your dad also sent his research notebook along with it."

Sergio looked back in the box and saw a large brown leather-bound notebook. He picked it up and perused its worn coffee-stained pages. They were full of chemical symbols, drawings, and medical jargon he couldn't understand.

"I sent that notebook and the letters to Ada and James when the package arrived," his mom continued, "and in turn they sent it on to some of your dad's colleagues at the WHO, but ultimately nobody could figure out the answers to the questions he posed in the notebook. After the doctors at the WHO made photocopies of everything, they returned the notebook back to me."

Seeing that Sergio wasn't quite satisfied with her answer, she added, "Your dad was incredibly smart. Even if he didn't solve the problem he went to Vietnam to solve, he still championed the important causes nobody would touch and made huge strides in medicine. All of that on *top* of being a war hero." She sighed. "But most importantly, he loved you and me with all of his heart. That will always be true."

Sergio smiled. Despite spending most of his life without his father, he still had fond memories of his dad and the happy days they had together as a family. Memories that fueled the lingering desire to know exactly what caused his father to go missing and why. Emily and Charlie were curious about their parents' battle in Vietnam during the war, but it was Sergio's father's second Vietnam story that most piqued his curiosity.

As he reflected on what he had just read, he heard a loud "aha!" come from his mother in the corner of the attic, where she stood holding a blanket in a dusty plastic bag with a satisfied grin. "I knew it was up here!"

Sergio couldn't help but smile back.

"Why don't you pack up those letters back in their box, and when you're done, I'll take you out to dinner," she said. "A fancy meal before you, Emily, and Charlie pig out on junk food for the next few weeks."

She started making her way back down the creaky metal ladder, dusty blanket bag in tow, leaving Sergio alone in the attic. He looked back at the Vietnam letters and leather notebook.

What were you up to, Dad?

He closed the boxes he'd opened and turned off the overhead 40-watt bulb whose light barely covered a quarter of the attic crawl space. As he made his way to the opening in the attic floor, he turned and glanced back at the box. As the seconds ticked by, his curiosity got the better of him, and without further deliberation he grabbed the Vietnam letters and notebook out of the box. He held them carefully as he shimmied down the ladder before folding up the ladder above him. A poof of dust misted off the ceiling when the ladder fully tucked inside the attic hatch. He snuck the notebook and letters into his room before grabbing his worn-down tennis shoes.

"Ready for dinner, Mom!"

Chapter 5

The late-spring sun was already beginning to shine as three identical black SUVs rolled up to Maria Santos's home at exactly 7:00 a.m. the morning of May 6th. Given her house had the longest driveway, it was chosen as the rendezvous point for the beginning of the Vietnam trip. Maria sipped her second cup of coffee of the morning as she watched James, Delia, and Emily Lewis step out of the first car and Ada, Bill, and Charlie Tillman climb out of the second.

"Sergio!" she called down the hall. "Everyone is here!" She heard the sound of a door slowly opening and then turned to see her groggy-looking son trudge to the front door.

"Good morning, sleepyhead," she said, smiling as she ruffled his hair.

"And here I was thinking once I finished high school, I wouldn't have to wake up before seven," he replied.

"Oh hush. You kids can take a nap as soon as we're gone," Maria replied as she opened the front door, continuing "Good morning, everyone!"

"Good morning, Maria! Good morning, Sergio!" James Lewis shouted from the driveway.

"Good morning!" Ada echoed from slightly farther away.

An officer wearing dark sunglasses walked towards the front door. "Good morning, ma'am. I can go ahead and grab your bags for you."

Maria stepped slightly to her side. "Thanks, they're right here. And don't forget the small backpack there as well—it's got my travel blanket in it," she said, turning around and winking at Sergio, who rolled his eyes and shook his head as the officer collected her bags and walked back to the cars. The Lewises and Tillmans started towards the front door, with Emily and Charlie leading the pack. They were the first to step inside the house.

"Hey Em, hey Charlie," Sergio said.

"Morning!" Emily replied in a cheerful but sleepy voice.

"Hey hey. My dad insisted on grabbing some doughnuts for us as a little treat before the parents ditch us," said Charlie, holding up two large paper boxes.

"Awesome." Sergio turned towards Emily's and Charlie's parents. "Good morning, everyone. Oh, and thanks for the doughnuts, Uncle Bill."

Bill Tillman had a huge grin on his face. "You're welcome, Sergio!" He turned to his wife. "See Ada, I knew they would like them!"

"Just remember to eat a few healthy breakfasts while we're gone, kids," Ada said with a smile.

"Why don't you three go put those in the kitchen? Sergio, you can grab some plates after we leave," Maria added. As the kids scurried down the hall, Maria turned back to the group. "How was the ride this morning?"

"It was good!" Delia Lewis replied. "I always love sunrises this time of year. Something about the dawn light really makes all the monuments look that much more beautiful. And James made a good point—they'll look even better once we're in the air."

35

Maria nodded. Depending on what side of the plane you were on flying into either National or Dulles, you really could have some spectacular views of Washington. It reminded her of how José, who was a bit of an aviation geek in his spare time, would dutifully look up the type of plane in which the family would be flying to make sure they had seats with the best views.

"It doesn't hurt that we can move around this plane freely, either," James joked. "Though I still wish we'd get a cool call sign like 'Air Force Two' when we're on it. I'm thinking, 'Air Force Lewis.'" I'll have to take it up with the president when we get back."

"Don't let the secretary of the Army hear you say that—I think he still has the power to bust you back down to private even after all these years," Ada said with a smirk. "Any plane is better than those old troop transports they put us on, though. Do you remember how cold it got inside, James?"

"My teeth didn't stop clattering until 1987," said James, feigning a shiver.

The group smiled, and out of the corner of her eye Maria saw another person walking up the driveway towards the house. Officer Molly Pak was moving quickly, holding a clipboard with some documents.

"Good morning, Molly," Maria said. "How's Bilbo?"

"Hi Mrs. Santos, great to see you! And Bilbo is doing excellent, thank you. I just got him a new toy, so my hope is that it'll last at least the duration of your trip."

For as long as Maria had known Molly, she had been obsessed with two things: *The Lord of the Rings* and her all-white miniature schnauzer Bilbo. Sometimes when her shift was over, Officer Pak would bring Bilbo over to Maria's house for the kids to play with.

Just one of the many reasons why Emily, Charlie, and Sergio liked her best of all of Ada's officers.

"Where are the kids?" Molly asked.

"Oh, they're just getting into some doughnuts Bill bought them," Ada replied. "Charlie, Emily, and Sergio—Officer Pak is inside now!"

A rustling came from the kitchen, followed shortly by Sergio, Emily, and Charlie making their way down the hallway back to the front parlor.

"Hey Molly!" shouted Sergio, wiping some powdered sugar off his cheek.

"How are my favorite new high-school graduates doing?" Molly asked.

"I think we could use about eight more hours of sleep," said Emily, "but otherwise we're good."

"I'm coming towards the end of a twelve-hour shift, but no, you all *definitely* need more sleep than me. And to think, you didn't even offer me a doughnut—I see how it is," Molly said as Ada gave her a lighthearted pat on the shoulder.

Despite her youthful appearance, Officer Pak had been working for Ada for the past eight years and had grown close to the Santos, Lewis, and Tillman families as a result. The kids treated her like an older sister, and due to her intelligence, tenacity, and drive, Ada viewed her as her protégé at the Agency.

"Well looking at the time here, Molly, I think you can go ahead and start," Ada noted.

"Absolutely, Director Tillman," said Molly, turning to the kids. "Right. As you know, your parents will be out of country for the next two and a half weeks. Through discussion with Director Tillman, Secretary Lewis, and Mrs. Santos, we've determined I will be your main point of contact during the trip. Should you need to communicate with your parents, or need anything during the next few weeks, you can give me a call either at the office or my house. I will be coordinating with your parents' security detail and the in-country officers in Vietnam from here in Washington. I have the full breakdown of their schedule and travel details at my disposal. Any questions so far?"

"How'd you get stuck with us instead of this luxurious trip to Vietnam?" asked Sergio.

Officer Pak laughed. "As much I love you three, I'm actually staying here in Washington because I'm coordinating a few other efforts on top of this trip. But of course, I volunteered to help watch over you all as soon as Director Tillman put the opportunity out to a group of us officers. Not that you all need babysitting, of course."

"Will you be coming by our houses, though?" asked Emily.

"I'll check in with each of your over the phone periodically, but won't need to come by in person unless you specifically need me to do so."

"And playing with Bilbo does not count as a specific need," Ada jumped in.

Molly smiled. "You all can take turns watching Bilbo when I go on my vacation after your parents get back. Any other questions?"

Maria scanned the room, but saw everyone shaking their heads in response to Molly's question.

"Okay great." Molly passed each of the kids a sheet of paper from her clipboard. "I know you all have it already, but I've taken the liberty of printing out all my contact information so it's all in one place for you. Please don't hesitate to call if anything comes up."

"Thank you, Molly. I appreciate your initiative as always," said Ada. She turned and nodded at James.

"Okay kids," James said, "it's time for us to head out."

The parents embraced their children.

"Stay safe, and have fun. Love you," Delia told Emily.

"I will, Mom. Love you. Bring me back some cool souvenirs!"

Ada and Bill hugged Charlie as Ada said, "Don't hesitate to call Molly if you need anything at all. She's got you covered. We love you."

"I love you, too," Charlie replied.

Maria turned to Sergio and gave him a long hug. "I love you, Sergio. Keep Emily and Charlie safe, and try to have some fun while we're gone."

Sergio smiled. "I love you too, Mom. Enjoy your travel blanket, and take lots of pictures for me when you're there!"

Molly opened the front door and made a whirling gesture with her finger to one of the officers outside. The engines of the three SUVs revved in unison.

As the parents passed Molly on their way out the front door, Maria saw her turn back towards the kids and in a low whisper say, "You know I'm absolutely bringing Bilbo over here when my shifts are over, right?"

Charlie, Emily, and Sergio all grinned as Officer Pak winked and walked towards the awaiting vehicles. Maria and her fellow parents gave their kids a final wave as they entered the cars, and like clockwork, the vehicles pulled out of the driveway at exactly 7:20 a.m. They would have only a short commute to Andrews Air Force Base once the Capitol Police escort joined the caravan.

Chapter 6

The first few days of the Vietnam trip proved to be no different than those in a typical summer vacation for Emily, Sergio, and Charlie. They watched movies, played video games, stayed up too late, and slept in. Occasionally they would even turn on the news to see coverage of their parents' trip, but most of all, they lounged by the pool at Sergio's house.

On the afternoon of the sixth day of the trip, Charlie and Emily had once again migrated from their respective homes over to Sergio's pool. As they often did, Emily picked up Charlie in her dad's old car and drove to Sergio's. When they entered his house using Charlie's keys, they walked past the living room television to find CNN's reporting on the Vietnam trip. Pictures of their parents with Sergio's dad in the early nineties flipped past on the screen, with the caption *"Miraculous Three" remembered today in Vietnam*. After lingering a moment in front of the screen, the pair continued on through the house towards the backyard where Sergio had already gotten a jump start on the day's pool session.

"Serge, do you just live out here now?" Emily asked, sliding the glass door behind her.

"Pretty much," he replied, turning to look at his friends. "Sometimes I think this pool chair is more comfortable than my bed. Honestly."

Emily and Charlie laughed as they laid out their beach towels on the sun-bleached vinyl pool chairs positioned towards Sergio. The day's heat had already brought out the strong smell of chlorine from the water. "I am starting to get a little sick of pizza, though," Sergio continued. "Unfortunately there just aren't as many good places that deliver out here."

"Luckily, we read your mind...mostly because Emily and I are feeling the same way. I made Emily stop so we could pick up some subs," replied Charlie, taking a sandwich out of his bag and handing it to Sergio.

"You two are the best!" Sergio said, finally leaning up from his chair and turning to the small side table between him, Charlie, and Emily.

She had a big smile on her face. "We know."

"What have you guys been up to today?" Sergio asked between bites of his turkey and roast beef on multigrain bread.

"I mean between waking up at 11 a.m. and picking up the sandwiches, it's been pretty busy," Charlie said lazily.

Emily, still laughing at Charlie, replied, "We did see CNN talking about our parents as we walked through the house."

"Oh yeah, I forgot I left that on," Sergio said. "I was watching some of the coverage earlier today. Looked like they had a good visit to the old battlefield."

"Yeah. They were showing some nice pictures of your dad with my dad and Charlie's mom. From the Medal of Honor ceremony."

"The ones that Charlie's mom has in the hall? Those are some good ones. I think my mom has a few copies as well with some of my dad's old stuff."

"Yep, exactly," Charlie said.

The group continued to eat as the *Getz/Gilberto* bossa nova album played through the indoor/outdoor speaker Sergio had rigged up at the start of the summer. After a few minutes, Sergio crumpled up his now-empty sandwich wrapper. "You know, speaking of old things, I was up in the attic with my mom the day before she left, and she showed me a bunch of my dad's old letters."

"That's cool," Emily said. "What were they from?"

"Mostly his trips related to his work. Like apparently, he wrote my mom every time he went to a medical conference or one of his WHO trips. He even wrote a few on his last trip to Vietnam."

Charlie looked over at Emily. Sergio didn't often talk about his dad's disappearance, but when he did, they wanted to be as supportive as possible.

"Oh yeah?" Charlie replied. "What did they say? Anything funny?"

"That's the thing...they were honestly super weird. I read some of letters up there he'd sent before I was born and they were just like I remembered him—cheery and lighthearted. But the three he sent from Vietnam on his last trip were really odd."

"How so?" Emily asked.

"The word choices he made were just strange. Like it was definitely his handwriting, but the tone didn't sound anything like him or his other letters. Plus, he had a few spelling mistakes, and my mom always said he was a stickler for grammar and spelling... Anyway, when I asked her about them, she said he'd been under a bunch of stress before and during the trip, so that's probably why the letters were weird. But I still find it strange. Also"—Sergio paused to wipe some yellow mustard off his chin—"he sent his medical journal back with his last letter."

"That's interesting. Wasn't he only a few days into the trip when they...last saw him?" Emily asked delicately. After all these years she still never knew the best way to talk about the disappearance.

"Yeah, it was like day three or four. Pretty early into what should have been a much longer trip." Sergio paused, pensive. "I don't know...My mom said she gave the letters and notebook to your parents to take a look, but they didn't know what was going on. Neither did the WHO doctors who saw them next. There was some disease my dad was digging into but hadn't quite solved before the trip."

"My dad never told me that," Emily said.

"Neither did my mom," Charlie added.

"To be fair, I didn't even remember that my dad had sent them," Sergio continued. "My mom said she used to read all the letters to me, but we were pretty young at the point when any of them arrived in Washington. And I don't think I would have clocked how weird these ones were anyway. Still, I haven't been able to stop thinking about them." Sergio paused, then said, "Do you two want to see them?"

Both Emily and Charlie, curiosity piqued, nodded.

"Cool, I snuck them out of the attic into my room."

Emily and Charlie scarfed the rest of their sandwiches, which had so engrossed the hungry teenagers that they didn't have a chance to jump in the pool. They brought their trash into the kitchen, washed their hands with the peppermint soap by the sink, and made their way to Sergio's room.

As the three walked into the bedroom, Emily scanned the multiple bookshelves Sergio had positioned throughout his space. Despite her having been in his room many times when hanging out with him and Charlie, each time she entered, she always found something new that she'd never noticed before—some piece of art or Army memorabilia that was tucked into a corner, a new book, something historic. Every little component revealed a different facet of Sergio's interests and their progression over the years. His collection of items nearly rivaled hers, though hers mostly consisted of local art or craftworks she picked up on State Department trips with her family. She was a sucker for small, suitcase-friendly paintings from vendors on the street.

Emily's attention snapped back to the room when she heard one of Sergio's desk drawers slam shut as he plopped a large manila envelope down on top of his desk. "There are three letters total."

"Let's take a look," said Charlie, grabbing one of the letters out of the larger envelope. Emily and Sergio followed suit, grabbing the remaining two letters. When they each finished reading, they each passed their current letter to the person next to them—Charlie to Sergio, Sergio to Emily, Emily to Charlie—until they had each read all three letters.

"Pretty odd, right?" Sergio asked.

"It's like he thought someone other than your mom was going to read them," Emily replied. "The words sort of make sense, but it doesn't really feel like he's saying anything specific."

"Agreed, Em. Charlie, what are you thinking?"

Charlie sat silently over by the desk, skimming through each of the three letters and pointing to each word as he read.

"Hello? Earth to Charlie, do you read us?" asked Emily.

"Oh...sorry," he replied. "Hey Sergio, do you have a piece of paper and a pencil I can use?"

"Sure. What's up?" Sergio asked as he grabbed some blank copy paper from a lower desk drawer and a pencil sitting in the NASA Space Camp cup that Charlie had gifted him years ago.

"So, I agree with both of you that these letters are strange..." Charlie started, "but then Emily's comment made me start to think...What if, for whatever reason, these letters *were* monitored by someone? Or at least, they were when they were sent?"

"But by who?" Emily asked.

"Oh, I have no idea. But let's just assume they were, or at least that your dad believed they were."

"Okay," Sergio replied. "Let's assume. So what?"

"Well, what if your dad was writing in some kind of code? Maybe that accounts for some of the weirdness."

Emily and Sergio looked at each other. They both knew, like his mom, that Charlie had always been fascinated by cryptology and its usage throughout history. Growing up, he often told them about things like the spy ring that helped George Washington gather military intelligence during the Revolutionary War, or how agents in the Cold War were able to secretly pass information from person to person. Charlie and his mom would even write messages to each other in code, though mostly to discretely generate birthday and Christmas present ideas for Charlie's dad.

"I don't really remember my dad ever doing that," Sergio said, "but I suppose they would have learned how to encode messages during Special Forces training. What type of code do you think it could be?"

"I don't think it's anything complex. There's nothing like a key or cypher anywhere in the envelopes. Here, hand me the first letter," Charlie said.

Emily grabbed the first letter and put it in front of Charlie, adding, "I did notice that typo in the letter Sergio mentioned."

Charlie unfolded the letter and looked it over quickly.

> *Hi Maria and Sergio,*
>
> *I tried having interesting notes kaptured in a moleskine, but each is no good. Will attempt to create here extra details. With it lucky, learning lots on site each time here. Everyone makes it nice to have enough jerky, ultimately, not gonna lie. Easy here outside, provided I not go off the dark field. Really, I envy nobody doing stuff within inside lab/library. Hope all very excellent/cool (underscore _really_ excellent).*
>
> *Love,*
> *José*

Charlie grabbed his pencil and started to tap the words in the letter with the eraser end. "Is it a skip code?" he mumbled. "No, that doesn't fit... Maybe an Atbash cipher?" He started writing on a piece of scrap paper.

From what Emily knew of codebreaking, Charlie appeared to be replacing letters in each word with their opposite in the alphabet as he scribbled.

"That's gibberish too. Hold on." He grabbed another piece of paper and resumed writing while Sergio and Emily read over his shoulders.

ITHINKIAMBEING

Charlie stared at it for a second, then drew slashes between the letters he had written.

I / T H I N K / I / A M / B E I N G

Emily was shocked at what she was seeing. "Keep going, Charlie!"

He wrote the rest of the letters down, and after taking some time to add slashes, Sergio and Emily looked down in amazement at the final product.

I / T H I N K / I / A M / B E I N G / W A T C H E D.
/ W I L L / L O S E / T H E M / I N / T H E / J U N G L E. /
H O P I N G / O L D / F R I E N D S / W I L L / H A V E
/ C U R E.

The teenagers were stunned by what was written on the page. After a minute, Sergio broke the silence. "Do the other letters!"

Charlie grabbed the second letter and, using the same technique, wrote a message down on the paper.

C L O S E / T O / O L D / S I T E. / W I L L / T R Y / T O /
M A K E / C O N T A C T.

Without hesitating for commentary from his friends, Charlie decoded the third and final letter.

E N E M Y / N E A R. / G I V E / F R I E N D S /
N O T E B O O K / − / T H E Y / H A V E / T E C H / T O
/ H E A L.

On the bottom of the page, Charlie rewrote each of the messages and put his pencil down.

Letter 1: I think I am being watched. Will lose them in the jungle. Hoping old friends will have cure.
Letter 2: Close to old site. Will try to make contact.
Letter 3: Enemy near. Give friends notebook—they have tech to heal.

Sergio grabbed Charlie's shoulders and gave them a shake. "Great work, Charlie! I can't believe it."

"Charlie, how'd you figure this out?" asked Emily, still shocked.

"I ran through a few of the most common code types I've read about, but none of them fit. The fact that Dr. José used a different greeting and ending each letter also threw me off. But ultimately, it was really the typo on the word 'captured' that made me think he was using the first letters of each word intentionally," Charlie replied with a satisfied grin.

The three looked on at the messages on the paper in front of them, and as the initial elation of their code-cracking began to fade, the full weight of what they were seeing set in their minds.

"So Em was right: my dad was being watched by somebody. And clearly whatever or whoever he was looking for, someone was after it or them as well," Sergio said. "But why? He was just a doctor..."

"Let's try to break it down based on what your dad wrote across all three letters," Charlie said, matching Sergio's more serious tone. "As you two have pointed out, Sergio's dad *was* being watched or followed, and I think it's safe to assume it was whoever he referred to as 'enemy.' We don't know who that is, so we can mark it down as an open question."

"And the jungle part," Emily jumped in. "We know Dr. José was near the battlefield our parents all fought in, right, Serge?"

Sergio nodded and Emily continued. "The reference to 'old site'—that's got to be the battlefield. I think he was making his way back to the battlefield area. In '93, there wasn't a real path or anything like that leading to the site, so it makes sense he would have to trek for a few days to get there. Unlike today."

"Agreed," Sergio said. "Our parents had to do a two-day hike before the battle took place, so that makes sense. The only piece left of the letters is this reference to 'old friends.'"

Sergio glanced over Charlie's handwriting again before continuing. "At first I thought it could be Aunt Ada and Uncle James, but he wouldn't need to go to Vietnam looking for them, and they don't have any special medical knowledge."

"Following that same logic too, he would have asked his WHO colleagues if he needed their help," Charlie added.

"This is a wild guess," Emily said, "but my dad always talks about how they had help from some locals during the battle. That they wouldn't have survived without it. You think 'old friends' is referring to the villagers who helped them?"

"Honestly, it would make sense," Sergio muttered. "When I was little, my dad told me that after the battle, but before the Army came to rescue him, those villagers used some unheard-of technique to quickly treat his injuries. That sounds pretty friendly to me. Actually...yeah! That totally makes sense!

"I vividly remember after a conference in Montevideo, my dad shared with me that scientists in Brazil were finding new medical uses for plants that grow deep in the Amazon. Basically, the indigenous people of Brazil—the Caribs I think?—had been using the plants for centuries, but the knowledge of them had only just been making its way to scientists. I used to always laugh thinking about what that process would look like in reality—people in crisp white lab coats cutting through the thick jungle with machetes until they found some magical plant."

Sergio trailed off for a second before looking back at Emily and Charlie. "In any case, from the notebook my dad sent back to my mom, we know that when he went back to Vietnam, he was attempting to cure a disease that nobody had been able to treat. If we're taking wild guesses, my guess is that he was trying to find those local villagers—his 'old friends'—to get their help and see what natural 'tech' they could share. Maybe he thought whatever treatment they'd used on his wounds could be the missing piece to his research."

"Okay," Emily replied. "So to summarize: we think your dad went to Vietnam with the intention of going back to the battlefield, contacting the villagers who helped our parents, and seeing if the cure they used on his injuries could be used to help cure the disease he was researching."

"Yes," Sergio said. "Which still leaves the question of who this 'enemy' is and how come the villagers were never contacted."

"Well, our parents engaged with the Viet Cong, right? They were clearly adversaries during the war," Charlie said. "Maybe it doesn't make as much sense for after the war, but when the North Vietnamese unified Vietnam, tons of former Viet Cong joined the new national government. Unless..."

"What?" Emily asked.

He paused. "I guess this is my turn for a wild idea: there was and still is some anti-American sentiment in Vietnam because of the war, so maybe someone was holding a grudge against our parents for surviving the battle and getting so much attention for it. I hate to say it, but maybe they found out Dr. José was making his way back to the country...and they decided to try and find him."

"Charlie! That's a dark line of thought," said Emily, glaring at him.

"You're right, Emily. Sorry, Serge, I went too far. I know that's a pretty bleak theory."

"I mean the idea is pretty harrowing," Serge replied. "And I hate to consider it, but Charlie, you might be onto something." He paused for what, to Emily, felt like an eternity before continuing. "I know I don't always talk about my dad's disappearance with you two, and truthfully, I've mostly accepted that he really is just...gone. But there's always that voice in the back of my head asking, 'What happened?' And as dark as this line of thought is, if it gets us answers... it might finally help me get the closure I need."

Emily grabbed Sergio's shoulders and held her friend for a moment.

"Thanks, guys," he said. "Right. So now that we've painted this grim picture, what do we do with it? I mean as smart as Charlie is, I'm thinking Aunt Ada may be a little bit smarter and probably cracked this code when she first saw the letters. Right, Charles?"

Sensing that Sergio was trying to lighten the mood, Charlie replied playfully. "I'll happily concede that she is, in fact, much smarter than me. I've got no doubt that she figured it out and shared it with Emily's dad."

"Definitely," Emily said. "I mean I know that our parents tried for years to locate Dr. José using any clue they could get. My dad said they used every State and Agency resource within their control to research what happened, but they couldn't find any evidence. It was like he just vanished."

"Hear me out on this before you two shoot it down," Sergio said. "I know this may sound crazy, but based on what we've just worked out, I think it tracks: what if our parents' trip to Vietnam wasn't just for the thirtieth anniversary of the end of the war? What if they found something recently and needed cover to discretely visit the battlefield? I mean think about it—Emily, how long do your dad's official trips take?"

"No more than a few days typically," she answered. "But let me play devil's advocate here for a second. They're also treating the trip as a vacation. It's not completely unheard of for the Secretary of State to extend an official trip for some personal holiday time."

"That's true I guess...but why would they choose to vacation at a resort so close to the battlefield? And for so long?" Sergio replied. "Look, I'm not saying they solved the mystery or anything like that, but it feels like they're looking for something specific."

"I don't know, Serge. I suppose it's not out of the realm of possibility. I mean Aunt Ada is the head of a spy agency, so she definitely knows how to keep a secret or two," Emily said. "Here's what I'm thinking—we should ask them about it after they come back from the trip. We can show them Charlie's decoded message, explain our theories, and ask them to share what they know. I think we're absolutely on the right track, but I don't know what we can do until they come home."

"I just wish we had a way of knowing what they know right now. This is the most I've learned about my dad's disappearance in years, and I'm going to lose my mind thinking about it without taking any action for two more weeks," Sergio said.

"There may be..." Charlie murmured.

Sergio looked over at Charlie, but Emily spoke before he could. "What do you mean, Charlie?"

"My mom keeps a safe in her office. I've never seen what's inside, and she always told me it was just tax documents and boring stuff like that whenever I asked her. I didn't have any reason to disbelieve her, so, I've never cared to look."

"Okay..."

"Right. Well, the other day, before the trip, Uncle James was over at the house when I got home from some errands. They were chatting in my mom's office when I walked in, and on the desk, I saw my mom holding a big file folder with 'Dr. José Luis Santos' written on the top tab. She quickly grabbed it and put it back in the safe. They were clearly talking about whatever was in that folder. And based on everything that we've learned today, I think Uncle James and my mom put together a dossier on Sergio's dad."

"Can you get us into that safe?" Sergio asked.

"I think so," Charlie replied optimistically.

"What have you got up your sleeve, Chuck?" Emily asked.

"From her time on the road, my mom always told me the best way to hide something important is to put it in the most boring spot possible. Somewhere out in the open, but where nobody would care to look even if they saw it—cabinets with cleaning supplies, drawers with kitchen utensils, etcetera. I'm guessing for convenience's sake she wouldn't have hidden the key to the safe outside of her office, so I bet I can find it."

"Let's do it!" Sergio exclaimed. "And if it helps you justify it, we don't need to go snooping for anything else—just stuff related to my dad that we'll ask our parents about anyway."

"I'm okay with that. Em, you good, too?" Charlie asked.

"Yep, sounds good," she replied. "Wait, Charlie—I just realized...is that why you were always opening the cabinet in your laundry room when we were growing up?"

"Yeah! That's where I hid all of my allowance money," he said with a big smile on his face.

"Charlie, have I ever told you how much I appreciate that your mom inadvertently trained you to be a spy?" asked Sergio.

"I don't know how inadvertent it was," Charlie said, "but I could certainly stand to hear it from you more."

Emily grinned. "I'll go grab my stuff from outside and then head over to Charlie's. Sergio, since you'll need to come back here anyway, why don't you drive yourself and Charlie."

"Yes! Sounds like a plan!" Sergio replied as he started looking for his keys.

After grabbing their belongings and Charlie's sheet of decoded messages, Sergio went to the living room to turn the television off. His dad's face was being shown on the repeat broadcast from earlier in the day. Sergio smiled, hit the power button on the remote, and then ran outside to lock his front door. Emily, Sergio, and Charlie's two-car caravan backed down Sergio's driveway, just as their parents' caravan of government cars had done only a few days prior, and made its way towards Charlie's house.

Chapter 7

As they weaved through D.C. traffic to keep up with Emily's car, Charlie was enjoying the breeze coming from the rolled-down windows of Sergio's gold sedan. His mom had pulled some strings to get the three kids into the CIA's defensive driving course as soon as they received their licenses, which in addition to making them safer drivers, had the added benefit of helping them move through rush-hour gridlock on the District's many one-way streets. Sergio was playing a new jazz CD his mom had gotten him—*Page One* by Joe Henderson—and the music only helped add to the excitement of their quest. Charlie had always liked solving puzzles, and helping one of his best friends figure out what really happened to his father seemed like the ultimate challenge. As they neared his house, it was all he could think about.

From farther down the road, Charlie saw Emily pull into his driveway. However, instead of walking straight inside with her key as she usually did, she stood near her open driver-side door and turned back to face Sergio and Charlie as they slowed into park behind her. The troubled look on her face caught Charlie off guard.

"I'm surprised you aren't inside already, Em! With how hot and humid it is today, I would have expected you to have run straight inside to the A/C," Charlie said as he hopped out of Sergio's car.

"You didn't forget to shut your front door when I picked you up today, right? I mean I know I was rushing you along, but I feel like you locked it," Emily asked, with what Charlie felt was a touch of stress in her voice.

"I always lock that door. I step on the welcome mat, check my pockets for my wallet, house key, and cell phone, and then lock the door. It's a habit. Why?" But as soon as Charlie responded, he saw what was stirring Emily.

"What's going on?" Sergio asked as he got out of the car.

"My front door is ajar, and I know for sure that I locked it," Charlie said. He squinted as he tried to see in the bright afternoon sun, but after a few seconds, recognized the front door had clearly been kicked in.

"I'm calling Molly. Nobody move," Emily said as she pulled out her phone. All of the teenagers had added Officer Pak to their phones' speed dial a few years ago, so within a few seconds she had her on the line. Sergio and Charlie watched Emily as she spoke, only hearing her side of the conversation:

"Hey Molly."

...

"I'm with Charlie and Sergio at Charlie's house."

...

"Yeah, we're all okay. We just got here and we noticed that Charlie's front door was ajar—looks like somebody kicked it open."

...

"It doesn't look like anyone is still here, no."

...

"Okay, yeah, that's perfect, thanks. See you soon."

"What did she say?" asked Sergio.

"Molly is going to head over here right now. Said she can be here in about ten minutes and that we shouldn't go inside until she arrives," Emily replied.

"Forget that—it's my house, I'm taking a look now," said Charlie, already starting to move towards the door.

"Molly figured you would say that, so she asked that we at least try to listen for anyone inside before we go in, and then wait in the living room if we don't hear anybody."

"I'm right behind you, Charlie," said Sergio, squaring his shoulders as if ready to fight.

The three started towards the front door, but only after Emily made the boys hold their keys between their fingers in improvised claws. Once they were on the front patio, Charlie stuck his head past the open doorframe.

He listened. There were no sounds of movement coming from inside the house, other than the faint rustling emanating from the air-conditioning system which was in overdrive to counteract the warm summer air rushing into the house from the open door. He noticed some wood fragments on the ground—presumably from the doorjamb when the door had been kicked open.

"I don't hear anybody. I think whatever happened is over," said Charlie, fully opening the door to his home while still holding his improvised key-claw weapon in a defensive position. "Until we're sure though, let's grab things from the kitchen to protect ourselves."

Sergio and Emily followed Charlie inside, shutting the door behind them. Like Charlie, neither one of them heard anything which might indicate that another person was inside the house with them.

As the three walked through the house, Charlie noticed all the classic signs of a ransacking—flipped-over furniture, items flung across the floor from inside drawers and cabinets, and broken glass from picture frames knocked maliciously on the floor. After arriving in the kitchen, they each grabbed a knife from the block sitting on the black quartz countertop.

Charlie did a quick walk through each room in the house on the main level, especially curious to see how badly his room had been damaged, and then with Emily and Sergio, he checked the other floors. Upon not finding anybody in the house, they made their way back towards the kitchen.

"Whoever did this made a huge mess," Charlie said, "and obviously we need Molly to confirm when she gets here, but after a quick look, I didn't notice anything missing. Disheveled, yes, but nothing taken. The TV was still in the living room, computer still in the office, things like that."

"This is strange," Sergio said, still gripping the paring knife he had chosen from the knife block. "Do break-ins even happen on your street?"

"Never. There are a lot of Agency and government officials in this neighborhood, so generally speaking, security is pretty solid," Charlie replied, shaking his head. "It never even—"

"Hey, what's that on the dining room table?" Emily interjected.

Sergio and Charlie turned towards the open doorframe which led into the brick-walled dining room. They scanned the room before each noticing what she saw just moments before: a small white envelope was sitting perfectly centered on the maple dining table.

Emily was the first to enter the room, followed by Sergio, then Charlie. She grabbed the envelope off the table and showed it to each of them.

"Go ahead, Em," Charlie said.

She placed her knife down on the dining room table and opened the envelope. Inside was a piece of heavy stock paper on which someone had neatly written a message. Emily read it aloud.

"We have taken your Secretary of State, your CIA Director, and all those unfortunate enough to have chosen their company as our hostages. They have stolen what rightfully belongs to us, and have failed to deliver as promised. Unless you deliver the đi qua to us in seven days, we will kill them all. Then, we will kill you. If you cross us, you will fail. The site of their greatest triumph will become the site of their greatest defeat.

– Casus Belli –"

Emily's hands were shaking by the time she finished reading the note. She put the thick paper down, then covered her mouth with her hands as she said, "Oh my god. OH. My. God."

Charlie put his hand on Emily's shoulder to comfort her as he looked over at Sergio, who reread the note. Fists fell to Sergio's sides as he read it over and over again. "Who is Casus Belli?"

"I don't think it's a person...I think it might be a group," Charlie replied with shakiness in his voice. "It basically just means 'an act justifying war.' Traditional rules of engagement would say that a nation needs casus belli in order to declare a war. For us in World War II, it was the attack on Pearl Harbor."

"This is a declaration of war then?" asked Sergio, visibly frustrated that Charlie hadn't really answered his question. "And what the hell is the đi qua?"

"I have no idea," Emily replied, still shaking a bit, "but that looks like Vietnamese to me."

Surely I've seen this item referenced before...I could have sworn I just saw it, Charlie thought.

He tried to remember the Vietnam War books he'd skimmed ahead of his parents' trip, but still, nothing came to him. Adrenaline was making it hard for him to focus.

"How could anybody even do this?" Sergio asked. "I thought both Aunt Ada and your dad had full-time security?"

"They do," Emily replied, "but on the vacation portion of their trip, they were only going to have a few officers with them, something they had negotiated with the president on an exception basis."

"But surely other people would know they'd been taken, right?" Sergio continued. "I mean they had limited security immediately near them, but there were lots of officers nearby. I'm sure one of the officers would have radioed into the field office."

Sensing the stress level in the room was rising, Charlie spoke up. "Here, let's check the news quickly." He turned on the small TV in the kitchen just off the dining room door. Flipping through channels, he landed on CNN.

"Anything?" Sergio asked.

"No. I mean they're talking about how much of a diplomatic success the trip was, but nothing mentioning a kidnapping. Let me check a few others." Charlie continued switching through news outlets, but like CNN, none of them showed any news which might validate the threats in the disturbing letter sitting on his family's dining table. He turned off the TV and returned to the dining room.

"Look, I have no clue what's going on," he told his friends, "but if I've learned nothing else from my mom, it's that in stressful situations, you have to just work the problem. I don't know if this is a threat or a legitimate ransom note, but let's remember we're not alone. We can figure this out."

Through the window in the back of the dining room, Charlie saw a government-issued vehicle pulling into the driveway. "Molly just got here. She'll know what to do."

◊◊◊◊◊

Molly knocked on the door, but seeing it was unlocked, she opened it without hesitating, holding her sidearm in her hands as she stalked into the foyer.

"Kids? Are you here?" she shouted, hearing her voice reverberate off the brick walls near her.

"We're all in the dining room, Molly. Everyone's okay. We think we're alone," Charlie shouted back.

"Good! I'm going to do a quick sweep of the house regardless. Give me five minutes."

Molly kept her sidearm out just in case, but with each room she checked, she grew more confident that she wouldn't need it. She inspected the basement first, checking the locks on the two exterior doors that led to a back deck area. After shaking the door handles and seeing that the deadbolts were intact, she checked the window locks.

Those are okay, too, she thought, moving through the mental checklist she'd established.

She continued up to the second floor, inspecting each bedroom, closet, and bathroom. All appeared fine, though she noticed the mess the intruder had left behind. It was clear whoever had broken into the house was looking for something specific.

Jewelry? That doesn't fit. Maybe it was documents.

Given the nature of her boss's job, it wasn't out of the realm of possibility for someone would attempt to break into the house. Though the attempts would be foolish as any and all sensitive materials would be locked up, either at Langley or behind multiple layers of digital encryption.

She finished her inspection of the house's upstairs area and made her way back to the main level, doing a quick walkthrough of each room. She passed the living room, Charlie's room, and then Director Tillman's office. She noticed the doors to the closet where the director kept her safe were ripped off the hinges, but the safe overall looked intact. Random documents were strewn over the floor as well, but after perusing a few, Molly determined they were normal household papers—bills, junk mail, invitations to a few weddings—nothing out of the ordinary.

Confident there was no immediate danger, Molly returned her sidearm back to its holster and calmly walked into the dining room through the kitchen, calling out, "All clear! Though every room looks like Charlie was living in it with the amount of clutter everywhere."

She thought her jab at Charlie would put everyone at ease, but when she saw the distressed faces staring back at her and the knives they had laid on the table, she changed to a more commanding tone.

"Everything's okay now, team. From what I can see, whoever broke into the house was looking for something specific. What that is, I can't say, but they got out of here when they couldn't find it."

"No, Molly," Sergio said as he handed her the white envelope. "There's something more."

Molly took the letter out of Sergio's hand and started reading. Sergio, Emily, and Charlie could all see her smile fade with each sentence she read. When she got to the last line, she stood silently, staring at the piece of paper. Sensing the three sets of eyes looking at her, waiting for some sort of reassurance, she lifted up her head and said, "You three should have a seat."

Chapter 8

The chairs squeaked against the floor as Sergio, Emily, Charlie, and Molly each grabbed the closest dining chair near to them and sat down.

"Okay," Molly began. "First of all, thank you for calling me so quickly—you did the right thing. I'm glad that you all weren't home when this break-in happened. Second..." She exhaled slowly. "...I think it's time you all learn what specifically I do for Charlie's mom."

The teenagers looked around at one another following Molly's comment, but quickly turned their attention back to her.

"As you know, I joined the director's team eight years ago. I rotated in to cover for another officer who unexpectedly left the Agency. That 'temporary' assignment ended up lasting two years, at which point Charlie's mom created a special position for me within her office in which I could continue working directly for her. For the past six years, that special position has also entailed me working alongside the State Department—well, more specifically, Emily's dad—to help investigate Dr. José's disappearance.

"My new assignment was technically off the books, but the mission was clear: find out who took Dr. José. Evidence of the disappearance was slim, and as you all know, no body was ever recovered. However, two years into the investigation, we found information suggesting that he had been kidnapped by an underground terrorist group operating in Vietnam."

Molly turned to Sergio and placed her hand on his. "There was *very* little to go on, Sergio. We knew he had been taken, but found no specific demands or ransom notes. Mostly just whisperings of what name the group was known by. As you might have guessed by now, that name is written on this piece of paper."

"Casus Belli..." Sergio muttered.

"Yes. Local intel told us this group was responsible for other kidnappings in the area, and their membership likely consisted of former Viet Cong soldiers, but even that detail was shaky. As in the case with Sergio's dad, limited evidence was left behind at the scenes of the other kidnappings to provide better insights into the group's location or motivation. Now, Sergio's mom did show some letters from Dr. José she thought were odd to the director and the secretary. Turns out the letters were—"

"Encoded," Sergio said.

"We just found the letters today, and Charlie was able to decode them. That's actually why we were coming back to Charlie's today," Emily added.

"You three really are quite clever, you know that?" Molly said. "But yes, those letters were a big help in understanding he was indeed kidnapped and had not, for example, gotten lost in the jungle. Without more evidence though, the pace of the investigation became painstakingly slow. I shared anything and everything I could find with the director and the secretary, but we reached a point in the investigation where it felt like we'd need to suspend the search. That is, until a few weeks ago."

"What happened a few weeks ago?" Emily asked.

"One of my in-country contacts found a burned-out WHO truck in the countryside not far from where your parents' famous battle occurred. It was the first solid clue in years to give us a probable location for your dad's kidnapping, Sergio. It took a few weeks to vet the intel and confirm that it actually was the vehicle Dr. José had been traveling in on his trip, but once we did, I shared it with the director, and she informed me she intended to share it with the secretary."

"Maybe that's the conversation you caught the tail end of, Charlie," Emily said.

"It's got to be," Charlie replied.

"Two months ago, when your parents received the invitation to represent the US in Vietnam, they'd already planned on an extended stay in country to try to explore a few possible locations of the kidnapping. They saw the official visit as a way to explore around Vietnam themselves without drawing unnecessary attention. The WHO truck find was a lucky break that helped them pinpoint their search. The real reason I stayed behind in Washington was to share any additional information I could drum up for your parents and to coordinate logistics."

"Did my mom know of this plan?" Sergio asked, "And Charlie's dad and Emily's mom?"

"They knew the high-level details and of course wanted to be there in case Director Tillman and Secretary Lewis found anything, but they don't know specifically about Casus Belli—just that a group kidnapped Dr. José. The director and secretary were not planning on bringing anyone else in your families on their search mission until they got close, though."

The teenagers were silent as if they were trying to process everything they just learned from Molly. Charlie cleared his throat, and then said quietly, "So what does this note mean then?

And how come we didn't see any stories about the kidnapping on the news?

"Unfortunately, it means two things: first, my officers—the security detail protecting your parents—are dead. The only reason they wouldn't have called in the attack on your parents is if they were killed before they got a chance to, so I don't think anyone realizes yet that the kidnapping happened. The second thing is that your parents are in real danger. This ransom note is not a hoax."

"I'm sorry, Molly. What are they even looking for, though?" Emily asked. "Why would my dad or Aunt Ada have this—what does it say on the note—the *đi qua*? I'm assuming that's Vietnamese."

"It is Vietnamese, you're right. That's how I knew this letter was legitimate. The *đi qua*, roughly 'the passage' or the 'go past' in English, is the name for an object that our investigation kept coming across. Nobody at the Agency knows for sure what it does or how it got its name, but it's supposed to be otherworldly, and I mean that literally—my assets in Vietnam say it came from outer space. We assume that it's a piece of a meteorite. Something of that nature, even just a small piece, could go for millions of dollars in the right market, more than enough money to completely change someone's life, or, if what we know of Casus Belli is true, continue funding terrorist activity.

"To your other questions though, Emily—why someone would think your parents had it? In the chaos and destruction of the Vietnam War, there were a lot of war trophies taken. It's not a new phenomenon—people having been looting things from their adversaries for as long as war has existed. But beyond basic mementos, people often steal things of cultural significance as a way to further demoralize their enemies. I'm not saying your parents specifically did that. However, despite the US pulling out of the war without a clear victory, your parents' triumph at the battle brought them a lot of international attention. People who know nothing else of the war know about the Miraculous Three. So maybe because of the war, the prominent roles they've held since, or both, Casus Belli believed that your parents were in possession of the *đi qua*."

"Do they though, Molly?" asked Sergio.

"Let me be clear—whether they have it or not, we are going to use the full resources of the federal government to go get them back. I have the specific coordinates of where your parents were scheduled to be when the kidnapping occurred, and with the location of the WHO vehicle, we can create a targeted search area. We will get them back.

"But with that said, neither Director Tillman nor Secretary Lewis ever mentioned anything to me about having the *đi qua*. When I asked about their time in the war, they told me they'd picked up some enemy rifles and flags to bring home. Pretty standard stuff, and nothing against any rules of war. However, if any of you have heard anything that might indicate otherwise, it could be a massive help. We may be able to negotiate their return more easily with the *đi qua*."

The three looked down at the table while Molly hoped they could remember any key parts of the numerous war stories their parents had shared with them.

"I've never seen anything like that around my house," Sergio said. "I was just up in the attic with my mom a few days ago looking through some of dad's things—those letters we mentioned, specifically—but there wasn't anything that looked like a meteorite. We have all his old military things and medals framed downstairs. So, between those spots, I don't think it's at my house."

"I'm in the same boat," Emily chimed in. "My dad has a lot of old military maps that he got in Vietnam, and definitely a few of those flags you mentioned, but nothing that sounds like the *đi qua* as you've described it. I mean maybe he has something tucked away in his office, but he likes displaying things from the war out in the open. He told me it helps him remember the sacrifice of the troops who didn't make it home."

Molly nodded. "That seems right to me, Emily. I've been to your dad's office a lot and talked with him about his collection. Nothing like the *đi qua*." Molly turned to Charlie. "And I've been in your mom's office the most, but likewise, I've never seen anything there."

"Same here," replied Charlie. "Nothing really out around the house, either."

"Charlie, what about the safe?" Emily asked.

"Thanks Em, you're right," Charlie said. "In all of the commotion, I forgot the whole reason we came over here. Molly, the other day I thought I saw my mom showing Uncle James a dossier on Dr. José. She put it in her safe as I walked in the room. So, after we decoded the letters, we were going to try to get into the safe and get more answers for Sergio. I guess you're aware of that dossier, but maybe there's some additional information we could find in there?"

Molly looked confused for the briefest of moments, but composed herself before replying. "I didn't know Ada—sorry, the director—kept a dossier at home. She told me all of our work would exclusively stay in the office. Do you really think you can get into the safe?"

"I felt more confident before my house was ransacked, but I'm still willing to try if you think it'll help," said Charlie.

"Yes, I absolutely think it will."

There was a cacophony of squeaks as all four dining room chairs scooted back in unison. The group tiptoed over the slew of objects scattered unceremoniously across the home's floors and made their way to the mess awaiting them in Ada's office.

"Alright Charlie, what are we looking for? Where should this safe key be?" asked Molly.

"Well, I told Sergio and Emily earlier that my mom is a fan of hiding important things out in the open. Something she says she learned in the field," Charlie replied.

"That's a good strategy. It's something she taught me as well."

"That means places like desk drawers or cabinets aren't a good place. Luckily our would-be thief already saw to dumping those out for us," Charlie said, scanning the room as he talked, carefully stepping over the items thrown about the floor.

"Knowing my mom, there are a few potential choices. First, the inside of the shredder bin. Why search for things where they would've already been destroyed?" Charlie asked. "Em, could you take the lid off that thing that looks like a trash can please? To your right."

Emily shuffled over to the shredder, took off the lid, and looked inside. "Nothing in the bin, and I don't see anything near the shredding mechanism in the lid."

"Okay, no worries. So, in that case, my second thought is...the fireplace," Charlie said in Sergio's direction. Sergio put his foot up on the brick base of the fireplace and looked inside the flume until Charlie spoke again. "Sorry Serge, not in the fireplace. You see that fire extinguisher to the side?"

Sergio turned his head to the plastic stand on which a small fire extinguisher sat.

"Can you take a look underneath the base of that thing? Looks like there's a small gap," Charlie said.

Sergio lifted up the fire extinguisher, examined the base, and then shook his head at Charlie.

"Okay, okay. Let me think this through—you'd not only want the hiding place to be ordinary, but easily accessible so it's not a pain to get into the safe every time you need to use it." He continued to scan the room until his eyes locked on the large printer sitting on the shelf behind him. "I feel good about this."

Molly watched Charlie as he moved his hands around the printer, studying it for a moment. He slid the internal paper tray out of the printer, removed the paper, and then shouted, "Aha!"

He turned back to the group and held up a thick metal key. "Molly, I'll let you do the honors."

"Great work, Charlie!" Sergio said.

"How did you know it would be in there?" Emily asked.

"My mom rarely prints anything at home, but whenever my dad says that we should take the printer to the recycling center, she always shoots him down," Charlie smiled. "I guess now we know why."

Suddenly a loud *kerchunk* was heard from the back corner of the room. Molly opened the safe door and immediately began perusing its contents. Charlie, Sergio, and Emily joined her at the front of the open safe.

"Is this the dossier you saw?" Molly asked Charlie.

"Yep, that's the one," he confirmed.

She took the dossier over to Ada's desk and flipped through its contents. Inside, Molly picked up a small, faded green field notebook with the words *US Army* written on the front. She started to read through that one first.

"What's that, Molly?" Charlie asked from near the safe.

She flipped through a few pages before responding. "It's your mom's field notes from the days leading up to and immediately following *the* battle. I've never seen this before."

"Wow. She never mentioned she still had that. But I suppose you don't get appointed director without being able to keep a secret."

If his mom could keep documents like this hidden from someone working high up within the CIA, I wonder what other secrets she's guarding... Molly thought before turning her attention back to the open safe, where Sergio and Emily were inspecting its many internal drawers.

In the bottom-most drawer, they found a few gold and silver bars. Moving up, in a slightly smaller drawer, they found what looked like an Army-issued pistol alongside a few boxes of ammunition. In the largest drawer, in the middle of the safe where the dossier had been stored, they found additional documents which, upon a cursory review, appeared to be related to the search in Vietnam. Sergio and Emily each grabbed a document and began to read. Before Charlie could grab one, Molly spoke up from near his mom's desk.

"Okay, I think I've got something interesting here. It's a journal entry from the day after the battle, when your parents were back at base awaiting their next orders." She started reading the entry.

"Sergeants Lewis, Santos, and I have returned back to HQ. I assisted cataloging the cache of documents and items recovered from the enemy outpost. Items detailed future troop movements,

so I'm hopeful that the information will lead to some strategic victories. And especially to honor the lives of those soldiers we lost to recover the information...I don't know that I will ever forget the carnage I witnessed yesterday.

For our efforts, Major Kaywood said he expected General McComb to approve multiple commendations. In the interim, Major Kaywood also said that we could pick an item or two to keep from the recovery site. Sergeant Lewis selected a map which had already been photographed and logged. Sergeant Santos took an NVA medical supply kit he found at the site while looking for supplies. I selected the Viet Cong flag we captured when we finally took the outpost, and had Sergeants Lewis and Santos sign the flag. However, I also took an additional item.

Prior to our exfil from the site, I walked around the battlefield to collect the dog tags of our troops who were KIA. As I approached the body of a Viet Cong soldier, I noticed a small flat metal disk on the ground. It had some kind of design or stylized text in small characters running around the perimeter, but what was most interesting to me was the shine of the metal. I have never seen anything like it—it is matte in appearance, but can reflect the sunlight as brightly as a mirror. And it oddly remains cool to the touch, even after being left in direct sunlight for some time. I'm not familiar with traditional Vietnamese jewelry, but perhaps this was an ornament given to the soldier by his family. In any case, given it has no apparent military purpose, I decided not to report it to the major and will take it with me back home following my deployment.

I expect we will receive our honorable discharges in the next few weeks. It will be nice to leave this war behind us."

"Is it just me, or does that metal disc Aunt Ada described sound a lot like an object from space?" Sergio asked. "Molly? What do you think?"

The group looked back at Molly, who was rereading the description of the object. Without missing a beat, she replied, "Did you three check all of those drawers yet?"

"All but this one up here," Charlie replied. Taking a hint from Molly's stare, he proceeded to open the small top drawer. Inside he found a flat square wooden box with a label printed on top reading *Vietnam*. He took it over to the window near him to inspect it in better lighting. With Molly, Sergio, and Emily staring at his hands, he opened the box.

The shock of the bright light hitting Charlie in the face made him jump back, momentarily confused at what had happened, until he realized that the light in his eyes had been a reflection of the sunlight pouring through the window. When his sight readjusted to the dim light in the room, he saw what he was holding.

"I can't believe it—this is it!" he exclaimed.

"Bring it here!" Molly replied, matching his excitement.

Charlie walked the box over to his mother's desk, with Sergio and Emily joining him and Molly, who took the flat, matte metal disc out of the box and inspected it closely. As she slid her finger over the symbols engraved in the disc, Charlie noticed that she was silently mouthing along, as if she was reading the markings.

"Can we see it?" Emily said before he could say anything.

"Absolutely," Molly replied.

Emily took the disc from Molly's hands and showed it to Sergio.

"It's much heavier than it looks," Emily said, "and I see what Aunt Ada meant about the shine. I've never seen anything like it."

"Molly, you said the *đi qua* was likely a meteorite, right? Isn't there a history of space metals being refined into weapons or..." Sergio paused, inspecting the disc again. "...jewelry? I imagine something like this would be easier to transport and sell than chunks of space rock. Though I bet it probably took a long time to refine it to this point."

"You're not wrong," Molly said. "And an object like this, one that's been refined and decorated, would be significantly more valuable. It's like diamonds—they become more expensive once they're expertly cut and polished." She looked at disc, now currently in Charlie's hands, before saying quietly, "I never thought I'd ever be able to hold that in my hands."

Charlie continued inspecting the disc. "I can't get over how smooth this thing's surface is—there aren't any visible cuts or imperfections hinting at how it might've been smelted and cast."

"I noticed that too, Charlie," Emily said.

"So how are we going to get this to Vietnam?" Sergio asked. "Obviously Casus Belli are going to be willing to trade it for our parents, but I'm guessing there's some kind of protocol for this type of thing."

"There is, and that's exactly why you three can't make the trip with me," Molly replied.

"Hold on, hold on," said Emily, straightening her posture. "They're our parents. We helped find the thing that's going to save them. We should be able to go."

"You read the note, Emily. This isn't like some adventure story—your lives and the lives of your parents are actually in mortal danger. And I'm sorry if this is coming across as harsh or scary, but I need you three to understand the risk. We minimize that risk by getting the *đi qua* to the kidnappers while keeping you all out of harm's way, and in my experience, being an ocean away from your enemy is a pretty effective method to avoid harm."

Emily looked back at her, terrified.

Molly sighed. "Look...you know that I care about all of you, right?"

All three nodded.

"You've made an invaluable contribution to the effort of saving your parents. But when we rescue them—and we will rescue them—what are they going to say to me? 'Molly, thank you so much for bringing our children this close to the terrorists. That was a wise decision befitting someone of your education and experience.'"

"Probably not..." Sergio said.

"No, probably not," Molly said. "In addition to keeping you and your parents safe, I also value keeping my career—for which I've worked very hard—so that I can provide Bilbo with the high quality of life he deserves."

"You need to get this disc to Vietnam *and* keep us safe, right?" Charlie asked. "If you leave the country, who will be around to protect us? Just think about it—if we hadn't been at Sergio's pool today, who knows what would've happened. Like you said, people want us dead, and clearly, they have people in this country who can get to us."

"Yeah!" Emily added, nodding.

Molly considered what Charlie had just said. "You know...I really hate it when you make valid arguments that counteract my points." She started pacing around the office. "Why don't I just lock you three at Langley under guard from a few of our officers then?"

"You could," said Emily, who looked like she was eagerly waiting for her chance to add to Charlie's argument, "but surely somebody is going to ask why the children of the secretary of state, the CIA director, and a missing war hero are in need of guarding, especially when these prominent government figures are currently on a highly publicized tour of Vietnam and nobody knows they've been kidnapped."

"Alright, alright, you've made your point," said Molly, still pacing.

"So, your decision is...what?" Charlie asked.

Molly shook her head. *"If*—and it's a big if at the moment—I get permission from my superiors to do this, this is how it'd go down: we arrive in Vietnam, we make the trek towards Pele Ketan, and then I drop you off with the officers near your parents' resort, where you'll stay with the officers until I personally come back to pick you up. Is that perfectly clear?"

Molly was generally lighthearted with the teenagers, but when she was serious, they knew she meant business.

"Yes," Charlie, Sergio, and Emily replied in unison.

"Good. I'm going to go make a phone call, and then we'll see."

Molly stepped out into the hallway, shutting the office door behind her. She heard the teenagers move close to the door, trying to eavesdrop on her conversation. With the thick door in the way though, she knew they could only barely hear the tones of her voice.

I don't blame them...I would have tried the same thing.

After a few minutes on the phone, Molly reentered the room and delivered the news.

"You have permission to travel with me to Vietnam."

The teenagers let out a loud cheer at the verdict.

"Charlie, go pack a small carry-on bag with a week's worth of clothes. Don't forget your diplomatic passport. Emily and Sergio, when he's done, I'm going to drive all of us to your respective houses where you'll do the same. When we're done, I'm driving us to the airport. We're hitching a ride on a series of diplomatic flights heading that direction tonight."

"Admit it, Molly, you actually think this is a pretty good plan," Sergio said, with a sort of playfulness that was unique to their relationship.

"I won't admit anything," she replied. "But what I will say is that I don't imagine Casus Belli will expect me to keep you three so close. It'll give them less reason to try and catch you."

"Well let's hope they don't need to catch us at all," Emily said.

Charlie could be heard coming downstairs as they walked from the office into the hallway. Molly closed the wooden box containing the metal disc and put it in the zip-up pocket of her windbreaker. "All ready," he said at the base of the stairs. "One thing though. Who's going to take care of the house? I can't leave it like this with the broken door and everything."

"I'll send some Agency guys over to clean and make repairs. We have a team of people for that," Molly replied.

With Molly's assurance that the house would be looked after, the group headed outside, and despite the broken lock, Charlie made an effort to wedge his front door closed.

After the teenagers piled into Molly's car, Molly backed the car out of the driveway and made the turn towards Emily's house. Then Charlie's home slipped out of view, and Molly wasn't sure what would come next.

Chapter 9

The whir of the C-40C's jet engines provided a soothing white noise throughout the cabin that Emily appreciated after the past twenty-four hours. What had started as a normal day at the pool ended with her sitting on a practically brand-new diplomatic plane to Ramstein Air Force Base with her two best friends and the increasingly mysterious Molly Pak. While her parents had flown west to Vietnam, Emily and her compatriots had to go the long way around through Europe. They arrived in Germany early the next morning, and after a quick meal and shower on base as the plane refueled, the group reboarded the jet with a fresh slew of diplomats and government workers for their next overnight flight to Da Nang.

She knew that most diplomats had to fly commercial, so without her dad or Charlie's mom present, Molly had to have pulled some serious strings to get the four of them on these flights. Emily looked down at her watch—they were only five hours into the eleven-hour flight to Vietnam.

Despite her exhaustion and the luxurious accommodations which the new diplomatic aircraft provided (*this might be nicer than my dad's plane*), Emily could not fall asleep. As she shuffled in her chair, breathing in the fresh leather smell emanating from her seat as she moved, the sharp contrast between her current comfort and the misery of those who'd been kidnapped was not lost on her. Her thoughts were first and foremost with her parents. She trusted her dad's and Aunt Ada's experience in the field—especially in Vietnam—and knew that Molly was going to do everything within the Agency's power to get them back safely. However, Emily couldn't shake the terror of something happening to her family.

Likewise though, she could not stop thinking about the metal disc sitting in Molly's black travel bag. In her restlessness, she tried to unravel the enigma surrounding the *đi qua* and why Casus Belli were so willing to kill for it. Conceptually she understood the item's worth (if it was indeed made from rare minerals), but struggled to imagine how something so small could bring so much chaos into her world.

Emily was no stranger to world conflicts, especially those over resources. It was the bulk of her father's work, and he always mentioned the latest crises to Emily and her mom at the dinner table. But as she only got the snippets he had clearance to share, there was always a distance between her and the subject matter, which led to the stories feeling academic.

This current crisis was real, though. Tangible.

All those hours I spent at the library and model UN don't really seem helpful now.

As a good student and overachiever in high school, she was typically confident (Sergio and Charlie would say "cocky") in her knowledge and choices. But everything she'd experienced in the past three days was humbling her. Out in the real world and without her parents, she was being put to the test.

And there's no study guide for this.

As she stared at bulkhead of the plane in front of her seat, she heard something rustling behind her. She turned around, and in the dimmed cabin lighting, she saw Charlie and Sergio thumbing through a 2001 edition of the CIA World Factbook.

"You two couldn't sleep either, huh?" Emily asked in a hushed voice over the back of her plush seat.

Sergio replied, "Barring the fact that we drank probably a liter each of German soda on base—"

"It's got real cane sugar in it!" Charlie softly butted in, still coming down from his sugar rush.

"—we were both too mentally preoccupied with what's going to go down in Vietnam when we land."

"Same here," said Emily.

"I'm glad Charlie thought to grab this book before we left."

"Obviously the facts they have for the different countries are great, but these books also always contain detailed maps. I figured that'd be useful, too," Charlie replied.

He flipped to the Asia section of the Factbook and found a map of the Indochina Peninsula. The subsequent page had a zoomed-in map specifically focused on Vietnam.

"My dad has a map where he's pinned the locations of all of his unit's battles," Emily said, "so I recognize a few of the names. But his map was produced during the Vietnam War. Nice to see a modern one."

Sergio put his finger on the map and traced the path from Hanoi to Da Nang, and then over towards Cambodia. He tapped his finger when he stopped on Pele Ketan, and, looking at Charlie and Emily, said, "That's where we're heading."

"I've personally always preferred globes to get the scale right," Molly murmured, "but I suppose they're a bit more cumbersome to carry around than a paper map."

Emily turned back to the seat next to her where Molly was sitting.

"I thought you were asleep this whole time!"

"I was," Molly replied. "One of the benefits of extended time in the field is that you learn how to catch up on sleep wherever and whenever possible." She winked at Emily, who smiled back at her.

"Charlie, Sergio, and I were just talking about what our plan of action is for when we arrive in Da Nang," Emily said.

Molly rubbed her eyes to wake up, then folded out the oversized tray table from her chair's armrest. Through the gap between her and Emily's seat, she turned to Charlie and Sergio. "Why don't you two join us up here. Bring the map."

Sergio and Charlie unbuckled their seat belts and came around to the bulkhead area in front of Emily and Molly, placing the map on the open table. Molly gestured at the foldout footrests in front of them which doubled as additional seating, and as they flipped the seats down, Molly began.

"We'll be touching down in Da Nang in about five or so hours. Unlike in Germany, we're landing at a civilian airport this time, so you won't have a chance to shower until you arrive at the makeshift HQ set up in the area neighboring your parents' resort. I'd recommend changing clothes and freshening up in the plane bathroom here before we land. It'll be a few hours on the ground before you'll get the chance for a proper bathroom experience.

"We'll then clear passport control relatively quickly with our diplomatic credentials, even with your emergency-use one, Sergio. Just follow Emily. She's done this a bunch and knows the process."

"It's pretty easy honestly," Emily replied.

Molly nodded. "Once we're on the ground, we'll connect with Officer Omar Peterson. He's been the director's and my main in-country contact for years now, and he knows nearly as much about

Dr. José's disappearance as I do. He's also the one who helped the director and the secretary gear up before they headed into the jungle from the resort.

"He'll be driving us towards Pele Ketan, but obviously time is of the essence here in order to rescue your parents—we're going to try to make the six-and-a-half-hour drive in one go with only essential breaks. From there, I'll rendezvous with a few others from the security HQ who will join me on the trek through the jungle towards the area where we believe your parents are being held. Finally, once I've confirmed their location, I'll radio for backup to pick us up."

"This sounds oddly like our parents' mission thirty years ago," Charlie said.

"The greatest way to learn is from experience, right?" Molly replied. "You're not wrong, though. They're in almost the same area where they fought and they're once again relying on the success of a stealth mission for their safe return. But the good thing is we have a lot more advantages than when they fought: we're not at war, we have better technology, and we have what Casus Belli want the most—the *di qua*."

Charlie nodded.

"Is Officer Peterson going with you in the field?" Sergio asked.

"No. I want him staying with you three to keep you safe. He's got a lot of experience from his time in the military, and on top of him being inside in our operation here, he's one of the people I trust most at the CIA. If you three stick by him, he'll protect you."

"But he's not as funny as you, right, Molly?" Emily asked sarcastically.

"Nobody is, unfortunately. Makes things a bit dull at times, you know?" Molly replied with an even tone, though Emily could see the smile forming at the edges of her lips as she tried to keep a straight face.

"Now once we reach HQ, Officer Peterson will show you around and make sure you're comfortable. I'll also be in direct communication with him throughout my rescue mission—no need for any radio silence like when your parents were fighting." Molly moved her hand and patted her coat pockets. "Do one of you have a pen or marker I can borrow?"

"I've got one," said Emily, fishing a black permanent marker out of her bag and handing it to Molly.

"Charlie, do you mind?" asked Molly, pointing to his Factbook map with the marker.

"Not at all. We have a million copies of these at home," he replied.

"Thanks," Molly said as she uncapped the marker in her hands and began to draw. "Okay, this is the route we're taking from Da Nang to Pele Ketan." She circled Da Nang's airport on the map, then drew a long line following Highway CT02 towards the city located not far from Cambodia's border. "This," she said in a hushed voice, circling an area farther into the jungle, "is where the battlefield is. And over here"—she added another circle—"is where we believe your parents were kidnapped."

Charlie, Sergio, and Emily could see how close the circled areas were to each other on the map.

"Geographically speaking, those areas, and where we suspect your parents are being held, aren't too far away from one another. However, the jungle there is pretty thick, not to mention that there are still a lot of undocumented tunnels from the war. That's in part how we think Casus Belli have been able to remain in hiding for so long. In any case, it'll be slow going, but don't worry, my team and

I will have plenty of time to find your parents before the seven days are up."

Molly put the cap back on the marker, folded up the map, and handed each item back to its respective owner.

"When this is all over, I promise we'll have a real sit-down and share everything that Secretary Lewis, Director Tillman, and I have learned over the years. And after their ordeal, you three will be a welcome surprise for your parents for sure. Now," she said, shifting in her seat, "I recommend you all try to get some rest. I think the flight attendants serve breakfast about ninety minutes before we land, so you'll have time then to eat and change. Okay?"

All three of them nodded.

"Okay good," Molly said as she folded her tray table back into its armrest storage area. Charlie and Sergio flipped up the footrests behind them and made their way back to the row of seats behind Emily and Molly, and Emily turned around and saw Sergio turning off the reading lights above Charlie and himself, signaling that they were actually going to try and sleep. As Emily turned around and sat back in her seat, she looked over at Molly to ask her a question— but Molly was already fast asleep. Emily smiled and shook her head, jealous of how easily her travel companion made resting on planes look.

Then Emily turned off her own reading light, reclined her chair, and took one look at her watch before letting the white noise and pressurized air in the cabin lull her into an uneasy sleep.

Five and a half hours to go.

Chapter 10

The plane's massive wheels screeched as they made contact with the hot tarmac at Da Nang International Airport, and a woman's voice came through the cabin over the intercom. "Good morning, folks, this is Major Bradley. I want to be the first to welcome you to Da Nang, where the local time is 0 seven hundred hours. Current weather is a pleasant twenty-eight degrees centigrade."

Some noises from the interior of the cockpit could be heard over the intercom before Major Bradley continued.

"We will be arriving at Gate A1, alpha one, where a shuttle bus will be waiting to take you to the diplomatic and crew passport control area. Once through, pre-hired cars and shuttles will be waiting just outside the doors of baggage claim. Taxis are just to the left. I hope you had an enjoyable flight—it was certainly our pleasure flying you here—and we wish you productive travels ahead here in Vietnam. Again, good morning, and welcome to Da Nang."

Sergio lifted up his window shade and got his first glimpse of Vietnam as the intercom crackled off. Heavy commercial aircraft were taxiing on the runway to his right, and beyond the planes, the sun hung low over some far mountains. His parents always made a point to travel for vacation, even after his dad disappeared, wanting Sergio to experience other cultures firsthand. He had seen a great deal of the world, almost as much as Charlie and Emily, but had never seen Vietnam. The place had always been present in his mind, perpetually dancing through his thoughts—and now, finally, here he was looking at it. He could hardly believe it.

It made him miss his dad, and made him worry about his mother's safety that much more.

As Molly had promised, making it through diplomatic security was significantly faster than his experience with passport control as a tourist. Within twenty minutes of stepping off the plane, he, Charlie, Molly, and Emily were walking past baggage claim towards the passenger pickup area outside. When the terminal's automatic doors opened, the warm, humid air hit Sergio's skin. "Compared to Washington, this really isn't too bad," he told Charlie.

"Isn't too bad *yet*," Charlie replied with a wink.

As Sergio followed Molly, he noticed she was leading them past the rows of chauffeur-driven cars that the other diplomats on their flight seemed to be using.

"Hey Molly, did the consular office send a car for us?" Emily asked.

"No. Omar—Officer Peterson—is picking us up himself so we can make our way straight from here," Molly replied.

They walked until they neared the regular-arrivals parking lot, where Sergio saw a man leaning against a slightly scuffed white vehicle. He couldn't quite make out the model of the vehicle but noticed dozens of similar cars in the parking lot. When Molly continued walking straight towards him, Sergio deduced that this was Officer Peterson.

"Hey Molly, how was the flight?" Omar asked as the group came within a few yards of the vehicle. He was a stern-looking man, probably a product of his years of service both in the military and at the Agency, but like Molly, appeared surprisingly youthful for his age.

"It was good, Omar, thanks." She gave him a long handshake, then reached inside her duffle bag and pulled out a bag of candy, tossing it to him.

"German gummy bears! They really just have better flavors over there. Thanks for grabbing me some on your short stint on base," Omar said.

"I know they're your favorite. Almost grabbed the American version from the Postal Exchange by accident, but the clerk steered me straight," she replied, then turned to the three teenagers. "Folks, I want to introduce you to Officer Peterson. Omar, meet Emily, Sergio, and Charlie, Ada's son."

"It's nice to finally meet you all," Omar said. "I've heard so much about each of you I feel like I know you all already."

The teenagers smiled in reply.

"As requested, I got them to pack light so we can all fit in the car," Molly said.

"Thanks, Molly. It may be a little tight, but we've got space in the back here. You all can leave your bags there and go ahead and get situated in the car. I've got the air-conditioning running already," said Omar, making his way to the back of the car.

As the three shifted their duffle bags off their shoulders and placed them near the now-open trunk, Sergio waited for a moment. He took a deep breath, and as the smell of warm grass and jet fuel hit his nostrils, he looked at his surroundings.

I can't believe I'm finally here.

Sergio made his way towards the left-side back door that Emily and Charlie had climbed through already. He noticed Charlie had chosen the middle seat.

"I made Charlie play rock paper scissors for the middle seat, but as you know, I'm incredible at it. The result," Emily said with a grin, "well...you can see for yourself."

"You hustled me, huh? Is that what our friendship means to you?" Charlie asked.

"Don't worry, Chuck, I'll rotate with you during one of the pit stops, because I'm a *real* friend," Sergio replied, sending a cheeky smile in Emily's direction while he pulled the passenger door shut. Emily laughed while a visibly grumpy Charlie squeezed into the middle seat.

As they joked, Sergio glanced up at the rearview mirror and watched as Omar loaded the last of the luggage into the open trunk area behind them. While shuffling items around to make space, Omar slid a long, hard-shell case towards the back of the car. He opened the lid, showed Molly the contents, and quickly refastened the case's lid. Then, shutting the trunk, he talked to Molly out of earshot of the teenagers. Her expression turned more stoic as he spoke, but Sergio couldn't make out what the two of them were saying. After a moment, Omar and Molly walked to the driver's and front passenger seats respectively and entered the vehicle.

"You all ready? Everyone buckled?" Molly said as she looked in the rearview mirror. "And sorry to see that Emily hustled you, Charlie. You should know better by now than to let her trick you into a game of rock paper scissors."

Sergio and Emily laughed, and even Charlie let loose a small smile.

"We're good to go," Sergio said.

And at Sergio's word, Officer Peterson put the car in gear.

◇◇◇◇◇

Once the group had gotten away from the airport and suburbs of Da Nang, the mountains Sergio saw through the plane's windows were coming to life in front of him. The emerald hills rolled by as the car passed rice field after rice field, following the bends and curves of Highway CT02. Although Emily and Charlie had nodded off in the seat next to him, Sergio was captivated by the vibrant colors of the passing Vietnamese countryside .

"I can't believe how beautiful everything is here," he murmured to Molly and Omar.

"It really is," said Molly, staring as intently out the window as Sergio. "I'm happy that most of the vegetation has come back. There was so much destruction here during the war. Bombings...Fires...It tore up the landscape. Just awful."

"I've read there are parts of France and Belgium that are still scarred from World War I, even though it's been almost a hundred years since the fighting stopped. Glad it isn't like that here," Sergio said. "Officer Peterson, did you choose to come here to Vietnam or were you just assigned this post?"

"I chose it when the position came open," replied Omar, glancing back and forth between the road and the rearview mirror. "Like you, my family has a strong connection to this place. When the opportunity to work here presented itself, I couldn't turn it down. It's what my parents wanted for me, too. And please, call me Omar."

"He's been invaluable to the investigation into your dad's disappearance, too," Molly told Sergio. "A lot of what we talked about at Charlie's house—the knowledge we have on the kidnappers, their motivations, everything—came directly from his work."

"I...I don't know what to say. Thank you for your help," Sergio said.

"Trust me, Sergio, I want to bring Casus Belli to justice as much as you do," Omar said. "The pain they cause to this part of the world needs to end. And with the *di qua*, we'll be able to flush them out."

Omar's reply confused Sergio—he didn't think that he or his friends had spoken directly to Omar about the ransom note or the *di qua*. *I'm probably just jet-lagged...surely someone mentioned it.* Sergio was just thankful that he had a team of people who were dedicated to helping him and his friends get their parents home safely.

The car continued on until they had been driving for about three hours or so, when Molly decided it was time for a short lunch stop. Though Omar purchased a few snacks for the group prior to their departure—protein bars, granola, and fresh fruit—the teenagers and Molly gobbled them up before they had even made it out of Da Nang. Sensing their hunger, Omar agreed that a proper meal was in order and pulled over to a small roadside stand near Thác Đắk Chè. The car rocked into park as he pulled the emergency brake up, waking Emily and Charlie up in the process. The group got out of the car and sat at a table overlooking the large waterfall. They felt the spray of water in the breeze as they enjoyed papaya salad and bowls of spicy beef noodle soup.

Like himself, Sergio knew that Emily and Charlie were stretched to their limits. Between finding out their parents were missing, flying to the other side of the world at a moment's notice, and jet lag, the teenagers were trying their best to keep up and not snap at one another. Judging by the looks on his friends' faces, Sergio could tell that the break for some warm food had certainly helped.

◇◇◇◇◇

Wrapping up their early lunch, the group packed themselves back into the car. Much to Charlie's delight, Sergio dutifully honored his earlier offer to switch seats. Sergio didn't mind.

Easier to see the road in front of us, anyway.

As they continued down the highway, the hillsides became progressively more forested. Sergio saw the thick jungle vegetation growing with each mile that passed underneath the car's tires.

After three more hours of driving, according to his watch, Sergio looked over Charlie's shoulder and saw the Sa Thầy River flowing down below them on the highway. From Charlie's map, he knew that the river formed part of the Cambodian border with Vietnam.

They were close to their destination.

Almost as if on cue, Omar flipped on the turn signal and steered the car towards an exit ramp leading them off the highway. With only a simple roundabout waiting at the end of the exit, Omar barely decelerated the vehicle as he looped them around the curve to turn left. While plenty of cars had passed them on the highway during the drive, Sergio noticed that there were no other cars on the country road they now cruised. Tall trees hung near each side of the road, blocking any view farther into the jungle. Where he had before seen mountains and rivers, Sergio now only saw thick vegetation. They were moving farther and farther away from any clear signs of civilization.

After twenty minutes, Omar turned the car off the main paved road to one of dirt and gravel.

"Is this a shortcut to the HQ?" Charlie asked.

"Most people coming to this area head up from Ho Chi Minh City on another main highway, so the government has less of a desire to spend money to keep this route paved," Molly said.

Sergio noticed she was gripping something near the side of her leg, which after a few moments he realized was her sidearm. She was looking out the window now, more frantically than she had earlier in the day, scanning either side of the road. Sergio also heard the car's engine revving.

Omar had picked up the pace.

Sensing that something was off, Sergio looked through the window on Emily's side of the car and watched the tree line beside them. Between the small gaps in vegetation, blurring due to the car's increased speed, Sergio caught deeper glimpses into the jungle. Birds perched on branches, insects flew in the warm air, and for a moment, it almost looked like there was the outline of a man staring at the car.

Wait a minute...that can't be right.

Sergio's turned himself back towards the rear window to look for the man again, but before his eyes could fully focus on the jungle, a blinding flash of light shined out from the edge of the tree line. In an instant, the electronics in the vehicle shut off and the car began barreling out of control.

"Hold on!" screamed Omar, grappling with the steering wheel that had suddenly lost its power steering. Using all of his strength, he strained to keep the vehicle on the road while slamming on the currently non-power-assisted brakes. Sergio felt the car fighting against its own momentum, only barely responding to Omar's efforts to slow them down.

Just as the car began to lose velocity, it hit a patch of loose dirt and gravel, thrusting the car into a skid. The car drifted to the left slide of the road and with a loud *thump,* crashed into a tree, and all of the passengers were thrown hard against their seat belts as the car came to a complete stop.

Chapter 11

While the seat belt had largely done its job holding him to his seat, Charlie's ears were blaring from the impact of his head hitting the headrest in front of him. When he finally managed to open his eyes again, he saw stars. In his confusion, he looked over at Sergio and Emily. Both looked banged up, but generally fine. He heard a muffled shout coming from the front of the car, and in the rearview mirror he could see Omar's lips moving.

"Is...back...?" Charlie thought he was saying, reading his lips.

"Is everyone doing okay back there?" Omar shouted again, Charlie hearing the full sentence this time.

"We're okay back here," Emily said frantically. "Are you two okay?"

"We're okay. We're both okay," Molly replied.

Charlie assessed the damage in front of him—the entire forward part of the car was wrapped around a tree. Charlie noticed trails of wispy white smoke coming from underneath the car's damaged hood. Thanks to Omar's efforts in slowing them down, the tree damage didn't appear to go any farther into the vehicle. His driving had saved their lives.

"What the hell was that?" Sergio asked. "I thought I saw someone in the woods, and there was this bright flash of light, and then—"

"You saw someone?" Molly asked pointedly.

"Only a glimpse of what looked like a man standing just past the road in the vegetation," Sergio replied, turning to look around, "way back there."

Molly and Omar looked at one another before she continued. "You three, get out of the vehicle slowly. On Charlie's side."

Charlie opened his passenger door and was beginning to slide out of his seat towards the vegetation on his side of the car when rapid, loud metallic *pop pop pop* noises came from the other side of the road.

"Get out now and lay down!" Omar screamed as he also exited the vehicle, pulling his sidearm out of its holster. All three teenagers threw themselves out and took cover against the side of the car.

Molly drew her weapon and after exiting the car, came running around to join them. Both she and Omar started firing rounds into the jungle in the direction of their assailant's automatic gunfire.

His heart pounding, Charlie heard the rapid whizzing sounds of the bullets from as they passed over the car. He crouched down further, and from his position on the ground, he saw four pairs of legs creeping closer to the car.

"What can you see, Charlie?!" shouted Emily, wiping sweat from her forehead.

"It looks like there's a couple of them!" he shouted back, then crouched again to carefully take a look around the back of the car. There were four men standing in the road shooting at them, with a fifth shouting orders at the group from his position slightly further behind in the jungle. Two of the men held AK-47s—he recognized the infamous rifle's distinct shape and banana clip from the Vietnam War books he'd read—but the other two held weapons he couldn't quite place. They looked like conventional sniper rifles but had a distinctive glowing purple line running down their silver metal barrels. As they inched closer, Charlie thought he saw the purple line emitting sparks, pulsing rhythmically.

Suddenly one of the men holding the unidentified weapon took aim at their car and pulled the trigger. Charlie felt a static charge in the air, and turning around, he saw a small purplish fire burning in the side of a nearby tree. As it faded, he saw what looked like electric discharge lines emanating from the epicenter of the impact—almost as if the tree had been struck by a bolt of lightning. The man holding the weapon adjusted its small scope, then fired it in fast succession as his compatriots laid down suppressing fire with their AK-47s. The rounds were hitting the car with greater frequency now.

Molly and Omar rushed to take further cover behind the car, discarding their empty magazines on the ground beside them.

"I'm down to my last clip," Omar said loudly over the sound of gunfire. "You?"

"I'm out," Molly replied as Charlie, Emily, and Sergio looked on.

"I think it's time then."

Molly sighed, then nodded. "I didn't want to do this, but you're right."

She paused as Omar stood a bit higher and fired a few rounds towards their attackers, then turned to the teenagers. "Charlie, without standing up, can you open the car door and reach the lever for the back seat?"

Charlie gave Molly a confused look, but dutifully opened the car door currently acting as another barrier between them and the barrage of fire. He peeked inside and saw the lever to lower the seat, then turned back to Molly. "I think I can reach it."

"Okay, here's what I need you to do," she said. "While still crouched, you're going to flip down the seat. Once you do, I need you to feel around for that long hard-shell case in the trunk. One of its handles should be close to your seat. If you can reach it, give the case a yank and pull it out of the car. Understood?"

Charlie nodded and carefully reached inside the car, but a sudden spray of bullets forced him to duck back out of the car. After some suppressing fire from Omar, Charlie reached back in and managed to flip the seat down. Wiggling his hand through the open space to the trunk, he felt his bag, then Emily's bag. "I can't find it!" he shouted.

"You can do this." Molly said.

Charlie once more leaned into the car, and stretching his hand out as far as he could, he felt the cold plastic of the handle at the ends of his fingertips.

"I've got it!" he exclaimed as he curled his hand around the handle. The case was much lighter than he expected as he dragged it inch by inch out of the car door. When it was halfway out, Sergio and Emily yanked Charlie back to safety, yanking the case out of the car and over towards Molly and Omar in the process. Charlie kicked the door shut with his foot and scrambled over a large exposed tree root behind the car towards a better piece of cover.

Molly set the case down beside her, and with one more sigh, unlocked all of its latches. She opened the case's lid, and when Charlie saw what was inside, he gasped.

She pulled out a silver rifle from the protective foam liner inside the case, and with a twist of the weapon's handle, an electric purple light emitted from its side. Charlie heard the humming from the rifle and noticed the purple plasma buzzing around its barrel. She tossed the rifle to Omar and grabbed another from the case for herself.

"What...How, Molly?" stuttered Charlie.

She gave him a sympathetic look, then pulled silver cylinders out of the bag, handing one each to Emily, Sergio, and Charlie. They looked like the claves his drummer friends used in band class.

"If they get too close," Molly said, "I'm gonna need you to give the top of this a hard twist, sort of like a pepper shaker, and then throw it as far as you can in their direction. But not until I say so, okay?"

All three of them nodded.

"But who are they?" Emily asked.

"Casus Belli."

Molly then stood and joined Omar in firing her rifle at the attackers. Their increased firepower forced the enemy soldiers to take defensive positions. With each shot Molly and Omar fired, Charlie felt the hair on his arms stand up. He couldn't believe the awesome power that had been sitting mere feet behind him in the trunk of their car the entire drive from Da Nang, nor could he understand why both Casus Belli and Omar and Molly had the same weapons.

As two of the soldiers moved closer to their crashed car, Molly turned her head towards the teenagers and shouted, "Emily, get yours ready!"

Emily crouched, holding the cylinder in her hands.

"Now!" Molly screamed.

Emily gave the cylinder a hard twist, and using her upper body strength from years of swimming, threw it twenty yards—

precisely at the feet of the soldiers. It gave a loud electric crackle, with a purple light brightening the forested road. Charlie heard shrieks coming from the area where the cylinder had landed, followed by the sound of rifles and tree limbs crashing to the ground.

"Nice work, Em!" Molly said.

Emily returned to her covered position behind the car, hands slightly shaking from the adrenaline.

"Molly, there! By the tree line!" shouted Omar.

She turned her rifle towards the edge of the road, scanning from left to right, then pulled the trigger, and Charlie heard a man groan. By Charlie's count, that only left one more soldier in the street, plus the man he had seen farther back in the jungle.

"Molly, you're incredible!" Sergio shouted.

She turned back to smile at the teenagers when an immense *CRACK* rang out from the woods.

And Charlie saw a spot of red blossoming out from Molly's shirt, above her chest, near her shoulder blade.

"Molly, no!" screamed Emily.

"Omar, help!" shouted Sergio, getting Omar's attention.

Molly touched her shoulder with her left hand and Charlie could see the thick blood coating her fingers. She put her back against the car door and started to slump down to the ground. Omar turned his head and saw his friend slowly bleeding out.

"Oh god..." Omar said, before snapping back to the chaos in front of him. "Charlie, tie your jacket around her shoulder, under her armpit and around. Sergio, see that stick? Grab that too. The two of you are going to use it to make a tourniquet. I want you to make it as tight as you possibly can."

Omar's eyes darted across the trees, looking for the solider who'd taken the shot. "If the tourniquet doesn't hurt her a bit when you tie it, it's not tight enough."

As Sergio scrambled towards the edge of the woods, Omar fired off a few rounds while Charlie threw off his jacket and, with Emily's help, gently leaned the now-shaking Molly forward to wrap it around her. Charlie had seen enough war documentaries to know she was going into shock.

"Just hold on, Molly, you're going to be fine, you're going to be fine..." Charlie said, trying to reassure himself just as much as he was her. Sergio returned with a stick and the teenagers began tightening their makeshift tourniquet. Molly hollered in pain as they twisted the stick more and more. Charlie could see blood starting to soak through the jacket on her shoulder.

"*Cá nhỏ!*" Molly shouted up to Omar, who was firing rounds from his rifle. "*Cá nhỏ*—you can't take them to HQ anymore. You have to take them to Núi Giàu."

Omar glanced at Molly while trying to keep his eyes on the tree line. "We talked about this, *bà chủ*. We can still keep to the original plan."

"No," she shouted weakly. "We didn't think we'd have this much resistance, and it's clear they've gotten stronger. Take the kids to Núi Giàu—it's the only way to keep the *đi qua* safe."

Emily, Charlie, and Sergio were staring at Molly in utter confusion.

"There are two of them left. I'll take care of them and then we'll all go," Omar shot off.

"There are two left *at the moment*, but we don't know if there'll be more. We don't have a way to outrun them anymore..." Molly groaned in pain. "I'm done, but I've still got enough in me to keep them distracted for a while."

Emily, Sergio, and Charlie were frozen, speechless at what they were hearing.

Omar gave Molly a grave look. "This wasn't what we signed up for, *bà chủ.*"

"You'll be okay. You're ready," she said, then turned to the three teenagers.

"Kids...remember what I said to you in Washington? I still mean it now... I love you all."

Charlie felt tears well in his eyes.

"Follow Omar, and trust him. He knows what to do," she continued.

"We love you, Molly!" Emily shouted over the enemy gunfire, openly weeping alongside nods of agreement from Sergio and Charlie.

"And we'll take care of Bilbo for you," Charlie sniffled.

Molly gave them a soft smile, and they each gave her a hug, careful to avoid her wound.

"Sergio, Charlie, give Molly those cylinders back, and grab the bags out of the back," Omar said before shooting off a few more rounds in the direction of some AK-47 fire.

They each put their cylinders next to Molly as Omar gently pulled her into a standing position. She balanced herself with her rifle, giving him a reassuring look, and the two stared at each other for a few seconds.

Then she sighed, and murmured, "It's time for you all to go."

Omar nodded, then picked up his and Molly's bags, while Emily, Charlie, and Sergio each grabbed their own.

"We need to leave," Omar said. "Now."

Chapter 12

Charlie, Sergio, and Emily ran for almost twenty minutes straight before Omar agreed to let them rest for a moment.

Everything had happened so quickly.

Emily tried to play back the events in her head: one moment they were riding peacefully through the back roads of Pele Ketan, and in an instant, Molly was being left to die on the road behind them.

Poor Molly, Emily thought, unsure of how to process her grief. She felt like crying but couldn't seem to form more tears.

And now they were running through the Vietnamese jungle with a man they'd known for no more than ten hours, headed to a place she'd never heard of before.

What did Molly call him? Cá nhỏ? *More Vietnamese...*

Charlie and Sergio joined Emily on a log after washing their faces in the stream nearby. Both were silent, seemingly as confused and emotionally broken as Emily. Omar was off patrolling the immediate area around the stream, out of earshot of the teenagers.

"Do you guys remember the name of where we're being taken?" Emily asked, breaking the silence.

"Núi Giàu," said Sergio, not breaking his gaze at the ground in front of him as he put two fingers to his throat to check his pulse.

Charlie reached into his bag to grab the World Factbook map. *Forming a plan has always been his coping mechanism,* Emily thought. As he folded it open, she saw the markings Molly had drawn for them on the plane.

"This is where we were originally going," said Charlie, pointing to one of the circles scribbled in Sharpie on the page. "But this is where we were knocked off the road. I saw a mile marker just before we pulled onto the dirt road." Emily could see they were nowhere close to the temporary CIA/State Department security headquarters.

"It's late afternoon, right?" she replied. "Judging by where the sun is, my guess is we've been traveling northeast since we left the car." *It was hard to tell with all of the overhead vegetation, though.* "So that should put us...here." She pointed to another circle—the one for the battlefield on which her dad had barely survived.

"I don't see Núi Giàu written anywhere near here," Charlie said.

"Maybe it's a local name for another place. Or maybe I got our direction wrong. I'm not an expert, Charlie," Emily said, kicking a rock near her.

"No, you read the map correctly. It could just have another name," Charlie said. "But what I was getting at is that this Núi Giàu has got to be tiny. This map is fully accurate, and the CIA usually tries to include the local spellings of locations, but realistically, it won't have every little village or hamlet."

"Maybe Molly wanted us to go there specifically because it's so small. If Casus Belli aren't aware that it exists, then they can't track us down," Emily said.

"If that's the case, why was Omar so reluctant to take us there?" asked Sergio, lifting his head out of his hands and looking at Emily and Charlie. "I'm still not sure about him."

"You're right to be cautious," Emily said. "We don't know him. But Molly specifically said to trust him, and that's enough for me."

"It's enough for me too, I suppose," Sergio said.

"There is one thing I can't make sense of, though..." Charlie muttered.

"The laser rifle that Omar and Molly were using?" Sergio asked, and Emily nodded in agreement.

"Well, that's a mystery, too," Charlie replied. "I know the military loves hiring contractors to make crazy new weapons, so maybe they got their hands on something experimental. I don't know. But more specifically, what I can't figure out is why the Casus Bellis soldiers had similar weapons."

"What do you mean?" Emily asked.

"I don't think you two could see it from where we were taking cover behind the car, but I could actually see the men shooting at us. Two of them were using old AK-47s. Nothing special. But the other two...they were using, what did you call them, Sergio? Laser rifles?"

Sergio shrugged. "It's the most creative name I've got right now."

"Regardless," Charlie continued, "the other two soldiers had laser rifles that looked almost identical to what Molly and Omar had. Maybe a bit older or outdated, but operating on the same technology. Certainly way more advanced than anything I've ever seen."

"I mean, the simplest explanation is usually the best, right?" Emily said. "Maybe the same contractor sold it to different groups. Or maybe Casus Belli just stole it from someone. Could make sense as to why they only had two."

"Good point, Em," said Sergio, noticing Omar walking back to the group. "We'll figure this out though, Charlie. We figured out the code in my dad's letters, we can do this."

Omar approached them, still holding on to Molly's bag. He hadn't put it down since he grabbed it from the car. "We should probably get going. We're not far now."

"We're set to move, Omar. But I have to ask, where are we actually going?" asked Sergio, who looked down at his watch. "We've got less than five days now to rescue our parents."

Omar took a deep breath. "Where we're going, they'll be able to help. Look...I'll be honest, this was not part of the plan. Molly had worked it all out, but now we're basically improvising. She'd..." He paused. It was clear to Emily that Molly's death had affected Omar as much as it had her and her friends. "She'd been working this whole thing for years and was close to seeing it through. But we've come this far, and I still think we can end it the way she intended. We can get your parents back."

With that, all three teenagers grabbed their bags and started walking behind Omar deeper into the jungle. He kept his laser rifle ready in his hands the entire time, scanning the trees as they walked.

After ten minutes, they entered a clearing in the dense vegetation with a pair of trees, so symmetrical and evenly spaced they appeared to have been planted, at its center. Other than a lack of moss or grass near their trunks, however, there was nothing else that distinguished the trees from others in the jungle. Omar had been adamant that the teenagers walk between the trees and not around them. They certainly weren't near any specific trail or road, so Emily was a bit confused at the request, but honored it anyways.

As the group continued walking straight through the path beyond the twin trees, Emily noticed the vegetation was growing thicker on either side of them. Not just thicker—taller too. The path began to snake from left to right, often making it difficult to see more than a few yards ahead of Omar who was in the front of the group. The parallel walls of vegetation, now ten feet tall, were hiding everything else from view.

After one large bend to the left, the path both straightened and widened, and that was when Emily saw it.

About a hundred yards in front of her, Emily laid her eyes on a large, ornate stone gateway. The walls of the gate were inlaid with decorative red and yellow bricks laid in diagonal lines, and the gate itself—two solid stone doors—appeared to be inlaid with a silverish metal, forming a perfect circle split across both sides of the gate. A torch adorned each side of the main gate wall, adding light to the path which was naturally darkened by the high rows of vegetation leading to the gate. And just above the torches, she saw a large gatehouse which extended to either side of the path and past the vegetation on both sides. She had never seen anything quite like it in her life, and by the looks on her friends' faces, neither had they.

As they approached the gate, Emily noticed a series of engravings around the gate arch—they looked familiar, but she couldn't place how she knew them.

Omar stopped walking just in front of the gate doors, halting the teenagers behind him.

He placed his rifle on the ground in front of him, raised both arms, and in a clear voice shouted:

"I have ventured into the world and seen its troubles, but I return to you now having chosen the central path. I bring only those willing to learn."

Suddenly the flames in the gate's torches burned higher and brighter. A low-pitched bell rang out, and the gate's doors slowly and smoothly opened. Omar lowered his arms, picked up his rifle, and gestured to the teenagers to follow him inside. Emily could not believe what she had just witnessed.

As she passed through the gate, she was shocked by how large the city was. The group walked down a straight, paved pathway, and to her left and right she could see rows of identical houses, evenly spaced. Each was painted in beautiful reds and yellows, sitting on perfectly carved stone stilts, with large wooden beams supporting its curved and tiled roof. Decorations capping the beams on each house were unique—she saw birds, fish, water buffalo, but each delicately blended in with the design of the house. She heard laughing from within the nearest building to her left, and as they walked, singing from another home.

Passing by more rows of houses, she saw her first glimpses of the residents of the city. Teenagers, about the same age as her, Sergio, and Charlie, sat in a small courtyard drinking tea. Children ran by, giggling and chasing after a ball while mothers in beautiful red and blue dresses watched on happily from what appeared to be workshops. Emily only caught a brief glimpse into the nearest store, but saw its walls mounted with advanced electronics whose purposes she did not know.

After walking for fifteen minutes, the group made their way towards a large central square where their pathway connected perpendicularly with another equally large path. Each corner of the square contained large ponds, a quarter of a circle in shape, so that from above one might see a large circle divided only by the two pathways. The center of the square also housed a large, circular fountain, featuring similar engravings as those on the main gate. The breeze splashed some of the mist from the fountain onto Emily's arm, cooling the skin that had been growing warmer in the direct sunlight they now received having moved out of the thick jungle canopy.

Emily had read about imperial cities in Vietnam like Huế, but had never seen anything as impressive in both design and scale as what she saw around her now. Whoever designed the city's layout had masterfully woven together overlapping circular and square motifs to connect streets and buildings in both a logical and aesthetically pleasing way.

Passing by her, she saw open-top vehicles hovering above the ground, quietly and quickly zooming down Núi Giàu's beautifully appointed streets. Magnetic-levitation existed on high-speed trains, of course—Emily had seen it firsthand during a State Department trip to Japan—but she was unaware that a trackless version existed.

No, more than that, she thought, *it shouldn't even be possible.*

As the group continued on, Emily saw more individuals were taking notice of Omar, Emily, Sergio, and Charlie. Though each citizen offered a friendly smile or wave as they passed, Emily felt something was strange. Then the thought finally hit her...

Where are all the old people?

Everyone they encountered, especially those that greeted Omar as he walked, appeared, on average, to be middle-aged or younger.

After passing through the square, Omar led them straight to the large rectangular red-brick building directly at the path's end. In the shade of the structure's curved roof Emily saw four older individuals, the first she'd seen in the city, two men and two women, waiting for them on the building's covered porch. They wore simple but brightly colored red and yellow garments and identical necklaces with circular metallic pendants.

Omar led the teenagers up the steps, where one of the women stepped forward and turned to Omar. "Welcome home, *cá nhỏ*."

"Thank you, Lien. It is good to be back. With you and with the other elders," replied Omar, turning and bowing slightly to the three individuals near Lien.

"And to you three," Lien said, turning to the teenagers standing behind Omar. "Welcome to Núi Giàu. I am sure you have many questions, but I promise they will be answered in due time. For now, please join us inside."

Lien turned towards the ornate doors behind her and led the group off the porch inside the building. After passing down a short hallway to a dining room, Lien gestured to a large table. Taking Lien's hint, Omar guided Emily, Sergio, and Charlie to specific seats across from the elders. He sat down next to Emily just as two men pushing a trolley walked into the room. They offered the weary travelers ice-cold towels and pitchers of water, and shortly after, placed a plethora of warm and cool Vietnamese dishes on the center of the table.

"Please, rest and eat," said Binh, another of the elders.

Omar smiled at the three teenagers and reached toward the food on the table. Emily grabbed scoops of rice, spring rolls, and a bowl of beef phở. The food was some of the best she had ever tasted, and much to the delight of her hosts, she went back for additional servings. Charlie and Sergio matched her gusto as the elders spoke amongst themselves in Vietnamese.

After the meal, Binh guided the teenagers and Omar to a sitting room with bamboo wicker furniture, topped with comfortable red and yellow cushions. Once again, the elders sat across from Emily, Charlie, and Sergio. Tea was brought in, and Lien once again spoke.

"*Cá nhỏ*, or Omar, as you probably know him better, informed me that you three have no clue why you are here. Is that correct?"

All three of them nodded.

"But you have heard of Casus Belli, yes?" Binh said in his naturally low voice.

"We found a ransom from them in my home three days ago. They claimed responsibility for kidnapping our parents," Charlie said.

"Yes, Omar spoke to me of this," Lien said. "And just today, they fought you with our weapons."

The three teenagers looked at each other.

That solves one mystery, Emily thought as Charlie continued.

"Yes," he replied.

"The conflict between our people and Casus Belli is one that goes back centuries. It's a story of much pain and sadness," Lien said. "So much so, it's often hard to remember a time when we were not under attack. But our people have joyful beginnings, and it's on this that we try to dwell."

As respectfully as possible, Sergio raised his hand.

"Yes, Sergio?" Omar asked.

"Elders...Omar. Who are your people?" Sergio asked.

"We've been called by many names," Binh replied, but most commonly, we are called 'the Middle Way.'

"And our story began twelve hundred years ago with a gift."

Chapter 13

"Like so many others before them, our ancestors worked as simple farmers. They lived in a small village in this area, tying their livelihood to inconsistent crop yields which, more often than not, left them underfed and hungry. It was a hard existence, but by all accounts, they found joy in their living. Whenever possible, they stored surplus rice in a special silo and offered its contents freely to anyone in need. Furthermore, they established trade between neighboring villages, and by doing so, were seen as brokers of the peace in the area. They abstained from conflict as often as they could, choosing to fight only to defend themselves and those who most needed protection. They were content with their station, living and dying as honorable people.

"One day, the people in the village were preparing to celebrate the Lunar New Year. As the story is told, the men of the village were walking through dense jungle on a rainy day when they heard a crash come through the trees. As they walked in the direction of the sound, they came to a clearing and saw what looked like a circular stone structure, three meters in diameter. They had never seen this structure before, but noticed visible damage—cracks, burn marks—on the structure's stone walls. It was clear that the structure was the source of the sound they'd heard, but specifically how was unclear. And adding to the oddity of the situation, there was a man near the structure they did not recognize.

"Our people have always called him 'the Visitor.'

"The Visitor looked distressed as he desperately attempted to repair the damaged stone structure. The men of the village noticed he was gravely injured, walking with a limp as he moved around the structure. After observing him from the shadows for some time, the Visitor fainted in front of them. Forgoing concerns for their own safety, our ancestors ran to the Visitor, picked him and his belongings up, and rushed him to the village's doctor. As she worked on the Visitor throughout the night, the elders of the village searched through the man's bag, attempting to find some indication of who he was. The man's only possessions, however, were a series of slate tablets and a small flat metal disc covered in characters which they could not read.

"The Visitor was in and out of consciousness for a week, unable to communicate. Many feared he was close to death. However, the doctor and elders did not relent, working tirelessly to nurse the Visitor back to health.

"After a week, the man began to recover his strength, though he had yet to speak. The village elders brought in elders from nearby villages—those who spoke in different dialects—to see if the man could understand any of them. All attempts failed.

"The Visitor grew stronger as each day passed, and after some time, finally indicated that he was fit to walk again. The men of the village decided they would bring him along on a hunt near where they had found him. Straying away from the main hunting party, the Visitor proceeded to lead the villagers back to the stone structure.

The Visitor approached the structure's stones slowly, and after pressing a series of them in combination, a small circular opening formed in the structure's side. The Visitor removed the small metal disc from his bag and carefully placed it in the corresponding opening. Suddenly, from what appeared to be solid rock, a door swung open. The Visitor stepped inside the structure as the men watched on. After a moment, he returned to the men, now wearing a small circular stone near the base of his ear. And then he began to speak.

"Over the centuries, his specific words to our elders have been lost, but we do know this: the Visitor explained that he had traveled to Earth from another plane of existence—another dimension, specifically—but encountered an issue with his ship that caused him to crash and injure himself. He explained that his true nature was something beyond the comprehension of humans, and as such, he had chosen to take the form of a man. He sought not to draw unnecessary attention to himself, and believed that if he gathered enough resources around the crash site, he would be able make repairs to his ship.

"The hunting party, without hesitation, offered assistance in gathering whatever resources the Visitor required. While they did not understand how he had come to be in their midst, they recognized the Visitor's plight and knew it was their duty to offer whatever aid they could.

"Restoration went slowly, with the villagers offering personal items—metal jewelry, stoneware, whatever they had—when supplies could not be found. Eventually, the Visitor was able to communicate with others of his kind. He told the villagers that he would be unable to repair his ship, but that due to their efforts, he'd been able to share his location and would be rescued. The villagers were saddened that their new friend would be leaving them, but were happy he could return to his own kind.

"The Visitor, overwhelmed by the village's selflessness, offered the elders the only reward he could share: he would leave his partially repaired ship behind and teach the village how to utilize its technology. The Visitor's one condition was that knowledge of the ship and their encounter with him had to remain a secret. The five village elders agreed, confident that their people would never betray the Visitor's trust. It was on this day that the elders became the first humans to enter the stone structure.

"When they emerged, they spoke of having a deeper understanding of the world and the physical laws of the universe. While they could not fully comprehend the ship's technology, they were aware that they'd already begun to grow in wisdom. For one week, the Visitor continued these lessons with the elders, until, on the fifth day, a loud humming was heard coming from the sky.

"In the same clearing as the crashed ship, the villagers saw a large stone-like sphere hovering just above the ground. It was clear that this object—this ship—was the functioning version of the crashed stone structure around which they had first encountered the Visitor. He said goodbye to his friends, and before departing, gave them the small metal disc he had used to open the structure's door. Then, touching the floating ship's stone exterior, he opened a doorway and stepped inside. Before the villagers could even wave, a deafening crackling was heard, and before their eyes, the ship had disappeared."

◇◇◇◇◇

"Wanting to honor their promise to the Visitor, the villagers immediately constructed a camouflaged shelter around the crashed ship to ensure nobody walking in the area would find it.

As the ship was only a short distance away from the village, the elders periodically returned, eager to continue their lessons. Touching the stones the Visitor had touched and using the small metal disc he had left behind, they entered the structure to gain insights from the technology he had left behind. This practice continued periodically, though the elders were unable to comprehend much more than what the Visitor taught them.

"After a number of years, fearing that they might die before passing on the knowledge of the ship, the elders selected five villagers—those who would replace them as elders when the time came—and brought them to the ship. They showed them how to touch the stones, how to use the metal disc, and how to enter. Nervously watching from the outside, the elders stared as their five elect took their first steps inside the ship.

"After an hour, the five emerged. They looked dazed and were unable to speak. The elders, in their patience, sat in silence with the five and waited for them to process their experience in the ship.

"Finally, one of the five spoke up, saying simply, 'We understand now.'

"The elders smiled, knowing that the Visitor's gift would continue to enlighten their village well beyond their deaths. They had fulfilled their duty, and were ready to move on.

"But two decades passed, and death had only come for two of the five original elders. More confusing still, it appeared that the new five hadn't aged a single day. The elders called the five into a conference and discussed their suspicion: for those who enter the ship, time moves more slowly.

"In their first lessons, the Visitor taught the elders that time was relative, and in the decades following his departure, they had come to discover the role that large celestial objects played in weighing down space-time. But none of their discoveries could explain how this slipping of time could continue to occur after moving away from an object of that size. Especially confusing was that the ship could not possibly have the gravitational pull required to affect time in any remotely perceivable way. Regardless, it was clear to the elders and the new five that they would still eventually die—the two elders who had passed away from natural causes proved it as such—but they weren't sure how long they would live. They debated and wondered at the causes and limits of this effect, until a joint decision was made by this council of elders to test their theories with two new villagers.

"Like the new five who were chosen for their leadership in the community, the Council selected two young adults—a newly married couple in fact—who showed an aptitude for peacefully settling disputes between others. These two were taken to the ship, shown the ritual for entering, and allowed to step inside.

"Just as the others grew in wisdom after their encounter, the young couple quickly showed increased intellect and ability. In the years that followed, they met regularly with the Council, sharing scientific discoveries and discussing the nature of the Visitor's ship. In this time, they also gave birth to a child. But most importantly to the Council, and in alignment with their theories, the couple proceeded to age less quickly than their peers and their young child as the years passed.

"When the experiment ended, only one original elder still survived. She called a meeting with the new five and the young couple, and this Council debated the nature of the awesome responsibility the Visitor had left them. In this great Council, the original elder raised the main dilemma of our people: the ship could grant knowledge and longevity of life to those taught how to enter. For those seeking peace and justice, this meant increased knowledge and time to make a difference in the world. For those seeking selfish power and unjust gains, the ship created the possibility for mass suffering.

"After deliberation through the night, the Council unanimously decided that entrance to the ship should only be granted to those who had been trained to use its gift for good. The Council of elders, they determined, would initially consist of its eight living original members, then naturally decrease down to five upon the death of any three original members. The Council would train and approve all those seeking to enter the ship, and appoint replacements for themselves upon their deaths. And to protect the integrity of the Gift, the senior-most Council member would be the sole holder of the ritual knowledge on how to open the ship.

"Lastly, the Council decided that the ship needed to be permanently protected. In discussion with their community, they moved the entire village to the area around the ship. A permanent structure, the Temple, was erected to surround the ship and secure it from attack. After settling the villagers and building walls to protect themselves and the Gift, they decided on a name for their new village: Núi Giàu, or in English, 'Rich Mountain.' We are now sitting in the village they built."

"Following the establishment of Núi Giàu, our people were resigned to living a quiet, insular, and peaceful life. As more people received permission to enter the Temple, the village grew in wisdom and scientific knowledge. Individuals living longer meant they had time to experiment, to teach, and to debate. Progress was slow at first, but our technology began to rapidly advance. However, as the years passed, many felt guilty about their isolation from neighboring villages. The people of Núi Giàu realized they could not keep such a potential source of good in the world, the Gift—as entering the Temple was now called—a secret, so they petitioned the Council for solutions. The Council at that time was adamant that the existence of the Temple could not be shared with the world at large. However, they recognized the need to share their knowledge with the world. And so, a middle way, in line with the villagers' Buddhist philosophies, was chosen. We would help the world without being fully connected to it.

"The Council trained emissaries to go out into the world and indirectly teach those they deemed to be peaceful people—doctors, scientists, community leaders—how to develop advancements which had already been discovered at Núi Giàu. Each emissary had a clear mission: spread knowledge as widely as possible and make each target believe they had discovered the information themselves. Just as the ancient Greeks believed muses inspired great works of art and science, our emissaries would secretly inspire advancements that would help better the world. And because they had received the Gift and its benefit of extended life, emissaries traveled for decades at time, making treks to far-flung places which would have been impossible for any normal human to reach in one lifetime.

"Over the centuries, our emissaries met individuals who, like the founding Council, were great peacemakers. Recognizing the opportunity to increase aid to the world, select individuals born outside of Núi Giàu were trained and adopted into our culture. They too were given the Gift with the blessing of the Council. Our numbers grew, with emissaries living in and coming from all parts of the Earth. And with citizens now coming from different backgrounds, the Council voted that emissaries could take on a more audacious project: working to embed themselves into national governments to indirectly steer countries towards peace.

"The system was working exactly as designed, and the Council was pleased with the impact Núi Giàu had on the world. But as we worked for peace, there were those working for destruction."

Chapter 14

Across from the teenagers, another of the elders, Xuan, spoke up.

"Four hundred years after our village's encounter with the Visitor, the people of Núi Giàu had made significant strides in technological and scientific advancements. The city was filled with those who had received the Gift, and our network of emissaries was working secretly within almost every major world power across Africa and Eurasia. But the world at that time was filled with conflict and war. Violent religious and geopolitical conflicts became the norm, and our emissaries struggled to find new ways to broker peace. Ultimately, they were forced to take longer assignments—decades instead of just years—to build deeper trust and influence within the governments to which they were assigned. One such emissary was Duy.

"Duy's story began not so differently than those of other emissaries of his age. He was sent to Italy to spread medical knowledge throughout the cluster of feudal kingdoms in Tuscany. The remnants of the Roman Empire's network of roads and trade routes could still be traversed quickly at that time, allowing Duy to share information broadly in that region. In the city of Lucca, he encountered a man named Theodoric Borgognoni, a bishop and prominent surgeon. Surgery, while widely practiced, was largely unsafe at that time: surgical instruments would be reused from patient to patient, wounds would not be sufficiently washed, and patients' broken bones were incorrectly set. Duy, having studied medicine at Núi Giàu, took employment as an apprentice under Bishop Borgognoni. Duy shared his knowledge of antiseptic solutions, which Bishop Borgognoni slowly put into practice. Noting the success of this practice and others, the bishop published several books on 'his' groundbreaking medical advancements. His notoriety caught the attention of Pope Innocent IV, who requested the bishop as his personal surgeon. Knowing that he could not serve both the people in Lucca and the Pope simultaneously, Borgognoni sent his faithful apprentice Duy to work in the Papal court in his stead.

"Duy became a trusted advisor to the Pope, and guided him into using his office to reduce suffering in the world. When the War of Sicilian Vespers began in the 1282, the Pope personally selected Duy to travel to the conflict and report back on the conditions. Duy immediately traveled to Sicily, and took residence with a group of Franciscan friars at their monastery in the capital city of Palermo. In addition to corresponding with the Pope on the war, he used his knowledge and technology to treat injured soldiers, taking opportunities to speak to combatants on both sides of the conflict. He made efforts to work in secret, but the same passion which drove Duy to help as many people as possible also drew the attention of the malicious Sicilian rebel Ignazio Arcuri.

"As more and more soldiers in his unit returned home gravely injured from their time on the front lines, Ignazio Arcuri sought drastic solutions. He and his men joined the war for selfish reasons. Not for the king of Sicily, nor any figure of authority, but to take advantage of the chaos the war provided, destabilize the government, and ultimately, take charge themselves. They were committed to fighting to the death, but were running out of soldiers to keep the cause alive.

"Having heard rumors of the man who had secretly healed dozens in what the people were describing as a 'miraculous' fashion, Arcuri began to follow Duy's movements. Given that the Papacy was actively supporting his opposition in the war, Arcuri believed that Duy, under Papal mandate, would never willingly heal his troops. As such, Arcuri decided that Duy would have to be made to heal his men through coercion.

"Our reports tell us that Arcuri stalked Duy for weeks. Then, having learned his daily movements, he kidnapped Duy on his way back to the monastery during his habitual evening walk. He dragged the unconscious Duy into the cellar of his soldiers' safe house and, while waiting impatiently for Duy to come to, rifled through Duy's belongings. From a small dusty wooden container, he found Duy's correspondence with the Pope. He picked out a letter and began to read.

"While not formally educated, Arcuri could make out the gist of the Latin text he saw before him. He spat on the letter, disgusted by the Papal seal. Throwing it aside, he pulled out another letter from the bag. This letter, however, he could not read. Some of the text contained characters that looked like they were from the Latin alphabet, but the other characters consisted of symbols he had never seen. He put the letters and the wooden container on the ground next to him.

"Digging further into Duy's faded linen bag, Arcuri pulled out what appeared to be a refined piece of metal. It was smooth, inlaid with purple stones, and caused his hands to tingle as he touched it. Arcuri could not comprehend what he was holding, but suspected it was what Duy had been using to heal others. Not willing to wait for answers, he walked to the cellar and shook Duy back to consciousness.

"Arcuri interrogated Duy about the source of his healings and the letter with odd characters, demanding that he share the source of his technology. When Duy refused to relent, Arcuri and his men took turns torturing him. For days, muffled screams, which Arcuri told his neighbors were from the swine he kept in the house, filled the basement. But Duy gave nothing up. Finally, after nearly six days of torture, a frail Duy relented. In his weakened state, close to death, he revealed that there were others like him around the world. As pained breaths came from his lungs, Duy said that more would come from his home to heal and teach those seeking real peace. With his dying breath, he gave a faint smile, knowing he had successfully kept the existence of Núi Giàu a secret.

"Using the technology stolen from Duy, Arcuri healed his injured troops, and they abandoned their current war with the Pope, realizing then that a greater source of power could be captured. With his newfound knowledge that more emissaries with more technology existed, Arcuri and his group began a multi-generational quest to track down Duy's people, find their home, and steal their technology to inflict the group's will upon the world. This group ultimately became—"

"Casus Belli," all three teenagers interrupted Xuan in unison.

"Yes. Casus Belli," Xuan replied slowly as he looked at his fellow Council members.

"But as you are now aware from your journey here," said Quy, the fourth elder, in her delicate voice, "Casus Belli's story did not end in Italy.

"For centuries, members of Casus Belli tracked our emissaries—first in Italy, then farther around the world—and tortured them for information and technology. Like Duy, they bravely took the location of Núi Giàu to their graves. However, in line with the advancements made here over the years, each successive emissary killed carried increasingly more advanced technology than the next. Casus Belli were able to reverse engineer what they stole, develop weapons, and commit acts of terrorism wherever they roamed. We are not a warring people, but recognizing the exigent threat posed by Casus Belli, we took measures to arm and defend those we'd sent out into the world. We sent emissaries in pairs, each to protect the other, to more safely carry out our mission to help the world. But it became a game of cat and mouse.

"For every ten vile acts we prevented Casus Belli from carrying out, they successfully completed one. We helped significantly more people than they hurt, but each death, each act of destruction they carried out, was to us, a tragedy. Worse still, a tragedy for which we were ultimately responsible.

"As the world became more interconnected in the past two centuries through advancements we shared—steam engines, railways, aviation—we put more emissaries into the field than we ever had before. We were determined to overwhelm the evil that Casus Belli engendered. But the prevalence of large-scale international conflicts allowed them more access to global powers than had been previously available. The frequency of their emissary kidnappings increased, and ultimately, by the end of World War II, they had learned almost everything about us: the existence of Núi Giàu, our Gift, the Temple, and the key that the Visitor left behind. They also knew we were in Vietnam."

"By the time America's wartime involvement in Vietnam began, Casus Belli had become recklessly bold. Knowing they had a technological advantage over every other civilization but ours, they more actively infiltrated international militaries in order to find us. First it was with the French, using the period of colonization to embed themselves in this country in World War I. Then, when Ho Chi Minh started his independence movement in Hanoi, they placed themselves under his direction as soldiers willing to fight for his cause. Nobody knew how long the conflict might last, but their new leader, Aurelio Moretti, was eager to use the fog of war to his advantage. A descendant of one of the original members of Ignazio Acuri's troops, Moretti was hell-bent on finding the Temple and extending his life for the cause of global domination.

"His men, who had embedded themselves within the Viet Cong, searched all of Vietnam to find our village. As they traversed the jungle and dug deep tunnels, they strategically investigated places that they suspected could be Núi Giàu. And while in a clearing in a small outpost near Pele Ketan, they found small fragments of stone buried under the damp topsoil recently pulled up by bombed-out trees. To normal eyes, these stones would have meant nothing. However, Casus Belli's tools detected traces of radiation unique only to the Temple. From fragments of the Visitor's ship that had inadvertently been dropped from the Visitor's belongings, buried underground for centuries, Casus Belli had found the site of our ancestors' first village.

"They stationed themselves in the area and slowly fanned their way out in hopes of catching one of our emissaries returning home after a mission. For weeks they sat in the jungle, stalking villagers who looked as though they might provide a way in. Finally, they observed one of our women returning home as she passed through the twin trees at the start of the gate path. As she passed through the trees, the Casus Belli soldiers watched her disappear instantly. They walked around the trees, but finding nothing, decided to follow her through the trees. This is how they discovered our home.

"The soldiers took note of the gate's defenses, then hurried back to their outpost to call for reinforcements. Upon hearing the news, an elated Moretti decided to send the bulk of his forces—including his own son, Vincenzo—to bolster the soldiers' numbers and prepare for an all-out fight with our people. His troops gathered at the site of our old village, which is now nothing more than a clearing, and trained for their final raid. This unfortunately is when the fates of Casus Belli and those of your families became intertwined.

"The raid began just before midnight. The two Casus Belli soldiers who had originally found the entrance led the soldiers to a position just outside of the twin trees. The two entered the pathway and planted explosive charges on the gate, and just before running back through the trees, they detonated them. Our defensive forces, the Saolas, immediately responded to the explosion, running through the cracked gateway to chase the bombers down. Passing through the trees though, they were immediately brought down by the Casus Belli army that had amassed at our gate. The raid began in earnest then.

"Casus Belli troops rushed inside under the cover of darkness with Vincenzo Moretti leading the charge. He commanded his troops to hide, then, taking a small contingency of soldiers, charged towards the Council building—this building—to find the head of the Council in her quarters. Without mercy, he killed her in her sleep and stole the *di qua* off her corpse. Vincenzo ran outside, working his way back to his troops to begin a final assault when sharp sirens blared throughout the village. In response, the dim streetlights began to cast a light bright as the midday sun. From a speaker overhead, another elder announced that the *đi qua* had been stolen.

"Every available Saola ran into the street and immediately engaged Casus Belli. With our superior technology, our troops pushed Casus Belli back through the gate, onto the path, and back into the jungle. The Saolas chased them all the way back to the clearing, where they had left a small squadron of soldiers to hold the outpost. When our troops arrived, however, they saw that Casus Belli was engaged with American Special Forces—your parents' unit."

The jaws of all three teenagers dropped.

"What your government thought was a simple Viet Cong outpost," Xuan said, "was actually the meeting of the largest Casus Belli army ever assembled."

"It was a slaughter from the beginning," Binh added. "Even if they hadn't been outnumbered so greatly, the weapons the American troops had were no match for the advanced ones held by Casus Belli. You saw a taste of those weapons today."

"By the time the Saolas fully caught up to the fight," Quy continued, "the majority of the Americans were dead. Your parents watched as we fought off Casus Belli, killing most of their soldiers, including Vincenzo Moretti. We searched his body, then the entire battlefield, but could not find the *đi qua* anywhere. Assuming that one of the Casus Belli troops who'd fled had taken it for personal profit, we sent our troops after them. We left your parents with the cache of maps and documents Casus Belli had collected during their time with the Viet Cong.

"But your parents' bravery was not lost on us. We watched as Ada and James assisted José in trying to revive their downed companions, despite being actively targeted by Casus Belli. When the battle was over, we tried to heal as many of the Americans as possible, but the wounds of those who had not already died were too severe to be treated. And while we could not bring them to Núi Giàu, we knew your parents would honor our request to keep the details of our involvement a secret."

"For the past thirty years, we have been searching for the *đi qua*, unable to give the Gift to anyone new," Lien said. "We believed that it was in hiding with Aurelio Moretti and his few remaining troops. After a thorough investigation though, we suspected it had been inadvertently collected by your government and taken to the United States. We sent an emissary to Washington to investigate, but after eight years we were beginning to give up hope. That was, until Molly called us from Charlie's home three days ago."

Chapter 15

Ada felt the humidity clinging to her skin as a faint but growing light began to illuminate her cell.

Is this day three or four?

Between the beatings and the bare minimum of food provided to keep her and her companions alive, she couldn't recall exactly how long it had been since they were kidnapped. She dug deep into her military training, attempting to organize her thoughts around the key events that had occurred from the start of their captivity.

Okay. Day one, our security escorts were shot and killed mid-morning.

Her body shivered in response to this thought, not only in sadness for her killed men, but also out of the visceral fear she'd experienced when she heard the weapons fired upon her, James, and their security detail. The distinct electric crackling sound of the rifles had instantly transported her back to that day in the Vietnamese jungle in the 1970s, where she recalled the terror and carnage of the battle that had ultimately defined her life. Like James and so many other Vietnam veterans, she had sought out ways to overcome the PTSD she experienced through the war. Her "hero" status gave her access to the best therapy the VA office in

Washington could provide, which had taught her a variety of healthy techniques for coping with her trauma. And until three days ago, Ada was able to think about her wartime experiences without the same crippling anger, fear, and anxiety she first experienced upon shipping home after the war. But the sound—the horrible sound that had started the slaughter, the sound that she had not heard in thirty years—raised a primal sense of fear in her body. In her captivity the past few days, she'd worked through the techniques her therapist had taught her to calm her nerves. Only now was she able to process her trauma again.

They captured us, bound us, and dragged us blindfolded through the jungle for a few hours.

She remembered the sun being just past its apex in the sky when their blindfolds were removed.

James and I were pulled into one room. Maria, Delia, and Bill were put into another. Earthen floors, but a concrete ceiling and walls, and a heavy steel door.

The humidity in the air had only made the damp earth smell stronger, along with small rusty bars bolted to the wall on top of the small window grate currently serving as Ada's only source of light. She looked over at the table and saw the remnants of the rice and water they were served the day before.

Day two, they woke James and I up before dawn, pulled us into another room, and strapped us to old hospital beds. They asked us about José, about the battle, and something called a đi qua?

Her Vietnamese had grown a bit rusty in the years following the war, but she remembered being confused as to why they were asking about a doorway. When she and James had replied that they had no idea what the captors were talking about, the torture began.

They started with James—there was a device with a purplish glow which they pulled out of a smooth steel box, and when they pressed it against his neck, his whole body began to convulse.

She was quite familiar with weaponry of all kinds, conventional and unconventional, but had never seen anything this terrifying.

They alternated between the weapon and the old-fashioned beatings until James passed out, at which point they turned the weapons and hard questions on me.

In the dim morning light, Ada looked down at her wrists and saw bruises already forming. Painful reminders of the wrist restraints her body had fought against as she was subjected to the same torturous treatment that James received. She recalled their captors had alternated their aggressive attention between him and her throughout the morning, finally leaving the two alone for a few hours until the late afternoon.

How much time passed after the beatings stopped?

She assumed it was late afternoon. At least that was when a different man had walked into the room where James and Ada were still strapped to their hospital beds.

He was older than us, probably in his early eighties, with grey and white hair trimmed neatly in a tight buzz cut. He wore camo-patterned fatigues, but with no patches or ribbons.

Ada had an eye for obscure military traditions and dress, but could not identify any specific military affiliations this man might have.

He set down the tray he carried in with him, and from across the room I could smell that it was food of some kind. Finally, he pulled out the small metal folding chair tucked in the corner of the room and, placing it by both our hospital beds, took a seat where we could both see him.

Ada was stretching her memory's limits trying to recall what he said to them next. She recalled the scene like a distant movie.

"The boys tell me that you two aren't being very cooperative, but I suspect that it's more ignorance than obstinance," he said in a soft, but stern voice. "So I told them to take a rest and let me try.

"We know who you are," he continued, "we know what you did in Vietnam, and we know what you've been up to for the past ten years."

Ada looked over at James, who through a swollen black eye was trying to understand what their new visitor was implying.

"The same questions you've been asked today," the old man said, "we also asked of your comrade, Dr. Santos. Similarly, his answers were...well, let's just say they were unsatisfactory. And for years, as you looked for him, we've looked for you."

"You killed him, didn't you?" asked James, anger rising in his voice.

"We had no choice. He proved useless to us, and we knew that he would report to the two of you what he experienced. We could not let him go," the man said, coldly.

"You're a monster!" James screamed. Ada had never heard as much fury in his voice.

"I am one who fights for liberty, for which there is no cost too high to pay. What did your own Thomas Jefferson once say? 'The tree of liberty must be refreshed from time to time with the blood of patriots, an—'"

"'And tyrants,'" Ada said, glaring at him.

The man scowled. "My means justify the ends they will soon provide. You two can either support the cause of liberty as your country's government so often claims to do, or you, your spouses, and your children can take the same path Dr. Santos chose."

Ada shook against her restraints as he said this, screaming in reply, "If you touch them, I'll kill you!"

"See? You understand that death is sometimes the only way to compel someone to do what they should be willing to do for righteousness's sake. We are not so dissimilar," the man replied. "But I will not choose further violence unless it is necessary. I am giving you each the choice to answer my questions."

"Ask us already then!" James shouted.

The man stared at James, then turned his head back to Ada. "The day of your battle, you witnessed things that you did not comprehend, correct?"

"Yes," she replied impatiently.

"It's because you stumbled into a conflict you did not understand."

Ada had heard this sort of anti-American rhetoric plenty of times before. Many, both within the US and around the world, accused the United States of engaging in a conflict they should have avoided completely. Ada suspected this man had been part of the Viet Cong, or at least had been directly connected to the war.

"I'm guessing you were a soldier then? Is this revenge for America's part in the war?" James asked.

"No," the man retorted quickly. "You misunderstand me. War resets the balance in the world. The chaos your country's involvement caused only helped accelerate the plans we'd already made. But those you deem to be your deliverance—those mysterious soldiers who saved the three of you that day from certain death—were my enemy. Along with your soldiers, my own soldiers were destroyed. And we lost something we had rightfully claimed."

"The *đi qua*?" Ada asked.

"Precisely. The *đi qua*," the man said. "Imagine an item that can unlock avenues of power and knowledge unheard of in the world. That can make the world bend to your will. That is what was taken from us that day."

Ada and James looked equally puzzled.

"Your 'friends,' the Middle Way—or whatever other arrogant name they've chosen to go by now—slaughtered my people for stealing this prize from their midst. My troops were decimated that day, my son was killed, and the *đi qua* was lost to us." Frustration rose in the man's voice as he continued. "I've thought about that battle every day for the past thirty years, and as I've slowly rebuilt my forces, I've sought my prize relentlessly. We've waited and waited for a time when we could enact our revenge, needing only the *đi qua* to succeed. All this time we thought it was with our enemy...but it turns out it was with you."

"What are you talking about?" asked James. "All we took home was a cache of documents about Viet Cong troop movements. Just maps and papers."

"No. It was much more. To your eyes, it would have looked simply like a metal disc. Something the American military would have no problem photographing and then throwing in some storage box to rot."

"I remember the boxes distinctly," James said, shaking his head, "I helped catalogue the contents of everything we took."

"Oh god..." Ada murmured.

"What is it, Ada?" James asked quickly as the man slowly smirked.

"It's at home," she said.

"What? What are you talking about?"

"I found it on the ground when we were waiting to be evacuated from the battlefield. I thought it was just some decorative art one of their soldiers was carrying, and since I knew you and José were taking a few war trophies from the site yourselves, I decided to keep it. It never hit our military logs because I never reported it." Ada turned to the man. "Is this why you killed José? For some stupid piece of metal?!"

"You have no idea the worth of the item you stole that day," the main said angrily. "My organization and I will kill again and again—as many people as we have to—to get the *đi qua* back. But from what you've just told me, that sounds like it won't be necessary."

He paused for a moment, collecting himself, then said, "I am going to send someone to leave a message in your home, and then your children are going to bring the *đi qua* to me. If they do not, I'll kill you both. But if so, when I'm in possession of the *đi qua*, I'll let you two and your families go free. You will never see me again."

"You can't bring our kids into this. Let us go and we'll bring it to you," James pleaded.

"Now now, you've raised your children to be prudent. They'll understand that the threat is real and I'm sure we'll have no issues. Of course, if you're lying about the *đi qua*'s location, I will burn everything that you know and love, without mercy. So I want you to think carefully about what I've said."

"No...it's there..." Ada replied.

"Good." The man stood, signaling to a guard waiting next to the room's door. "I'll make the arrangements, and this whole business will be done soon. You two can go back to pretending to be war heroes in no time."

Before James and Ada could reply, the guard opened the door and let the man out of the room. Another guard quickly entered the room and re-fastened James's and Ada's hands. The two were escorted back to their original cell and given the tray of food the old man had brought into the interrogation room. After devouring their food, they both rapidly fell asleep.

So, if that was yesterday, I guess today is day three after all, Ada thought, turning and seeing her friend James curled in the fetal position, asleep on the earthen floor. Her thoughts continued replaying the words the old man had said to her and James. *What have I gotten the kids into? What will this group use the* đi qua *for?*

Her racing mind was interrupted by the sound of the metal door unlocking with a clunk. The thick hinges squeaked as the heavy door slowly opened. The sound brought James out of his own troubled slumber.

"Time to move," the guard said loudly to the pair inside the cell. Additional guards armed with the same purple-hued weapons walked into the cell, then grabbed and dragged James and Ada down a long hallway. Though they were fully bound before, the guards now allowed them to walk under their own power. The extra freedom was tempting. Even if Ada had wanted to fight back though, she knew she was too weak from the previous day's "enhanced interrogation" to put up a real struggle. For the moment, she accepted her fate.

At the end of the hallway stood a similarly sized steel door to the one they had just passed through in their original cell. However, when the guard opened this door, Ada could see that it was much better appointed than their last room. The floor was finished, and the room contained individual cots as well as a small bathroom with a toilet and sink. And that was when she heard something that really lifted her spirits...

"It's Ada and James!"

Ada immediately recognized her husband's voice, and tilting her head up, saw that Bill, Maria, and Delia were all inside the room. She also noticed another woman sitting in the back corner, and while she looked familiar, Ada couldn't remember if or how she knew her.

The guards threw James and Ada onto separate cots, filed out of the room, and shut the heavy steel door behind them. James and Ada were immediately embraced by their spouses and Maria.

"I'm so happy you're both alive!" exclaimed Delia, studying her husband's wounds. "Are you hurt badly?"

"I think most of the damage is done for now. Just thankful to be back with all of you," James replied weakly, with a soft smile on his face.

"We're thankful to have you back," replied Bill, similarly holding Ada.

"Are you all okay?" she asked.

"We're fine," Maria replied. "They threw us in this room when we got separated, and we haven't been allowed to leave. But they brought us some food and have otherwise left us alone for the most part. We heard screams coming from down the hallway though, and were worried sick."

James turned his head to Ada, knowing full well that the screams belonged to Ada and him.

She took his cue. "They interrogated us for a few hours, asking things about our battle, but it's done now." She wouldn't elaborate unnecessarily on the excruciating treatment they'd received the day before, especially in front of the mystery woman in the corner. Ada watched as the woman stared at her and James with great intensity, as if the woman was attempting to look past their injuries and determine their normal appearance.

"Good!" Bill replied. "And now that you two are back with us, we can introduce you to our new friend, Trinh. Trinh, this is who we've been telling you about, James and Ada. Trinh was out walking in the jungle when she got kidnapped. She's been here for a few weeks."

The woman alone in the corner of the room got up from her cot and made her way over to where the group sat. Trinh took a good look at both Ada and James, then said, "It's good to see you both again. Especially after thirty years."

And that was when it clicked for Ada. She did know this woman. Not just knew her—owed her life to her: Trinh had assisted James, José, and Ada after their battle all those years ago. But something threw Ada off—Trinh looked like she hadn't aged since they last saw her.

"I can't believe it…It's great to see you," Ada said. "But how are you here? And who was that old man who captured us?"

Trinh turned to the full group. "His name is Aurelio Moretti, and I think it's time you all finally learn the truth about what James, Ada, and José witnessed that day."

Chapter 16

Emily, Charlie, and Sergio sat in silence in the small private garden of the Council building's inner courtyard. Following their lunch, Omar had proposed that the teenagers take some quiet time away from the Council and the inner workings of the city to process everything they'd just been told. Lien, Binh, Quy, and Xuan graciously agreed, using the time to secure the *di qua* inside the Council building and prepare a plan to rescue the teenagers' parents. Omar, however, remained with the teenagers.

Sergio stared at the small waterfall across from him, watching as its droplets rippled the pool of water on whose edge he sat. Emily picked a long wooden bench, artfully painted in red, yellow, and purple, and laid on her back with her eyes closed. Charlie had taken to the edge of the garden and mindlessly played with the leaves of a plant in front of him.

Sergio heard Emily rustle behind him and turned his body around when she broke the silence.

"Omar, I'm going to ask you a series of what are probably stupid questions that I didn't feel comfortable asking the Council, but I'm going to ask you. Okay?" she said.

"Yes, that's perfectly fine." Omar replied.

"First—is basically every technological advancement we know of in the world a result of the Middle Way's emissaries?"

"Not exactly. As much as we'd have liked, we haven't had the capacity to send emissaries everywhere that might've needed them over the past few centuries. Honestly, it took a while to get the emissary program in the shape that it's in today...A lot of mistakes were made, and people suffered. But on balance, we've helped a lot of people who just needed the final push to make the same discoveries that Núi Giàu made first."

"Okay. So other than the weapons we've already seen, does Núi Giàu have technology that the world doesn't know about yet?" Emily asked.

"Yes. I'll take you three on a tour of some of the workshops later to see a few demonstrations if you'd like," Omar said.

"What does it feel like when you receive the Gift?" Charlie asked.

"It's hard to describe. There wasn't so much of a physical sensation. Maybe something like when you walk by a television and can sort of hear or feel the static. But the mental experience...it's something else. First there's a sense of euphoria, and then it's like a veil has been lifted and you can finally see all of the connections between seemingly disconnected things. I have to imagine it's how the Visitor's kind see the universe."

"Speaking of which," Emily said, "have there been other beings—other 'Visitors' that is—that've come to Earth since the original one crash-landed here?"

"We don't think so. To be fair, our ancestors were never supposed to know there were beings of that kind in existence, and at that point, never had the technology to check. But even with the deep-space scanners we developed, we've never gotten any indications that they've returned. We may just never see them again," Omar said.

As Emily pondered his answers, Charlie put down a pebble he'd been toying with from near the plants, then turned to Omar. "How many Núi Giàu emissaries are within the US government right now?"

"Fewer than you might think, actually," Omar replied, "and especially not at the high levels. Your parents were a special case since they ended up holding such prominent positions. I know it's hard to separate the type of work that your mom oversees from the type of things we do, but our aims are never more than just sharing our advancements and promoting peaceful restraint where needed."

Charlie continued looking at him, as if expecting more.

Omar spoke up again. "In the case of the US, most of our emissaries are in the surgeon general's office and the National Institutes of Health, with others working with prominent researchers at public universities."

"And so you and Molly were an exception?" Charlie asked.

"Yes. And in our case, Molly and I both have connections to the US. We grew up in Vietnam, but we each have family members that originally came from the States. They were adopted by the people of Núi Giàu after receiving the Gift, then remained in Vietnam. You'll find it to be a pretty common story here. A sort of United Nations really. In fact, that's ultimately where Woodrow Wilson's White House got the idea for the League of Nations."

He paused. "But that's a story for another day. In any case, Molly received the Gift before I did, but since we were so close in age, we were friends for most of our lives. When I found out that she was going to work as an emissary, I followed her down the same path. She's a great leader, and that's why I call her 'boss.'"

"*Bà chủ?*" Emily asked.

"Yeah! Hey, your Vietnamese isn't too bad," Omar said. "It isn't one-to-one with English, but it's definitely a term of respect."

Emily smiled. "And what did she call you again? *Cá nhỏ?*"

"It means 'little fish,'" Omar said. "Not as powerful of an image obviously, but it was our thing since, according to her, I was always following her in the proverbial pond."

"I'm going to name this little guy Omar then," said Sergio, pointing to the small koi fish swimming lazily in front of him.

Omar smiled.

"Omar, maybe this is indelicate, but I haven't been able to stop thinking about it," Sergio said. "If the Middle Way has known about Casus Belli for a while, how come you guys haven't just...I don't know a polite way of saying this...taken them out?"

Omar took a deep breath. "It's probably the greatest moral quandary that exists at Núi Giàu. As you heard the Council discuss, one of the core values of our people is peace. Put another way, we oppose the use of violence as a means to get things done. In practice, it just means that citizens of Núi Giàu will use any other tool at their disposal before ever considering using force. But what do you when there's an immediate threat to life? Our society has accepted that in these situations, use of defensive force is not only justified, but required."

"But what does 'immediate' even mean in that context?" asked Sergio.

"That's the crux of the debate. Where is the line, right?" Omar said. "For example, you could argue that, by their very nature, Casus Belli are an immediate threat to life. As long as they exist, people are at risk. To some in the city, Xuan included, using preemptive force to root out groups like Casus Belli is completely acceptable. You don't wait for cancer to spread before starting chemo, so why give violent groups a chance to plan?"

"Makes sense to me."

"However, there is a conflicting view, held by most of the current Council, that the moment we take preemptive action against a group, we become equally guilty. While any action against Casus Belli would be driven by the spirit of justice, there is fear that the standard for justice is susceptible to corruption."

"I think I understand," Charlie said. "Basically the fear of becoming judge, jury, and executioner in the world?"

"Exactly," Omar replied. "We can promote justice through existing governments around the world, but the moment we start directly enforcing our will, especially when we have the technological means to do so unchecked, is the moment we lose the soul of our peaceful community. Even with the best intentions, we're still human—we can be corrupted. The Council strongly believes there would be more death, more chaos in the world, if we changed our defensive stance."

"But what about the blood of the people in the interim? People who just wanted your help?" Sergio asked. "What about Molly?"

Silence filled the space between the group. Emily started to walk over to Sergio, but Omar waved her off.

"Sergio," Omar said, "this should have been said to you a long time ago, but on behalf of my people, I want to say it now: I'm so sorry that your father went missing before we could get to him."

Sergio looked up at Omar, sniffling as he wiped tears from his eyes.

"He was a noble man," Omar continued, "and he'd be proud of your sense of justice. That you care so much for others, especially those you've never met."

Sergio glanced towards his friends, then back at Omar.

"No, I'm the one who's sorry, Omar. I didn't mean to snap at you like that...I shouldn't have brought up Molly like that, either. I understand you're all just trying to help the best way you know how," Sergio said. "I'm sure it's a hard line for people here to walk."

"All good, Sergio, all good. And you're more right than you know," Omar replied. "It's caused tension between people in the city for centuries, particularly in those who lost family members to some willful attack. However, the debate became more intense after the attack thirty years ago, especially in the Council. Xuan used to be a champion for full restraint, but that attack...it rattled him...Afterwards, he became much more willing to consider force as a response to injustices around the world."

"Does that put him at odds with his peers on the Council?" Charlie asked.

"Definitely. The Council is an institution that knows how to hear and consider all perspectives, but they've given no credence to his ideas on the subject. If I'm him, I can't imagine being voted against constantly for thirty years feels great," Omar said. "Speaking of which, did you count how many Council members were present at lunch?"

"Four," Emily said.

"And how many has the Council had since the beginning?" Omar asked.

"...Five," Charlie said.

"Correct. As it turns out, the leader of our Council and the strongest defender of the reactionary stance, Trinh, was kidnapped in the woods by Casus Belli three weeks ago. I've been searching for her since then...Well, I was, until I got the call from Molly about what you'd found."

"You stopped the search for us?" Emily asked.

"You three proved to have a more pressing need," Omar said. "As much as it pains me to know Trinh is being held captive at the moment, the Council knows that Aurelio Moretti and Casus Belli will not harm her. They need her alive if they want to get into the Temple."

"What do you mean?" Charlie asked.

"The *đi qua* is the key to the Temple, right? But only the head of the Council and their appointed successor know how to use the key. The thing is, Trinh has not yet appointed her successor. With the *đi qua* missing for the past thirty years, she intentionally delayed passing on the knowledge until the *đi qua* was safely returned to Núi Giàu. Did Moretti know this when he ordered her kidnapping? Probably not. But Trinh is as clever as she is wise, so I have no doubt she informed him when she arrived. They may torture her, but they cannot push her too much, or they'll never receive the Gift."

"Pretty brave on her part," Sergio said.

"Definitely," Omar replied. "With the *đi qua*, Molly knew that you were in mortal danger. That's why she wanted to keep you directly under her protection, although she wasn't originally going to bring you to Núi Giàu. She was going to rescue your parents while you were with me and the other officers from their security detail, far away from any harm. Obviously, our experience in the car changed that."

Omar looked around at the group. "She also suspected Trinh and your parents were being held together, meaning we'd have a chance to get everyone back in one go. Moretti and Casus Belli haven't been this active since their defeat thirty years ago—especially since they lost the bulk of their forces. Molly figured they'd only act so boldly if they believed they could get Trinh and the *đi qua* in the same place."

"Were Molly and Trinh close?" Sergio asked.

"They were," Omar replied. "She was one of Trinh's students actually. They approached problems in similar ways, and Trinh's leadership style really inspired Molly to take whatever risks she needed to in order to help others. It's why she wanted to get out to the field as quickly as possible."

"That makes a lot of sense," Emily said.

"Molly really did care for you three…She would talk about you all the time whenever we spoke."

"She really was the best, wasn't she?" Sergio said.

"Absolutely," Emily agreed.

"The best," Charlie repeated.

Omar nodded with a faint smile, appearing to be fighting back tears. He sniffled, but did not speak.

The group sat in silence for a moment, with only the sound of a group of ducks splashing in the water in front of them.

"Well…" said Sergio, "I won't speak for the others, but I think I'd like to walk around Núi Giàu more if that's okay, Omar." Emily and Charlie nodded in agreement.

"Definitely," Omar said, wiping his eyes. "I'll take you to a few of those workshops I mentioned. We can—"

Then Omar stopped. From behind Emily, Councilwoman Lien and Councilman Binh approached the garden. As they drew closer, Sergio saw the concerned look on Binh's face as he held a piece of paper gingerly in his hands.

Omar turned and whispered to the teenagers, "Something has happened," before he stood and gave Lien and Binh a slight bow.

"This message was just picked up at the gates of the city. The messenger escaped before we could detain him, but we know where he came from," Binh said, pausing somberly. "Casus Belli have openly challenged us."

"Aurelio Moretti knows that the *đi qua* and the teenagers are here at Núi Giàu," Lien said. "He is bringing his forces here tomorrow, along with Trinh and the Americans, and says that if we do not open the gates, he will execute them in front of us one by one."

"Surely he can't think he will win?" exclaimed Omar. "Even if the Saolas were at half strength, Moretti wouldn't have the numbers to overtake us!"

"It isn't about strength. As much as he needs Trinh to survive to receive the Gift, he knows that we need her, too," said Lien. "He is counting on that to trade his way into the Temple."

"And the lives of James, Ada, Delia, Bill, and Maria are extra leverage," Binh said.

Seeing the stress on the teenagers' faces, Omar turned back to face them. "I promise you, we won't let anything happen to them."

"However, and this goes without saying," Binh said, "but Moretti and his troops *cannot* enter the Temple. If they receive the Gift, there is no end to the evil they would unleash upon the world. The power of Núi Giàu could not match their malice."

"We believe that we can rescue Trinh and your parents, but we will need to devise a plan," Lien said. "I've called a meeting of our Council and Saola leadership for later this afternoon. Normally, this would be a closed session, but as you three have a vested interest in its outcome, we are extending an invitation to you."

"Thank you for this honor," Sergio said on behalf of himself and his friends.

"Omar, see that these three are ready at the appointed time," Binh said.

"I will. Thank you, Council members," Omar replied with another slight bow.

Lien and Binh turned and walked slowly back into the Council building as the group watched on.

◇◇◇◇◇

As James, Trinh, and Ada sat near Trinh's cot, the steel door in the opposite corner of the room slowly opened. A guard, armed with an AK-47, rushed into the room and positioned himself beside the open door.

"What do you want?!" James shouted.

The guard said nothing, only staring at the wall in front of him, as the faint sound of a cane clacking against the floor grew louder and louder. Then, a few moments later, Aurelio Moretti entered the room and stopped just inside the open doorway.

"You'll be happy to know that you will be reunited with your families as early as tomorrow," Moretti said with a wicked grin.

"What do you mean?" asked Ada.

"Your children are in Vietnam, and they've brought the *đi qua*, as instructed." Moretti said, then turning to Trinh, continued. "And lucky for you, Trinh, they've been brought to Núi Giàu. No need for messy exchanges—we'll just walk in, and you can lead me straight into the Temple."

"You are much less wise than we estimated if you think my people are going to allow you to walk into the city, let alone the Temple," Trinh shot back.

Moretti's playfulness snapped into anger. "They may need you alive, but they certainly don't need these five. If you don't tell your Council to open the gates, their deaths, and the deaths of anyone else in our way, will be on your hands. I will no longer suffer the arrogance of your people. It ends tomorrow."

Without waiting for a reply, Moretti turned around and stormed out of the room as quickly as his elderly body allowed. The guard followed, and the prisoners listened as the steel door's lock engaged, leaving a heavy thud echoing in their cell.

Chapter 17

The "war room" (though Omar hesitated to describe it as such) was located in a side building connected to the Council building via a covered wooden bridge decorated in Buddhist motifs. Charlie noticed the lotus leaf patterns carved into the support beams on the short walk between buildings, with statues lining the walkway that he, Sergio, Emily, and Omar now passed. Everything they'd seen around Núi Giàu earlier in the day made it clear that the people residing here cared about the details—from the research they conducted to the technology they developed to the way they laid out their streets, every element was intentionally aligned with their beliefs.

Upon entering the large one-room building, Charlie was amazed at the artwork lining the walls all the way up to the high ceiling. As much detail as had been added on the bridge, this room contained even more. The center piece of the room though was what drew Charlie's attention. Standing in place of what might have traditionally been a battle map, Charlie saw an extensive mandala made of sand. The large circular table, ten feet in diameter, was filled with intricate square and circular designs made in red, yellow, purple, green, and white sand, and at its center, Charlie saw what was clearly a representation of Núi Giàu.

Gathered around the table were the Council members—Lien, Binh, Quy, and Xuan—but also a group of men and women whom Charlie had not yet met. Based on the patches on their sleeves each showing what appeared to be an antelope, he assumed these were the Saolas that Lien had mentioned would be joining.

Omar had explained to Charlie and his friends that the group was named after a native animal affectionately called the "Asian unicorn" due to its elusive behavior and distinct straight antlers. While only recently discovered by the rest of the world, the Saola was honored in Núi Giàu for centuries due its nonaggressive yet vigilant nature, an animal always watching peacefully but ready to fight to defend itself. The Council found this a fitting name for those tasked with protecting the city and its people from harm.

I hope I get to see one someday if we make it through all of this, Charlie thought.

Omar caught his attention and gestured to three empty chairs alongside the mandala table. Following Emily and Sergio, Charlie sat down. The low chatter in the room continued briefly until all the remaining individuals sat down, at which point, Lien stood and opened the meeting.

"As you all know, we have learned that Casus Belli will be marching its forces directly to Núi Giàu. Thanks to the brave women and men of the Saolas, our city has only ever been attacked once in its 1200-year history. And unlike thirty years ago, we know what our enemy wants and when they are arriving. However, Casus Belli come to us holding six hostages and the unyielding ambition to kill them at their earliest convenience. You have been summoned here today to identify how we will successfully save the hostages and defend the city. I yield the floor now to Anh."

A taller woman who appeared to be in her mid-forties stood as Lien concluded her introduction. The woman had shoulder-length black and grey hair, pinned behind her head with an iron clasp, and wore a simple grey and red dress. A knife sat on a belt around her waist.

"Thank you, Lien. I'll waste no time," Anh said, offering Lien a small bow in the process. "Núi Giàu was inadvertently designed as a fortress. Our ancestors mainly envisioned the high walls and jungle canopies as a means to keep the city hidden, but in the process, created a space with only two weak points—the front gate and the forest path leading to it. This gives us an incredible advantage in that we don't have to worry about assaults from any other position."

She gestured towards the center of the mandala, pointing specifically at the representation of Núi Giàu's front gate.

"To address this, since the last assault on the city, we've also built defensive positions in the clearing surrounding the entrance to the gate path. These positions near the twin trees are seldom used, but they are unknown to Casus Belli. They create a funneled route to the gate path which we can defend on all sides. However, as Lien has stated, this is not simply a military operation. Any false move on our part could risk the murder of the head of our Council, as well as the parents of our American friends here today. We need to devise a way to distract the Casus Belli forces, seize the hostages, and safely seal the city. If we can get the hostages inside, we can defend Núi Giàu indefinitely."

"An additional thing to note," Binh added, "is that Aurelio Moretti is specifically aiming to get inside the Temple. Above all else, he will let nothing stop him from receiving the Gift. Even if it means sacrificing all of his men."

"Thank you, Binh," replied Anh, pointing now to the path from the gate around the Council building to the Temple. "Should any one of Casus Belli's forces make it inside, they will lead a direct assault on the Temple, as their predecessors planned to do thirty years ago."

"Can we surprise them on the jungle roads?" Quy asked. "To keep the fighting as far away from our gates as possible?"

"It's something we considered," Anh said. "We have the numbers to make a guerilla-style attack possible, and such an attack would certainly create enough chaos for us to grab the hostages. However, the farther we step outside the city, the greater the number of variables for which we would have to plan. For example, the time it takes to get the hostages and our forces back to safety is directly related to how hard Casus Belli fights back. If they keep pushing during our retreat back to the city, we expose ourselves to a much greater risk of loss."

"I see. Thank you for the explanation."

Anh nodded in Quy's direction.

"Why not negotiate with Moretti directly at the gate?" Xuan asked. "As you've said, he needs our cooperation to get into the city and Temple as much as we need get the hostages back safely. We could potentially spare all of the bloodshed through diplomacy. I can't imagine he's the same man after his defeat thirty years ago—I bet he's willing to talk."

"We will certainly try. Negotiations might buy us additional time," Anh said. "With that said, my concern is that the hostages are still at risk should negotiations fail. We'd be relying on the restraint of a man and his troops who have shown no eagerness to deal in good faith."

"I would be willing to represent the Council and speak to him face-to-face. That may help," replied Xuan.

"It's truly noble of you to volunteer, Xuan, but we cannot risk you being taken as a hostage as well," Anh said. "Nor any other member of this Council for that matter. It only weakens our position."

"Anh, I respect your opinion, but as a member of this Council, I have a right to make leadership decisions, even if you might not deem them militarily prudent."

As Anh and Xuan continued to debate his proposal, Charlie turned his chair towards Omar and whispered in his ear. "I have an idea, but I don't want to speak out of turn. Could you share it for me?"

"We evaluate the idea itself, Charlie, not the person who says it. You can speak freely. Just wait for Anh's acknowledgement." Omar whispered back.

Both out of habit from years of school and from insufficient knowledge of war-room decorum, Charlie slowly raised his hand.

Anh finished making a point, then turning her head around, made eye contact with Charlie. "You may speak, Charlie," she said as Xuan looked on, arms now crossed.

"Are you all familiar with the Battle of Agincourt?" Charlie asked the room.

"You're referring to the fight between the English and French during the Hundred Years' War, yes?" asked Anh.

"Correct. The English forces under King Henry the Fifth were greatly outnumbered by the French forces. But King Henry used the land to his advantage—selecting a narrow battlefield, churning the field into mud, and hiding his archers in the surrounding forests—and ultimately won the day. Looking at Núi Giàu and its surroundings, is it possible that a similar tactic would work?"

Anh gestured to a man sitting to her right, bidding him to approach the mandala map.

"Quang, what do you think?"

The man stood and skimmed the map in front of him. Charlie discretely turned towards Omar and found he was already looking in Charlie's direction.

Quang is her number two, Omar mouthed silently.

"Thanks," Charlie whispered, turning back towards the map.

Quang took his focus off the map and turned to Anh. "We know Moretti and his troops will need to pass straight through the gate path to advance. To Charlie's point, it's reasonable to assume that, just like the French at Agincourt, Moretti's assumption is that the bulk of the Saolas will be centrally located. And since he's unaware of the defensive positions on the clearing, it's also fair to assume that he won't be expecting resistance from any other direction. That might be our opportunity."

"That could work, Quang. And thank you, Charlie, for the idea," Anh said. "Though we'll need to ensure the safety of the hostages first. Here's what I'm thinking."

Omar gestured to Charlie to sit back down as Anh continued.

"In Agincourt, the troops at the center of the battlefield were the bait to lure the enemy into indefensible positions. So," she said, reaching towards the gate path in the mandala, "we can position a smaller contingency of our forces just inside the twin trees. As Charlie said, these will be the forces Moretti expects, and if he sees that it's a smaller group, he'll be compelled to bring all his troops into the clearing. Knowing his ego, he'll probably be leading the column with the hostages close behind.

"If so, a second set of Saolas in the right-flank defensive positions can crash straight into the heart of his troops."

"Which will cause a lot of chaos," said Quang. "I think I see where you're going with this."

"Exactly," Anh replied. "In that chaos, our third set of troops, hidden in the left-flank defensive positions, can begin an extraction mission, making a run specifically for the hostages. Then, the bulk of our remaining forces, positioned just behind the city gate, can make a forward assault. They'll provide any additional support we need to rescue the hostages and bring them safely inside Núi Giàu."

"I've done a few exfils like this before, and I've read about even more of them," Omar spoke up from the other side of the table. "They can get messy quickly if the crowd-work isn't handled properly. How will we separate the hostages from the Casus Belli troops once the shooting starts?"

"Charlie's suggestion has actually given me an idea for that. I think we can use a mix of old and new technology on this one," Quang said.

"What did you have in mind?" Anh asked.

"Well just like we've done in other operations, I think we can tag the hostages with temp trackers." Quang turned to the teenagers, "The applicator looks sort of like a tranquilizer dart, but instead of knocking anyone out, the darts apply a tracking device to the target. You three can think of the devices like the microchips used for pets, except these don't need to pierce skin and can provide a broader range of things for us to monitor."

Sergio, Emily, and Charlie nodded, appreciative of the explanation.

"In any case, we'll tag them with the trackers," Quang said. "Then, we can use simple smoke bombs to muddy up the field of vision for the Casus Belli troops. We'll know exactly where to go, and the opposition forces will be scrambling to keep up. This has the added benefit of potentially reducing casualties on both sides."

Anh turned to look at Omar, and after a moment, he nodded in the affirmative.

"Well, that sorts us out for our initial approach, but Moretti is cunning. As such, we need to discuss defensive positions inside the city itself," said Anh, turning her attention back to the mandala map in front of her.

"30 years ago," she continued, "Vincenzo Moretti was able to make his way into the city center quickly due to the layout of our streets and buildings. The city's outer walls are strong, yes, but once inside, the gridded nature of our roads provides direct access to key sites. The same features which allow our people to walk freely—wide roads, open-plan parks—are the ones that make an enemy's advance easier. Fortunately, Vincenzo was prevented from making his way to the Temple, but we can't count on being as lucky again."

Mirroring Charlie, Emily raised her hand, and after Anh acknowledged her, said, "I think it's the same problem that art museums face."

"What do you mean, Emily?" Quang asked.

"Well, considerations for lighting and artistic placement aside, art museums typically display their artwork in large, open galleries, right? Easy for crowds to make their way through without disrupting patrons from viewing the art. However, some of the most famous museum robberies in Europe were facilitated by those same features. Since the thieves didn't have to weave through hallway after hallway, they could snatch art off the walls and run straight through the large galleries towards emergency exits. As a result, there's been a trend recently to build windy galleries that, while still large, prevent rapid movement to the museum's main points of entry and exit. I've seen it on a lot of trips with my dad. Consequently, that's also why you see more of those mini gift shops appearing inside galleries themselves in addition to the one at the museum entrance."

"That's a good analogy, Emily, and I think the museum solution is representative of what we'll need to do," Anh said. "Quang, how many of the electro-barriers do we have in inventory at the moment?"

"About one hundred or so," he replied. "Enough to barricade maybe half the city if we space them out."

"Yes, that'll work," Anh said, pointing to several streets on the map. "If we place them in the zones here, here, here, and here, once activated, those electro-barriers will force any Casus Belli troops to weave through the streets towards the Temple. It effectively triples the distance they'll need to cover to make their way through, and we can turn them on and off or reposition them as needed to allow our forces to make it through.

"We'll give the same treatment to the Council building path too, to ensure the *đi qua* remains safely stored away. I'm less worried about it being removed from its housing though, as it requires a Council member to take it out."

"The barriers shouldn't impact our citizens too much, and obviously there will be no impact to any of the standing structures," Quang added. "The people will want every measure in place to protect the Temple."

"They will," Anh said. "They trust the Saola forces to recommend whatever is necessary. As their head, I am going to order a general evacuation of the city to the network of tunnels and bunkers we built under fortified sections of Núi Giàu. We don't need a situation where additional people are harmed, and while I don't like invoking my authority this way, I believe it's the right move. Though for what I'm about to propose, I am going to need more than just my authority. I'm going to need the full support of the Council, too."

Charlie watched as Lien, Binh, Quy, and Xuan shifted in their seats.

"It is my sincerest belief that we need to place charges around the Temple building itself," Anh said gravely.

"Absolutely not!" Xuan shouted, his booming voice echoing off the walls.

"In the worst-case scenario, if Moretti receives the Gift, yes, his intelligence will increase. He will live a longer life. But that is that the crux of it—one life," Quy said. "We know that even those who receive the Gift at a young age still die. He is a villain, and we've seen villains come and go for centuries. His time will pass. If the Temple is destroyed though, we'd be ending the Gift forever."

"The Gift is the most precious thing we have, yes," Anh replied, "and that is why we would never use the charges unless we absolutely had to. But is it not our duty to let the Gift go if it's to be corrupted? Our desire to help the world drives us to do good, but if we are so attached to the Gift to be blinded by the potential evil it could cause, then I think we are lost."

"Those are strong words, Anh," Lien gently scolded.

"I'm sorry, Lien," said Anh, turning and bowing to Quy and Xuan. "I'm sorry, Council members. I meant no disrespect. But my point remains."

"We've never faced such a direct threat like this before," Binh said. "And I think that Anh's proposal, while containing some grave implications, is worth considering. Our ancestors were entrusted with the Temple due to their humility, not any supernatural ability or wisdom. We here appreciate the extreme responsibility of receiving the Gift, but our enemy does not. In that responsibility, we must consider preventing it from being used for evil deeds."

"I understand your sentiment, Binh," said Xuan, "but what would Trinh say if she were here? As soon as she was appointed head of this Council, she herself ordered an increase in emissary missions in response to the strife in the world. She values the Gift more than any Council chair in living memory. And I tend to agree with her."

"She did these things," Quy agreed, "but she also has held off on passing on her knowledge of the Temple's access until the *đi qua* was safely under our watch once again. She did not want to risk that anyone unprepared to receive the Gift could enter the Temple."

"I humbly defer to the Council's judgement on this, but will once again submit that we are not proposing destroying the Temple. Only creating a last-ditch defense," said Anh.

The room stood in a strained silence so quiet that Charlie could hear water dripping from the small fountain just outside the room.

"We will put it to a vote then," Lien said.

"All opposed to placing charges on the Temple complex?" Binh asked.

Charlie looked around the table and saw a solitary hand coming from Xuan.

"And all in favor of placing the charges?" Binh asked.

This time, Charlie saw Lien, Quy, and Binh raise their hands.

"Anh, you have the Council's permission to proceed. But you must guarantee that the charges cannot be detonated unless this Council grants permission," Lien said.

"I understand," Anh replied. "Quang, gather all members of the Saola forces in our chambers immediately. We must begin defensive preparations at once."

"We are adjourned then," Lien said.

As people in the room began to push their chairs back from the table, Sergio turned to his friends.

"Wait!"

The Council members paused what they were doing, then looked at Sergio.

"Forgive my tone," he said. "There is one request that I have for you all."

"What is it, Sergio?" Omar asked.

"I want to help defend the city and rescue our parents. My dad fought for what's right, and I can do the same. Emily and Charlie, too."

"We appreciate your courage, Sergio, and your willingness to defend this city and its people," Anh said, "but it is entirely too dangerous. You all have already helped in the proposals you've offered in this meeting."

Quang, who Charlie had already begun taking a liking to, spoke next. "I think we can find a place for them, Anh. They don't need to be on the front lines, but they can help scout and report movements of Casus Belli forces. We have more than enough Saolas to watch the three of them."

"I still don't think it's a good idea. It exposes us and the hostages to unnecessary risks," Anh said.

"While I acknowledge that they have a stake in the outcome of this fight," Binh said, "I agree with Anh that they should stay behind where we know they will be safe. If Lien concurs, then we will find a guesthouse for the teenagers on the periphery of the city where they're least likely to be exposed to any danger. The Saolas can escort them to the tunnels if anything goes wrong. Lien, you have final say."

Everyone turned their heads in Lien's direction. She was still for a moment, then slowly nodded. Sergio let out a long sigh.

"I will make arrangements for you three and share them with Omar later this evening," said Quang, patting Sergio on the shoulder.

"Thank you, Quang. And thank you Council members for your consideration," Sergio replied as everyone got up from the table and began to walk out of the room.

Omar walked over to Quang and led him to the side of the room. Charlie could see they were having a conversation but couldn't make out what they were saying to one another. He watched as Quang made repeated gestures towards the mandala table in the main chamber, then Charlie turned back to his friends as Sergio began speaking.

"I know I didn't really consult the group here before I suggested us being involved, so I apologize. It's just that you two had some great ideas in that meeting, and I know they'll need us when things start to go down...But even if we're not leading an assault, I genuinely think this plan is going to work."

"Thanks, Serge," Charlie said. "I really hope so."

"Me, too," Emily replied. "And thanks for asking for us to be involved. While I would've preferred to play some active part in it, I'm glad that we at least got to be a part of planning."

The three teenagers noticed Omar walking back in their direction.

"I can see why Molly was so fond of you three," he said, "though I can also see why she occasionally referred to you all as 'lovable rascals.'"

"There's no way Molly ever used the word 'rascal,'" Sergio replied.

"Let's just say the word she actually used was...less polite," Omar said with a smile, receiving even wider smiles from the teenagers in return.

"I know you all are probably frustrated with the Council's decision," he continued, adjusting his tone, "but please know you've already contributed in big ways. I've spoken to Quang, and while he's still making the final plans, he told me that you will be stationed with veteran Saolas. I'll personally inspect them in the morning before I head to my post, but these guys have seen a lot and know how to act when trouble comes knocking.

"The four of us have made it this far together, and along with the Saola forces, we're going finish it together. But now, I think it's time we get you all some dinner and then off to bed."

"That's not a bad idea. The jet lag is hitting me hard," Emily said.

"It's not every day that you cross twelve time zones *and* get shot at," Sergio added. "Usually it's just one or the other."

Emily snorted, and Charlie saw Omar cracking a small smile, too.

"Well regardless, I think you'll be pleased," Omar said. "Binh told me they've prepared quite the feast in your honor."

Chapter 18

By now, James was experiencing the same restlessness he'd felt when he was in the Army. While his last battle in Vietnam was his most famous, he was a veteran of several key conflicts during the war. The night before each of them had been filled with a mix of emotions—anxiety, excitement, and fear—and at the moment, those same emotions were playing out in his mind. Ada saw his leg tapping furiously on the concrete floor below his cot and immediately recognized his state of mind.

"Thinking about tomorrow?" she asked.

"How did you know?" he replied.

She smiled. "Your shaky legs gave you away."

"Oh," James chuckled. "I don't even notice this anymore."

"There's a reason they called you 'Jackhammer Jim.' Do you remember what your old CO used to say?"

Putting on a transatlantic accent, James replied, "'Lewis, you keep shaking your leg like that and I won't need any dynamite. We'll just set you up on the VC's roof and let you tap-dance your way through the ceiling!'"

Ada grinned.

"I miss the old man," James said. "He made me run until I puked, but he always cracked me up..."

James drifted off for a moment, then noticed Ada's smile fading.

"What's up?" he asked.

"Just thinking about everything Trinh told us. You and I are privy to some of the darkest state secrets in the US government, and what she told me is by far the craziest thing I've ever heard. I mean, we knew we were dealing with an advanced society when we fought here in the seventies, but one on this scale? It's mind-boggling."

"Well, that's definitely true...And the fact so many of the world's conflicts over the past few centuries have been promulgated by one group? I can't reconcile that. You've studied enough world history to know the work of a single assassin can shape geopolitics dramatically. Think of the first World War."

"Gavrilo Princip," Ada replied.

"Exactly. How many lives would have been spared, how many twentieth-century conflicts would have ceased to occur, had he not pulled the trigger on Franz Ferdinand that day? But to know that a militant group has lasted for this long and has had such a global impact...it's astounding. If we make it out of here alive, it's going to drastically change how you and I run our day jobs," James said.

"I hadn't thought about that piece of it yet. 'Hey Director Tillman, we think we've identified the group behind this terrorist plot.' 'Of course you have, it's Casus Belli! Let's go hit the Hawk and Dove to toast to a job well done.'" She shook her head.

"Speaking of work, any luck with getting a message out to your security detail?" James asked. "I know we've been tied up in the same rooms for a while, but I was passed out for a bit."

"No dice unfortunately. I spoke to Trinh to see if she had any means of communicating, but she said she was stripped of all her technology when she was kidnapped."

"I figured as much. I guess we'll have to play it out to the end. That was Trinh's plan, anyway."

"That's the thing that's been blowing my mind the most—we've had evidence of UFOs for years, but nothing like this 'Visitor' she mentioned," Ada said. "I'd hardly believe Trinh's story was true if she didn't look *identical* to how she did three decades ago."

"Nothing in all the training I've ever received prepared me for something otherworldly," James said. "Would you want to receive the Gift? I honestly don't know if I would."

"I...I don't know either," Ada replied. "I always thought I was the smartest person in the room, so it'd be nice to know it for sure. Plus, more time with the kids."

"That'd certainly be a plus."

"But I think we're past the point in our lives where we'd be ready to receive it. We've seen too much war and destruction, and I think that takes a toll. Alters how you think. What you're willing to do to survive."

"People can change though, right?" James asked, taking a moment to reflect on his own question. "Maybe you're right...As much as I'd want it, and I think I'd use it for good, who knows how I'd actually act if I got the Gift. As the good book says, 'pray you don't undergo the test.'"

"Well said, Father James."

He laughed. "Likewise though, I'm thinking of the national security implications of all of this. It's been easy to keep the details of our battle a secret all these years because, ultimately, we didn't actually know that much. Obviously, the Middle Way forces helped us, and an army receiving assistance from local people is not unheard of. But this—it changes everything."

"I've been having that same debate in my head since we talked to Trinh—at what point does global peace and security supersede our duty to the United States? Especially in the elevated capacities we serve. I mean, do we have to tell the president? I can't decide. And do the kids know? Presumably if they've made it to Núi Giàu, they've been briefed like we have," Ada replied.

"All good questions..." James said, turning his head to look across the room. "I wonder how the others are taking it..."

While the Americans and Trinh's cell was relatively small, based on the number of beds in the room, it had not been filled to capacity. The group decided early on to spread out their cots in a way that afforded them a bit of privacy. James and Ada currently sat in the corner of the room where Trinh had first revealed the truth of their wartime involvement. She now sat with Delia, Bill, and Maria, taking extra time to answer any questions they had about Casus Belli, the Middle Way, and the Visitor.

Ada glanced at the others across the room. "I think in her heart, Maria knew that José was dead the moment she found out he'd been kidnapped. From what I can tell, all of this extra information, while shocking, is actually giving her some comfort. She has irrefutable proof that her husband was a hero and that he died working to save others. And I don't know how Bill takes all of this in stride, but for as long as I've known him, he's been able to roll with whatever comes his way."

"That's something I've always respected about him," James added.

"Me too," Ada said. "How's Delia doing?"

"Her main concern is definitely the kids, so news of them being attacked on the road terrified her. But once she heard they were safe in some magical city, I think she was able to relax a bit. Plus, she's always believed in aliens too, so I think deep down she's actually really enjoying that aspect of it," James said with a small smile.

"We really married some resilient people, didn't we?"

"I'm thankful for it every day. I'm also glad the Army taught us how to compartmentalize. How we inform our government of what we've learned is definitely a discussion you and I'll need to have once we get out of here, but I'm putting that in a bucket for the future. Of course, I'm worried about the kids, too, but if Núi Giàu is as strong as we've been told, I'm sure they're safe. Which means for now, the most pressing question at hand is this: how do we actually get out of here?"

Delia, having seen James look over at her, waved at Ada and James. "You two should come join us now—Trinh has a plan for tomorrow."

James and Ada got up from the cot on which they had been sitting and walked across the room to stand near their respective spouses.

"Please continue, Trinh," said Bill, signaling to his wife to come sit beside him. James followed suit, sitting down next to Delia.

"Welcome, you two," Trinh said. "I was describing to the group here a little more about how Núi Giàu is laid out."

"Please, continue," said James, and Trinh nodded.

"The city is essentially impenetrable, with the only way in through the city gate. That means any chance of us making it safely inside will have to come through there. Once inside, my Saolas will have the means to protect us. I have no idea what they have planned for tomorrow, though. They train for many scenarios, but none of them has ever involved the enemy using hostages to bargain their way into the city. I am not worried, but I simply cannot predict the Saolas' strategy to get us away from Casus Belli safely. All of which means our focus should be on what we can do to escape when the time is right."

"You know Moretti and Casus Belli better than any of us. When will the right time be?" Ada asked.

"He needs me to show him how to access the Temple, but without the *đi qua*, he truly has nothing. He will bargain for it— your lives in exchange for the *đi qua* and passage inside to the Temple. He is so sure of his plan that, though he'll bring his full army, he assumes he will simply walk into Núi Giàu. He will brag about kidnapping me and tracking down the location of the *đi qua*. And that is our chance."

"How so?" James asked.

"He will be forced to negotiate before the city gate, and the gate path will limit the ability of Casus Belli troops to fully engage. Both the gate path and the gate itself will be heavily manned by Saolas, and my people will stall Moretti for as long as they feel they can keep us safe. We need only some distraction, a break in the conversation, and we'll be able to flee to the Saola force's protection," Trinh replied.

"Sorry if I sound unsure, but the plan is essentially just 'run'?" asked Maria.

"I understand your doubts," Trinh said patiently. "We are walking into a situation over which the six of us have very little control. But know this: my people will find a way to get us away from Casus Belli, and when they do, it is imperative you run as quickly as possible to safety. The faster you all enter the safety of Núi Giàu, the faster my people can expel Moretti and his troops."

Maria, still doubting the feasibility of the plan but acknowledging her responsibility in it, nodded.

Bill, who had been sitting quietly, now spoke up. "I trust that we'll be okay, but what happens if Moretti does make it to the Temple?"

"An outsider making it into the Temple has been my greatest fear since my appointment to lead the Council," Trinh said, "but the Council members are wise. They will not, under any circumstances, allow Moretti or his men anywhere near the Temple. We have been keepers of the Gift for more than one thousand years, and in that time, we have never granted entry to those unwilling to accept its burdens. That will not change tomorrow."

James listened as the word "tomorrow" echoed off the steel door to the cell. There was a strange weight to the word, and looking around the room, he could tell it was sitting with the others as well. He was lost in this thought for a moment until Ada's voice pulled his concentration back to the conversation.

"The people of Núi Giàu saved our lives in the battle thirty years ago, and they weren't even looking for us. I trust them and their plan," Ada said.

"And we have ways that we can help," James said. "Ada, José, and I have told you enough of our military stories over the years, and there's been one theme to all of them—force the enemy to make mistakes, then don't get in their way. Any bit of chaos we create might be just enough to disrupt their plans. Just follow our lead tomorrow. You'll know what to do."

"We will make it through this, and we will get back to the kids. I promise," Ada said confidently, keeping any private worries and doubts she had hidden from the others.

James looked at her, then Delia, and then scanned their grim surroundings. His foot began to tap the floor quickly.

He was ready to get out.

◇◇◇◇◇

Emily walked out of her bathroom towards the common room of the ornate guesthouse on stilts into which Omar had escorted her, Charlie, and Sergio for the evening following their dinner with the Council. Charlie and Sergio sat on the room's sofas in the red pajama sets that had been provided for them. She saw that they'd found the deck of cards in her book bag and were in the middle of some card game she didn't recognize.

"How do you guys get ready for bed so quickly?" Emily asked.

"We're boys—we washed our faces with the hand soap in the bathroom and quickly brushed our teeth," Charlie replied, and Emily rolled her eyes.

"Come sit down. We'll deal you in," Sergio said.

"No thanks, I'm falling asleep already. But I'll watch you play for a bit." Emily walked over to the open seat on the couch next to Sergio and watched his hands nervously shuffle the cards.

"You doing okay, Sergio?" Emily asked.

"I'm fine," he replied.

"Serge...let's be real," Charlie said. "The past few days have been insane. How are you actually doing?"

Sergio gently tossed the cards on the table, repositioned himself in his seat, and looked back up at Emily and Charlie.

"I've been...thinking about my dad a lot since we got here. And maybe it's just me being exhausted, but now that we've got this moment of calm, I feel like all of my emotions are finally catching up with me."

Emily and Charlie scooted forward, listening more intently.

"Finding my dad's notes the other day—was that yesterday? Geez, I can't keep track anymore—and then coming here and learning why he was kidnapped...it's just been hard to process.

Plus, Molly being killed in front of us, and now your parents and my mom have been taken. I trust the people here, but it's tough, you know?"

Emily put her hand on Sergio's shoulder. "Definitely. We've been caught up in this fight that's so much bigger than any of us. It makes me feel small and powerless."

"Yeah, exactly," Charlie added. "And here we are, having graduated high school approximately two seconds ago, needing to help save the world."

"Our biggest worry earlier this week was about where the best delivery food was from," Sergio said, and Emily and Charlie smiled.

"Maybe this is silly," she said, "but I feel like our parents actually prepared us for this. Not directly of course, but through their stories, the hobbies we got into because of them—in a weird way, they are supporting us, even if they're not with us right now. Including your dad, Sergio."

"You're right, Em. I've learned so much from your parents...and I know my dad's knowledge and sense of humor rubbed off on me," Sergio said, taking a deep breath before continuing.

"We've talked about it before, but after coming to Núi Giàu and learning about who he was up against, I feel like I'm finally ready to accept that...that my dad is dead. I'd love more than anything to be proven wrong, but as my mom always points out...he's still always with me. And maybe if we make it through this fight, we can celebrate his life more often."

"I'd love that. I know my mom has some crazy stories about your dad when they were in the Army. It would be awesome to get everyone together to hear them," Charlie replied.

"Especially now that we're older," Emily added. "I feel like they were saving all the inappropriate ones until we were headed to college."

Sergio smiled back at her and Charlie. "My dad was brave, and I'll be brave, too. Especially for our families."

Emily leaned over and gave Sergio a big hug, and Charlie stood and joined them.

As they ended their embrace, Sergio leaned back on the couch. "I'm really lucky to have you both in my life."

"Likewise," Charlie replied. "Particularly because you're so easy to beat at cards. We should have been playing for money."

Sergio laughed. "Low blow, Charlie. Low. Blow."

The three teenagers continued laughing and playing cards until Emily started falling asleep on the couch, at which point they all agreed to call it a night, knowing the next day would be the longest of their lives.

Chapter 19

What does one actually do on the morning of a battle?

Before their trip, Charlie thought he knew a good bit about war for someone his age. He'd learned about famous military campaigns, read diaries of common soldiers and generals alike. Yet in the cool pre-dawn hours, he still found himself mulling this and many other questions.

He felt a bit insecure about what he actually knew and how he could contribute to the coming fight. Nobody expected him to be a military expert, of course. He'd only just turned eighteen. But the doubt lingered, even if he hadn't let himself show it in front of Emily and Sergio. He just hoped he'd have the courage to help his friends.

After some restless sleep, he'd awoken earlier than the others, though whether it was from jet lag or nervousness, he wasn't entirely sure. After quietly perusing the small kitchen in the home, he showered, then put on his hastily packed clothes and shoes and decided to take a small walk outside their guesthouse. It was still dark out, but the dawn sun was just beginning to lighten the sky. During their tour of the city the previous day, he appreciated how manicured the paths and gardens were in the city. Those around their guesthouse were no different. The only change he saw around the city now was the addition of the small strips of metal coil that had been rolled across the road on which their building sat.

These must be the electro-barriers, he thought, studying a coil closely while taking care not to touch it. He'd worked with enough electronics (and had been shocked enough times) to know that you should always assume a wire is live until you know for sure that it isn't.

After watching the sunrise from a nearby wooden bench and pacing around for thirty minutes more, Charlie headed back to the guesthouse. As he walked in, he could hear Emily's shower running from the common room, and he also thought he smelled food in the kitchen. His stomach grumbled in reply.

"Welcome back, Charlie. I was wondering where you were," Sergio said.

"I had trouble sleeping last night...I think I finally understand pre-battle jitters now," Charlie replied.

"Had I not been so tired, I think I would've been right there with you, my friend," Sergio answered. "While you were out, Omar came by and brought us some breakfast. Come have some."

As Charlie approached the kitchen, he saw a wide variety of fresh foods laid out before him—sticky rice, banh mi, banh canh— and his mouth watered at the smell of the breakfast spread in front of him. He joined Sergio at the table and dug in. Shortly after, Emily came out of her room and sat down as well.

"Charlie was out on a walk, Em," Sergio mumbled, his mouth still full of sticky rice.

"Ah, that was a good idea. I should have gone with you," she replied, putting her foot up on a nearby chair and leaning to touch her toes. "We were in so many forms of transportation the past few days that I feel like my legs are still stiff. I suppose it doesn't matter now, though. Did you see any Saolas outside? Omar said he'd be back shortly, so I figured they may be here already, unless they're walking with him."

"Nobody yet," Charlie said. "Maybe this is a stupid question, but does anyone know when Casus Belli is supposed to arrive? I can't imagine their note was as formal as 'Hey, we'll be there to sack your city at precisely nine a.m. Please RSVP.'"

"Weirdly enough, Omar told me something similar this morning," Sergio replied. "Obviously when Núi Giàu was attacked thirty years ago, it was a surprise raid, so Moretti's men began the attack in the pre-dawn hours. But this is different—Moretti expects to just walk through the gate. Obviously Anh and Quang don't trust him to not try something, so they've ordered everyone to be ready as soon as possible. Before seven a.m. ideally."

"The old 'hurry up and wait' routine must be a universal military tradition," Emily said.

"That and giving the troops better food when commanders know the fighting will be horrible," Charlie added before taking another bite of his breakfast.

As the three began to clean up, they heard creaking footsteps on the stairs approaching their guesthouse, followed by a knock on the door. Watching the door open slowly, Charlie saw Omar walking into the common room carrying a large bag.

"Good morning, everyone. I hope you slept well."

"We did, thanks. Well, as good as we could have, considering..." Emily replied.

"And thank you for the food. We needed it for sure," Sergio added.

"You're welcome. I figured you three would be pretty hungry, even after the feast last night," Omar said. "And I'm glad to see that you all are already dressed ready to go. Thank you for your promptness."

"Of course," Charlie said. "The pajamas you gave us were incredibly comfortable, but we didn't feel it'd be appropriate to lounge around in them while a battle raged on outside."

"The optics of that would be bad, I agree." Omar smiled. "But I'm actually thanking you for another reason."

He put the bag he was holding on the now-clean kitchen table and opened its drawstring top.

"What do you mean?" asked Emily.

"Well just in the same ways that Molly rubbed off on you three, she rubbed off on me as well. She had a knack for disobeying the Council when she thought they were misguided, and after a long discussion with Quang yesterday, we've decided to follow suit. We're going slightly rogue."

"Are you saying what I think you're saying?" Sergio asked.

"Yes. We're bringing you three into defensive positions with us to serve as extra sets of eyes and hands. And we're leaving soon."

Sergio cheered and high-fived Emily as a jolt of nervous energy hit Charlie's system. He would have his chance to help save his parents.

"Now listen, right now only Quang and the four of us know the plan," Omar said. "Anh thinks I'm just here briefly to check on you before I return to my post. When we get to the front of the city, we're not going to have any time to mess around. As such, I want to run through a few things with you before we head out.

"First, you all have been unofficially assigned a specific Saola. Emily is going to be with Anh—and don't worry, Emily, we'll handle that conversation when we get there. Sergio is going to be with Quang, and Charlie, you'll be with me. You must do *exactly* what we tell you to do, even if you don't think it's right or fair. Even if we're breaking some rules, I owe it to your parents—to Molly—to keep you safe. Understood? I need to hear you all say it." His tone was as serious as when they first met him at the airport.

"Understood," all three replied.

"Good. Thank you." He reached into the bag in front of him. "On that note, I was able to get these for you all."

Charlie watched as Omar pulled out three rich green and brown camouflage jackets from the bag, handing one to each of the teenagers. Charlie held his up in front of him.

"They may not look like much more than standard-issue military wear, but these jackets are made of a material that's as strong as it is light. The closest equivalent you all might be familiar with is Kevlar, though the fabric in the jackets was developed here and is woven more tightly to protect against blades. We provide them to emissaries and Saola forces to help keep them safe when they're outside of Núi Giàu. Please, try them on."

Emily, Sergio, and Charlie each put on their jackets and checked the fit. Charlie was stunned at how breathable the material was, and how little his movement was restricted.

"How do they feel?" asked Omar.

"This is incredible! It feels like silk," Emily said.

"They're pretty special. These jackets have saved me more than once. We're able to customize the outer appearance, too. See this blue jacket I've got on? It's the same material—just needed a little tweaking to fit US standards."

Omar reached into the bag again, this time pulling out a small black box. After opening the lid, he removed three grey arch-shaped stones. He placed one in each of the three teenagers' hands, then took another one from the box.

"These are your communicators. You place them up behind your ears like this," he said, placing the empty portion of the semicircular object behind his ear. "It should stick right on."

Emily, Charlie, and Sergio placed them behind their ears. To Charlie's surprise, the smooth stone stuck firmly to his skin without the need to apply any pressure.

"Now unlike cell phones, you won't need to dial or anything like that to speak to someone. Simply press on the stone while you speak, and your intended recipient will hear the message," Omar continued. "I've got one, Anh has one, and Quang has one as well. You'll be able to speak to the three of us as well as each other. Emily, why don't you try sending a message to Charlie."

"Sure," Emily replied, then placed her finger on the stone communicator. "Charlie, can you hear me?"

"I can—but not just in the room—I could hear the message in my head. Is that normal?" Charlie asked.

"That's exactly how it's supposed to work," Omar said. "Bone conduction is a little unsettling at first, but you get used to it quickly. And for the sake of time, since the jackets and communicators all work, I'll move on to my second item: Your specific role in the plan. I took a guess at what your preferences might be and tried to incorporate them as best I could.

"Sergio," Omar said, turning to face him, "you and Quang will be part of the central column, positioned in the gatehouse. I know you wanted to be on the ground engaging with Moretti directly, but Quang agreed that you need to be safely behind the gate's defenses. You two will be directing the central column from there as you'll have the best viewpoint of the inner gate path, gate, and city walls. He'll give you more guidance when you're in position."

"Understood," Sergio replied.

"Emily, you and Anh will be in the outer defensives on the left flank. Like with Sergio, we decided to not put you directly on the ground. However, from the defensive post, you'll be able to point out the hostages quickly. If Anh comes around to it, she may also let you help throw smoke bombs into the field. Once the hostages have been tagged with the trackers, Anh will proceed to the ground with additional Saolas and retrieve them. Okay?"

"Sounds good, yes," Emily said.

"And that just leaves us, Charlie." Omar turned to look at Charlie. "As you can probably guess, that places us in the right-flank defensive position. Similar to Emily, you'll be remaining inside the defenses. Your task is an important one, though—you'll be working with Quang to signal when the team should detonate the explosives they placed as diversions on the ground near the right flank. Once you do, we'll signal to Anh as to when the extraction of the hostages can begin. I'll help in the communications and confirm every order before you pass it along. Does that work?"

"It does. Thank you for making a place for us in all this," Charlie said. *I can do this*, he thought.

"You're welcome," Omar replied before panning his head to look at each of the teenagers individually one last time. "Now the last thing is this—once we've recovered the hostages, we don't know where the enemy will be. Some of Casus Belli's forces may have made it inside the city, or they all may be in the gate path— we just don't know. At that stage, it's the job of you three to remain safe in whatever defensive position you can find. It'll be a lot easier for us to repel them if we know that everyone is tucked away safely.

"You three are incredibly brave, and I know deep down you want to help us, but you must stay safe. Okay?"

"Yes, we understand," Emily said on behalf of her friends.

"Good. I think—" Omar stopped suddenly mid-sentence, touching the stone behind his ear periodically, giving short replies to whoever was on the other end of his communicator.

"Yes, they are ready."

...

"Are you sure?"

...

"We're on our way." Omar said, taking his finger off the stone.

"What is it?" Charlie asked.

"That was Quang. Our scouts have just seen troops marching. Casus Belli is almost here."

◇◇◇◇◇

From the moment Omar shared the news that Casus Belli was on its way, everything felt like a blur. They were picked up by a Saola in what Charlie could only describe as a hovering golf cart with a covered trunk (*I'm gonna have to ask Omar what they're really called after this*, he'd thought) and the group was whisked away to the front gate of the city. Through a gap in the vehicle's covering, Charlie saw Anh looking at a map with Quang as the Saola put the vehicle into park.

Omar turned back from his uncovered seat towards the teenagers. "Hold tight for a second."

He swung his legs out of the cart and walked towards Quang and Anh. Charlie continued to peer through the gap in the cart's covering, listening to the group in front of him.

"Omar, good, just on time," Anh said.

"Quang gave me the call and I came right away." he replied.

"How are the teenagers? Are they in a safe position?"

"Well...they will be."

"What do you mean? I thought you left Saolas with them? Is there something wrong with the guesthouse?" Anh asked.

Charlie saw Quang touch the side of his neck, then heard Quang's voice. "Kids, you can come out now."

The teenagers slid back the covering on the cart, hopped out, and headed to the group.

Anh shook her head. "Whose idea was this?"

"It was mine, Anh," Quang said before Omar could reply. "I know the Council said no to their involvement, but you saw what they were able to contribute at the meeting yesterday. They've squared off with Casus Belli already this week and handled themselves perfectly."

"And with you and most of the Saola senior leadership up here, we know we can better protect them," Omar added.

Anh threw up her hands and started shouting at Omar and Quang in Vietnamese. Charlie had no idea what was being said but recognized a dressing-down from a commanding officer when he saw one.

After the discussion continued for a while, Charlie heard Anh tell Quang and Omar, "Fine, fine," while gesturing for the teenagers to come closer.

Quang and Omar really have our back!

"Alright, you three. Quang and Omar have explained their plan to me. I don't like disobeying the Council, and in particular, I don't like that this plan puts you closer to the front lines. But, it's too late to send you back to the guesthouse now, so I have no choice but to let you stay. However, I will not tolerate any further deviation from our battle plan—Quang and Omar will give you orders, but my orders supersede theirs. If I tell you something needs to happen, it's not up for debate. Do I make myself clear? I'm responsible, not them, if anything happens to you."

"We completely understand, and we'll act within any parameters you give us. We're just happy to help," Sergio said.

Anh sighed. "We have a job to do. Quang, Omar, get them into position. Emily, follow me."

As Quang shook Omar's hand, smiling at the acceptance of their unsanctioned plan, Sergio put his hand out in the middle of his friends, and Emily and Charlie piled their hands on as well.

"I guess this is it. I've never done a huddle like this before, so I'll just say: don't die," Sergio said.

"Really eloquent there, Serge. Truly. Inspiring stuff." Emily said. He stuck his tongue out at her, and she did the same in kind.

"Exactly what I needed, Sergio, so thank you...I love you guys. See you soon," Charlie added before Omar waved in his direction. They pulled their hands away and started walking towards the gate.

Charlie saw Sergio climb up the gatehouse's stairs with Quang, and then Charlie and Emily were led down opposing tunnels—each framing the left and right sides of the gate respectively—that ended in an electric lift to the upper defensive positions. A young (*though who really knows in this town*) Saola directed Charlie to a seat as Omar went down to meet Quang and Anh in Emily's tunnel. For the first time since their arrival, Charlie was now staring down at the twin trees that marked the path to Núi Giàu.

Looking directly across the clearing at the opposing tree canopy, he was shocked that he couldn't see the left-flank defensive position in which he knew Emily and Anh were currently located. He stared for another moment, looking for some sign, some indication of man-made construction, but found nothing. It quickly dawned on him why nobody had been able to find Núi

Giàu for centuries, though how and with what technology its citizens hid the city, he did not know.

Behind him in the defensive position were several Saolas. He recognized some of them from the war room the day prior, but had not yet learned their names. They were busy testing electrical connections and communicating with their colleagues in the left-flank and gatehouse positions. Charlie was continuing to scan the clearing in front of him when he felt a tap on his shoulder.

"Look over to the far side of the clearing—they're here," said Omar.

Charlie swiveled his head, and as he did, he saw rows of men, four across, start to march into view. He'd found a pair of electronic binoculars in the compartment in front of his seat when they arrived in the defensive position, and he used them now to scan the units of soldiers.

The men were not dressed consistently—while all of the soldiers had on some form of the classic green camouflage military uniforms Charlie had seen in movies, the patterns from uniform to uniform made it seem like they'd had to cobble together surplus supplies from different armies in order to properly outfit everyone. The only unifying feature between all of the different uniforms was a black chest patch, and at its center was a figure detailed in red.

"Omar, what's that on their patches?" asked Charlie, turning to Omar.

"It's the head of Ares. Greek god of war," Omar answered.

Charlie turned back to the clearing. Just like the men who'd attacked Charlie and his friends on the road, half the Casus Belli troops in each row carried electric purple rifles (which Omar had informed him at dinner were simply called "volt-actions") with the other half armed with AK-47s.

When the Casus Belli men finished arranging themselves in sections eight rows deep around the clearing, Charlie saw an older man walking through the center of the columns straight to the twin trees in front of him. Over his shoulder, Charlie heard Omar confirm what he already suspected.

"Quang, this is Omar. Aurelio Moretti has arrived at the gate path. Send out the central defensive squad."

After a short time, Charlie saw members of the Saola forces, armed with volt-actions, marching up the gate path. They took position inside the twin trees, stopping just short of the threshold between the clearing and the edge of the city, blocking the path. In the deafening silence that followed, he heard a man speak in a slow, deliberate, loud voice.

So...this is Moretti.

"In the past days, my thoughts have often centered on Ignazio Arcuri. A simple man, raging against the injustice and tyranny that surrounded him, fighting for a freedom he knew he deserved. And like so many of his time, he suffered oppression at the hands of his enemies, an oppression born from greed and violence. From royal halls, 'noblemen' sent those they deemed lesser to die on their behalf, their power stemming from the blood of others. Our founder knew his enemy was not the men in the street, but those in banquet halls.

"And one day, amidst the grit and grime of his righteous war, this truth was made clear to him: there are those in this world who have the power to end the reign of tyrants but choose instead to remain in secret, preferring to watch men suffer. How angry must he have been that day, discovering there was a hidden society that held the tools to keep his men alive, yet would not share those tools freely? I ask myself this constantly. But how did he choose to react? Did he cower in fear? Did he submit without opposition? No. He continued to fight.

"He made it his life's mission to find the associates of this society's 'emissary'—those who held the same technology, the same access to world-changing knowledge—and bring it to the people who needed it most. I am thankful every day for his unrelenting drive for the cause of true liberty.

"For centuries, our brotherhood has understood that there is no true peace when tyrants exist. No horror inflicted upon the world could ever be worse than the horrors devised by men who lord themselves over others under the guise of duty, honor, or divine right. And we have clawed, tooth and nail, for *years* to return the world to its natural state. We have shed our blood for this cause, and we have shed the blood of all of those who oppose it, as well. Yet there are those who still deny the world their gifts.

"It is said that every death is a tragedy. I have certainly mourned the deaths of all my fallen men. But I tell you now: no, there is joy in destroying your enemies. Joy in ridding the path to freedom of the overgrowth of injustice. Those deaths are not tragedies, they are rewards. And we know that there is no limit, no cost that we would not pay, to see our goals met.

"I, however, am a rational man. In the tradition of our forbearers, I always provide an opportunity for those who have wronged us to learn from the error of their ways. To see the path as we see it—clear as day in front of our feet. It is in that magnanimity that I come before you today.

"My son was stolen from me on this very ground. Brutally murdered for simply fighting for what he knew to be right. And so were his compatriots. I lost *generations* that day. Years of work and careful planning spent, wasted, in an instant. But today we correct past wrongs. I've come to claim the recompense due to my forefathers, my brothers, and me.

"I give you this choice: open your gates to me and my men. Take us to where you've hidden away your gift for a thousand years, and grant us the privileges that we—just as all human beings—are entitled to receive. Rectify the mistakes, the untold pain that your people have caused the world, and in doing so, the leader of your council shall be returned. And as an added present, these American 'heroes' and their children can return to lives of inconsequence and frivolity, a present that their doctor friend wasted by withholding information from us. He chose instead to rejoin his Green Beret colleagues rotting deep in Vietnam's soil.

"If you choose to defy us, the following will happen: the three spouses of the Americans will be executed here, slowly and painfully, right in front of you on the same soil where you executed my son. But not the American veterans. No...we will keep James and Ada alive until we capture their children, then, we will make them choose which child to keep alive. And after that, we will storm the city, kill those in our path, and take the Gift for ourselves anyway.

"I submit those options to you now, for your consideration."

Aurelio Moretti, using his cane to support himself, gave a small, mocking bow in front of the twin trees, then slowly righted himself and signaled to one of his men. From just outside the clearing, soldiers dragged six individuals to the center of Casus Belli's troop formations.

"I have eyes on Trinh and the Americans," Charlie heard Omar say from behind him. He felt Omar's hand grab his shoulder, providing some comfort against the disturbing imagery Aurelio Moretti had just planted in their heads.

"Charlie, can you see if your parents are bound at all?" Omar asked.

Recognizing this was his chance to support his family, Charlie overcame the terror of Moretti's threat and snapped into action. "It looks like only their hands are bound. My mom and Emily's dad look pretty beat up, though I think I saw them walk under their own power."

"Okay," Omar replied. "And now looking at the soldiers immediately around them, how are they armed?"

Charlie scanned the troops nearest his parents with his binoculars.

"Only AK-47s. I don't see any other weapons on them." Charlie listened as Omar echoed the message to Anh and Quang. Then, in his head, he heard Anh reply.

"Okay everyone, the Council is about to respond. We will listen for your signal before you begin the distraction."

Through speakers he could not see, Charlie heard a familiar voice speak out in a clear voice to the Casus Belli troops below him, immediately recognizing it as Lien.

"Mr. Moretti, you come here today under the guise of freedom, yet you yourself are holding hostages. You actively oppose liberty, and claim inheritance over a gift which was not given to you nor intended for you. And you provide options which are not only unfeasible, but unrealistic."

Through his binoculars, Charlie saw Aurelio Moretti looking gradually angrier as Lien spoke.

"As in all things," she continued, "our people search for another, more balanced path. And so, we offer you this: return our hostages to us and depart from these lands without violence. We do not wish to fight you, and would see that your retreat is protected from any threat. You may keep the technology that you've stolen from our emissaries, though we simply ask you use it for more peaceful purposes. You would honor the lives you've taken to acquire it by doing so.

"You speak of magnanimity, and as such, this is the gift that we offer you. Do you accept?"

Moretti stood still for a moment, shaking only his head. A wicked smile grew on his face, a crack in the thin veneer of composure hiding his building rage.

"I want you to take a look around this clearing now and remember the choice you've made today. The blood to be spilled will stain your hands for the rest of your miserable life!" Moretti shouted before turning to one of his men. "Bring me the doctor's wife!"

In Charlie's head, he heard Sergio scream, "NO!"

A gruff-looking solider grabbed Maria Santos out of the cluster of hostages, then, dragging her kicking and screaming towards Moretti, threw her down at Moretti's feet. With a swiftness that defied his advanced age, Moretti pulled out a revolver from the holster resting on his thigh and pointed it at Maria's head. Charlie heard screams from all the hostages, begging Moretti to stop.

"I am gracious beyond my years, and so I offer you this choice again," Moretti said in a cold, shaky voice. "Grant us passage or this woman goes to meet her husband."

"Anh, tell Lien to stall!" Sergio screamed into his communicator. "Omar, you've got to give the signal now!"

Charlie couldn't hear Anh's response, but he did hear the flurry of activity occurring behind him. Turning around, he saw Omar positioning the Saola troops to activate the explosives positioned at the side of the clearing. Omar started speaking in Vietnamese, presumably relaying orders he'd received from Anh and Quang. From down in the clearing, Charlie once more heard Lien's voice.

"I am willing to reconsider your proposal," Lien said calmly. "But I need you to show a sign of good faith."

Without moving his gun, Moretti replied. "I think my restraint at the moment is good faith enough. What more could you possibly require?"

With his eyes glued to the clearing, Charlie heard Omar through his communicator. "Anh, Quang, be ready. The diversion is coming."

"Let her walk freely to our troops in front of you," Lien replied to Moretti, "and we will create a path down which you can follow."

"Why would I do that?" Moretti said, anger building back in his voice. "I owe you noth—"

Charlie couldn't make out the end of Moretti's sentence as he heard Omar shout, "NOW!"

Charlie was blinded by a flash of light as bright as the sun in the clearing in front of him, then felt the defensive position shake underneath his feet as the explosive charges detonated, and mayhem ensued.

He saw columns of Casus Belli's troops lying on the ground, knocked over in the massive shock wave following the explosion, and saw the central column of Núi Giàu's forces charge forward as they opened fire upon the enemy. In the confusion, Aurelio Moretti dropped Maria and began returning fire at the Saolas. Charlie, remembering the task Omar had given him prior to the battle, reached for his communicator.

"Anh, Emily, do you have a clear shot to tag the hostages with trackers?" he asked.

A moment passed before she replied.

"Okay, all the hostages are tagged. We've got them now," Emily said.

"Anh, you're up," Omar said, joining the conversation. "Release the smoke grenades."

Charlie stared across the clearing, once again scanning the tree canopy in front of him with his binoculars. And that was when he saw it—from the largest tree trunks, just under the branches, he saw what he recognized as Anh's smoke grenades coming out of a small opening.

So that's where they are!

The clearing became increasingly obscured by greyish-white smoke. "From our vantage, the gate path and clearing are now completely covered by smoke," Omar said. "Quang— are you ready to provide backup?"

"We're ready. The gate remains closed, but Sergio is scanning the gate path and will give the signal when they're close by," Quang replied urgently. "You and Anh, send in your troops now."

This time, Charlie heard Omar's voice from inside the room. "Go, go, go! Draw their attention away from the hostages and make them concentrate their fire on this flank."

The troops inside Charlie's defensive position hurried down the electric lift to the battlefield, taking cover in the bunker at ground level. Amidst the smoke and gunshots, he saw bursts of purple electric light—the same that had been fired upon him and his friends on the highway—coming from beneath him towards the clearing.

"Here," Omar said, walking back over to Charlie. "Switch the binoculars to setting five."

Charlie took the binoculars away from his face and looked down to see a large "1" displayed on the screen sitting on the bottom of the binocular set. He tapped the screen until the number showed a "5," then put the set back to his eyes. Where only moments prior his view had been completely obscured by smoke, he could now see outlines of bodies running around the clearing, marked by their heat signatures. Scanning more from right to left, he then saw individuals with a purple "X" on their shoulders.

"Now that you can see the hostages, keep reporting on their location and confirm with Emily and Sergio as to their movements," Omar said before speaking more Vietnamese into his communicator.

"Emily, I've got a clear visual on our parents. Can you see them?" Charlie asked.

"I think I've got them, too," she replied. "I've moved down to the lower bunker and I'm waiting here for Anh. She's almost there."

Taking another look, Charlie saw the outlines of ten individuals running in a straight line from the trees across from him to the group of hostages. It was Anh and her troops.

"Anh, I've lost sight of Moretti, but your path looks clear from here," Charlie said into his communicator.

"Understood, almost there. Twenty more meters," Anh replied.

"Sergio, get ready." he heard Emily say.

"Ready," Sergio replied.

"Quang, Sergio, be careful," Charlie added, "I see more Casus Belli forces near the twin trees. Looks like they're trying to take cover beside them."

"Good spot, Charlie," Omar said in the room.

Charlie felt his confidence rise after Omar's comment. He also heard faint thuds coming from his chest and realized for the first time since the battle began that he could hear his own pulse. His heart was racing from adrenaline, making his hands shake the binoculars ever so slightly. He steadied himself, and then once more found the hostages in his field of view. Anh and her team were surrounding them.

"We've got them—making the extraction now!" Anh shouted, her voice straining from exertion.

"Come on, Anh, you've got this..." Charlie whispered to himself as we watched.

Without taking his gaze from the clearing, Charlie once again heard Omar in the room behind him. "Right flank, move closer to the twin trees. Their numbers are gaining."

Charlie stared as the outlined figures ran back to the tree line and its defensive left flank. Anh and her troops placed themselves on the sides of the hostages, making a perimeter around them with Anh at its head. They were almost back.

"Em, get ready to open the bunker door!" Charlie exclaimed into his communicator.

"I've got them!" she replied excitedly.

While the bunker wasn't appearing on Charlie's binoculars, he watched as the figures disappeared off his scope inside the tree line.

"One...two..." he counted to himself. "Come on...Three...four...five...ahhhh!"

Out of nowhere Charlie was violently thrown from his seat by a series of explosions on the battlefield. However, these sounded and felt different than the ones Omar and his men had set off as a diversion. Charlie quickly righted himself back on his seat and then turned to look at the twin trees in the clearing smoke. He was shocked to find lines of Casus Belli soldiers storming into the gate path. Behind him, Omar, who had also been thrown backward, stumbled toward the front viewing platform where Charlie sat.

"Quang!" Omar shouted. "Check in! They're storming the gate path!"

"No..." exclaimed a breathless Quang, the wind in his lungs likely having been knocked out of him in the explosions. "They've breached the gate!"

"What?!" Omar replied.

"Quang, engage all the electro barriers in the city and send your central squad forward!" Anh shouted through her communicator. "Omar, send the right-flank forces down the gate path to support! We need to seal this leak before any more of them make it into the city! We've got the hostages inside now."

Charlie turned to look at the tree line in front of him. The smoke had dissipated away from the edges of the clearing, and Charlie was high enough up that he could see the left flank without using the binoculars. While he still couldn't find the hidden entrance to the defensive bunker, he saw no Saola troops in that area.

"Emily, you got them all inside?" Charlie asked over his communicator.

"We've got them all!" she replied.

Charlie felt a wave of relief hit him.

"I count...Wait, hold on, that can't be right..." Emily muttered.

Charlie's brief moment of respite ceased, and he felt tension creep back into his shoulders.

"I only count five," Emily said. "Anh, you had all six, right?"

"We had six, yes," Anh quickly answered, "Charlie, what do you see?"

He picked up his binoculars again, and checking that they were still on the "5" setting, turned his gaze to the smoke-filled center of the clearing. He saw familiar outlines—troops on both sides fighting one another—but when his eyes saw the problem, his heart sank.

The outline of a person marked with a purple "X" was being dragged towards the twin trees by another outline holding a cane.

"It's Moretti...He's...he's got one of the hostages..." Charlie stammered.

And he heard Anh's voice follow his own.

"It's Trinh."

Chapter 20

Sergio couldn't believe what he'd just heard through his communicator, his nerves already shot after hearing Moretti's speech and seeing his mom being held at gunpoint.

"Anh, repeat that?" Omar said.

"It's Trinh...Moretti has Trinh!" Anh replied. "This is now our top priority. We need to separate them before he can get to the Council building. Where are the other Council members?"

Sergio heard Quang's reply both through his communicator and from next to him on the gatehouse. "I've just spoken to them over communicator and have informed them to continue taking refuge in the four corners of the city. Neither Moretti nor his troops will be able to find them."

"With the Americans secured, Trinh is the only leverage Moretti has," Anh said.

Sergio leaned over to Quang, who was currently firing shots from his volt-action through the gatehouse windows at the Casus Belli troops forcing their way inside the city.

"What does Anh mean?" he asked loudly, raising his voice to be heard over the cacophony of battle beneath them.

Quang turned away from the window to Sergio. "After the invasion thirty years ago, a new secure storage unit was devised for the *đi qua*. Nobody but the Council and a few Saola members know how to open it."

He paused, directing Saolas on the bridge near him towards a column of Casus Belli soldiers who were trying to break past the first electro-barrier.

"If he can't get the *đi qua*, it's over for him," Quang continued. "But since he needs Trinh alive to enter the Temple, he's in a tricky spot. Essentially"—he paused again, firing a few shots out the window—"he can't perform some 'smash and grab' operation like his son did. Without us or the Council, he's now fully reliant on Trinh to both get him the *đi qua* and get him into the Temple."

Sergio heard screaming on the city side of the gate below, and turned to see a Casus Belli soldier using an old-model volt-action on a pair of Saola troops who had rushed onto the scene.

"I'm headed your way now, and I'm bringing everything I've got," Anh said over the communicators. "Omar, you should do the same. There's no use fighting on the outside of the gate if people are already inside."

"Understood," Omar replied. "And what about the teenagers?"

"Let's bring them through the tunnel to the gatehouse. We'll get them out from there," Anh said decisively. "They're too close to the front lines now."

"I copy. See you shortly," Sergio heard Omar say. Shortly after, Charlie's voice came through.

"Emily, you're with our parents. Are they okay?"

"Yeah, Em, how are they?" Sergio joined in.

"They look a little worse for wear, but they're okay!" she replied. "I guess we're coming your way now.

"I'll see you all soon," Sergio said, a tear welling in his eye as he took his hand off his communicator. Amidst the fog of the battle, he gave himself a moment to appreciate that for the time being, everyone was safe.

"Sergio, did you play any sports in school?" Quang asked, bringing his attention back to the chaos around them. Sergio was puzzled by the question.

"I'm sorry, what?"

"Sports. Did you play any?" Quang asked impatiently.

"Ye...yeah. I played baseball. Why?"

Sergio watched as Quang pulled out a box of metallic cylinders, with a ring of the now-familiar electric-purple color around each cylinder's center. They were the same weapons Molly had given to Emily to throw on the road.

"Good, so you can throw," Quang said, putting one of the cylinders in Sergio's hand. "I'm going to need you to twist the tops of these and throw them for me whenever I say, and then I'm going to need you to not mention to Omar that I let you do this. I don't have time to give you a technical explanation of what they are, so I'm just going to say this: they're—"

"Grenades," Sergio replied to a now-confused Quang "We had to use these with Molly and Omar when we were attacked on the road."

Quang put a hand on Sergio's shoulder and with a soft smile, said, "Well then, you're already a pro. More Saola troops are making their way to the gate from both sides, so for now we need to clear a path for them and slow down the pace at which Casus Belli can advance. The more jammed up the gate path is with our people, the more difficult it will be for Moretti to make it through. I'll lay down some suppressing fire, then you'll throw them as hard as you can where I'm aiming. Understood?"

"Yes."

"Here we go." Quang turned towards the city side of the gate, and looking to his right, began firing shots towards a company of Casus Belli troops who were attempting to break through an electric barrier. "Throw!"

Sergio stood up over the gatehouse's ledge and threw the grenade as hard as he possibly could, then crouched back down immediately, nearly missing some AK-47 fire from one of the Casus Belli soldiers in the process. He didn't look back at where the grenade had landed. His imagination was more than enough to picture the grenade's gruesome impact.

For the next few minutes, Sergio and Quang continued their routine, switching from the city side to the path side of the gate as needed to slow down Casus Belli's forces. Sergio felt himself getting the hang of battle, finding his rhythm amidst the fight, when suddenly a grenade flew through the open gatehouse window just down the hall.

"Quang, duck!" he shouted, pulling the man to the floor behind a stone bench.

A deafening electric crackling sound filled Sergio's ears as the grenade exploded down the hallway, scattering pieces of stone debris from the now-fragmented gatehouse windowsill all around them. More explosions were heard underfoot, followed by shouting and more gunfire.

Pulling his head just over the nearest windowsill, Sergio saw Moretti—still dragging a bound Trinh—moving into the city while surrounded by a company of his troops. They blew past the first electro-barrier down the main road, having targeted it (or at least Sergio assumed) with one of the grenades that had exploded underneath them. Before he could say anything to Quang, he heard Quang shout out, "Do not hit Trinh! Aim for the squad and only take a shot at Moretti if Trinh is out of the way!"

Quang picked up his rifle from its resting spot on the ground following the explosions and quickly took aim at Moretti. Charlie saw the electrified shot miss Moretti's shoulder by mere inches as Casus Belli's leader moved out of eyesight beyond a row of manicured trees. In pure frustration, Quang threw the rifle down on the ground and stewed for a moment. Sergio threw the last grenade in the box out the window, then turned to see Quang touching his communicator.

"Understood," he said, turning his attention to Sergio. "Everyone is here. You did great."

From over Quang's shoulder, Sergio saw Charlie and Omar approaching from down the gatehouse's corridor. Upon seeing his best friend, Charlie sprinted over and gave Sergio such a forceful hug that the two nearly fell over.

After righting himself, Charlie grabbed Sergio's shoulder. "I can decidedly say that no amount of video games prepares you for real war."

Sergio snorted. "We're doing okay for our first time!"

Omar walked up, gave Sergio a pat on the back, then turned to talk to Quang, who was still periodically directing the Saolas on the ground. Omar's expression turned more severe as Quang spoke. Sergio could only assume it was because of the news that Moretti was now fighting his way into the city.

"What do you think happens next?" Charlie asked, "I'm not ready to stop helping."

"Agreed," Sergio replied. "And I feel personally responsible— Moretti made it through the gate three minutes ago."

"No, don't think like that," Charlie said sharply, "We still have the upper hand. He..."

Sergio watched as Charlie's eyes shifted over his shoulder. Afraid of another grenade, Sergio spun around, but as he was about to duck, he saw her.

"Sergio!" Maria shouted at the top of her lungs.

"Mom!" he shouted back.

She rapidly closed the distance between them, grabbing Sergio and holding him tightly in her arms.

"I'm so glad you're okay, Sergio."

"I'm glad you're okay too, Mom," Sergio replied, hugging her tightly back. "I've been worried sick about you since we found the ransom note at Charlie's house a few days ago."

"A ransom note?" she replied, stunned.

"It's a long story, but we figured out Dad's weird letters," Sergio said. "He was leaving us a code about this place, Mom. Charlie, Em, and I figured it out, and with Molly's help, we made it to Vietnam."

Maria looked shocked. As Sergio looked back, he remembered what Moretti had said about his father's death. "And Mom, we'll get justice for Dad. But not Moretti's way...not vengeance. Real justice."

Sergio reached out to Maria, now crying as well, and hugged her again.

"Mom! Dad!" said Charlie.

Down the same hallway into which his mother had just walked, Sergio watched as Charlie ran to embrace Ada and Bill. Maria and Sergio, still holding each other, watched as the Tillman family reunited.

Ada looked up from her son towards Omar. "Officer Peterson, I think there are a few details of your background that you left out in the job interview," she said with a wink.

"Yes, ma'am. Just a few," Omar replied.

Sergio watched as a smiling Emily came up the stairs to the gatehouse, arm in arm with her parents a few minutes later.

Behind them, though, was a stoic-looking Anh. She signaled the Lewises to follow her towards the center of the gatehouse where the Tillmans, Sergio, Maria, Omar, and Quang stood.

"I am genuinely happy that your families are back together," Anh said, "but unfortunately, we need to postpone formal reunions until the current crisis is fully resolved."

Sergio let go of his mother, taking on a more serious posture.

"Quang, I received word from the Saolas in the city center," Anh continued. "Moretti has been bogged down by the electro-barriers in place, giving our people more time to engage. However, he's pulled additional reinforcements from somewhere else and is still pressing forward. I want to send you around the perimeter to the Council building to head the defenses there. Go now, and take one of the ibises in the gatehouse's garage."

Quang nodded before running down the hallway as Anh continued.

"As for you all," Anh said, looking at the newly freed hostages, "we can't keep you here in the gatehouse. From everything we've seen so far, we can no longer trust that it's secure. As such, I'm going to have my troops escort you to the edge of city. Councilwoman Quy will take you into her home. You'll be safe there."

"We can fight," James spoke up.

"I can't ask that of you," Anh said.

"James and I know this enemy," Ada interjected. "And unlike the last time we faced them, we know what we're walking into."

Anh still looked unsure.

"We don't need to be leading the charge anywhere, but put us to use," James pleaded. "Please...we owe you that much."

"Now I can see where the kids get it from..." Anh said, shaking her head. "Okay. But I'm keeping you off the front lines."

"That's fine!" Ada replied, her excitement evident.

"We're coming too, Anh," said Sergio.

"Absolutely not," Maria replied.

"Agreed," Ada said. "While we appreciate you helping, you kids should never have been in this position in the first place."

"And why not? We've gotten this far, haven't we?" Emily said.

"Because you're not trained, that's why," James said curtly. "War is not a game. You could be killed. And we'd be the world's worst parents if we allowed you to continue to put yourselves at risk."

"You two joined the military when you were our age," Charlie shot back. "Not only did you join, you enlisted. You know how I know? Because you both proudly told me you felt like people needed your help and you didn't want to sit around and wait for someone else to do the job."

"Son...please..." Bill replied.

"Exactly right, Charlie!" Emily said, scuffling away from her parents towards Charlie.

"He's right, Bill..." Ada murmured. "I'd be a liar if I said I didn't have this exact same conversation with my parents. I was planning on running away from home if they'd said no..." She turned to Charlie. "I still don't like this, though."

"Emily, we're so proud of you and the boys," Delia chimed in. "You're trying to do what's right. But this isn't the way."

Sergio couldn't take it anymore. "If I don't help them fight, then my dad—your friend—will have been murdered for nothing!"

The group stood in stunned silence, the air filled only with the sounds of intermittent gunfire.

Maria walked slowly to Sergio and put her hand on his shoulder. Then she turned to Anh. "Anh, can you keep them off the front lines?"

"I can't guarantee their safety," Anh replied quickly.

"Can you keep them off the front lines?" Maria reiterated patiently.

"I'll do what I can," Anh said.

"Mrs. Santos, I'll personally look after Sergio," Omar added.

Maria looked over at Ada, who in turn gave her an assuring nod. "He's one of our best, Maria."

"And Director Tillman, you and James can take Emily and Charlie, right?"

Delia shook her head at James, but James replied anyway. "We've got them covered."

Anh spoke up. "Okay then, this is what we'll do—Bill, Delia, and Maria, you three will go with one of my Saolas to Councilwoman Quy's home. Ada, James, Charlie, and Emily, you four will ride with me to the back of the city to our defensive position in front of the Temple. The fighting hasn't progressed that far yet, and hopefully it won't, but if it does, we'll need all the help we can get to make a last stand. And as for Omar and Sergio, I need you to buy us more time. Staying away from the core of the fighting, I need you both to activate some of the traps we arrayed near the electro-barriers. If we can separate Trinh from Moretti, then this will all be over. But we need to move, now."

Shouts of "understood," "yes," and "agreed" were heard from the group.

Sergio glanced over at his mother. He knew she would have preferred he stayed by her side, not wanting to risk losing another loved one in the same jungles that took her husband ten years prior. But instead of protesting further, she grabbed Sergio's arm and gave him a gentle look—and he knew it meant, simply, *make it back to me.*

"Good," Anh replied. "We have little time. You have your orders."

Without hesitation, the group sprang into action and split off in different directions. Ada, James, Charlie, and Emily loaded into another, larger model of the same transport (or, as Sergio now knew, an "ibis") the teenagers had arrived in earlier in the morning. Emily turned and gave a wave to Sergio as they sped off.

"Sergio, you have to promise not to tell your mother about this..." Omar said, handing him a small metal box with a black, rubberized grip, "but since we're going to be closer to the danger, I'm giving you this. It's essentially our version of a Taser."

Sergio smiled to himself discreetly, not letting Omar onto the fact that he'd been throwing grenades with Quang just moments prior.

"If things get bad and someone gets too close," Omar continued, "point the non-grip end away from you, and then swipe your thumb in a circular motion over the center of the casing. It's nonlethal, but will temporarily do some serious danger, so please be careful, okay?"

"Understood," Sergio replied.

Omar pulled out a small tablet-shaped object and fastened it to his arm. After double-tapping its surface, a screen was projected off his wrist. Sergio saw a map of the city, with colored dots blinking all over its surface. The dots moved in front of Sergio's eyes, and he quickly surmised the green dots were Núi Giàu forces and the yellow dots were Casus Belli forces. The lone "X" on the screen was Trinh.

"Take a look. These purple lines are the electro-barriers, and you can see they've mostly bottlenecked Moretti and his troops in one specific area, but you've probably noticed that some of the barriers are moving. My best guess is that Casus Belli's forces have repurposed them and are now using them to block Saola troops from making a clear attack."

"How can we stop them though? I thought those barriers were impenetrable," Sergio said.

"They are from their base up, but not from underneath," Omar replied, touching a button on the side of the map projected off his wrist. Sergio now saw the underlying view change, highlighting the city's roads in light blue. "These are the drainage and sprinkler systems that run underneath the city's roads, meticulously designed to collect and redistribute the massive amounts of rain that falls on the city...And today, we're going to blow some of them up."

"We're going to do what now?" Sergio asked.

"We can remotely seal sections of the pipes and then override the pressure sensors our engineers built into them. If we do it right, the result?"

"Boom," Sergio replied.

Omar nodded. "Not enough to do any serious damage, but it'll be enough to knock over their troops and the electro-barriers they've grabbed. Just enough to allow our people to close the loop around Moretti."

"How sad," Sergio said. "Their shoes will be completely ruined."

Omar winked as he touched his communicator. "Quang, everyone is accounted for, but we can see that electro-barriers are getting repositioned in the center column. Anh and I think the forecast calls for a *Winter Monsoon*."

"The Council isn't going to too happy about it, but I think it's the right call," Quang replied through their communicators. "Take the back route over here and stay dry."

"Understood. Sergio and I are making are way to you at the Council building now," Omar said.

The two ran to grab a small motorcycle-like ibis, and with Sergio securely sitting in the rear seat, Omar kicked the vehicle into action and the two took off like a shot.

As they sped through the streets, Sergio was shocked by how the city had changed in the last hour. Given its relatively open layout, Sergio could see purple electro-barriers fully illuminated on all of the main roads, even from the periphery of the city. Those in their path temporarily deactivated as Omar steered them straight through, barely reducing the ibis's speed. From his seat, Sergio watched in terrified awe as Casus Belli clashed with Saola forces, and he ducked as errant shots from volt-actions periodically strayed in Omar's and his direction. Had they not been hovering above the ground on the ibis, he would have felt the ground shake as the initial water pipes exploded on certain key roads to their left.

Rounding a row of neatly decorated trees, Sergio could see the Council building slowly coming into view. From the stress preceding his arrival into the city, he hadn't fully appreciated how large the building was when he, Emily, and Charlie had first entered it the day before. The bushes and small plants ornately placed around the road made the contrast that much starker. Even now, when the building appeared so close at hand, he realized they were a little more than half a mile away. Glancing down at Omar's arm, he could see that they were riding closer and closer to Casus Belli's forces, too.

Due to the sound of the wind rushing by them, Omar took one hand off the steering controls and touched his communicator.

"When we get there, I'm going to need you to follow my lead. Good cover positions will be few and far between, and we'll probably need to run from place to place."

"Okay." Sergio felt a tingle on his skin, assuming it was adrenaline still coursing through his veins from the morning's events. But suddenly he heard a familiar electric buzzing before a purple flash of light flew dangerously close to his head. Spinning in its direction, he saw three Casus Belli troopers hiding behind some bushes off the side of the road in front of them. They raised their rifles again, taking aim.

Charlie frantically touched his communicator. "Omar! Look out ahead!"

A torrent of volt-action fire flew in their direction, and Omar swerved the bike around it erratically. "Hold on!" he shouted into the wind, not bothering to use his communicator. Using his free hand, Omar pulled out a small pistol, similar in style to the larger rifles Sergio had seen around the city, and fired back at the enemy troops in front of him.

Sergio ducked low in his seat, clenching the sides of the bike as the barrage of shots flew near them. Weaving the bike hard to the right, Omar fired a shot across his body and took out one of the three Casus Belli soldiers. The soldier next to him, acting particularly reckless, ran out from his position and fired at them from the middle of the street. Omar repositioned the bike, then took aim again and fired a shot that brought the soldier down.

"Nice shooting!" Sergio shouted, beginning to feel invincible with Omar on his team.

"One left!" Omar yelled, turning his head slightly backwards to look at Sergio.

He patted Omar on the shoulder, then turned his attention back to the last soldier, partially obscured by the bushes he crouched beside. The other soldiers were focused on firing as many shots as possible in Omar and Sergio's direction, but this soldier was aiming his rifle carefully. Waiting. Sergio assumed this man was planning on surrendering now, having watched his compatriots be so easily brought down.

But then Sergio heard it: an electric whiz that flew not at Omar's or Sergio's head, but at the front of their bike.

The bike's engine exploded in a burst of purplish-blue flame, forcing the nose of the ibis to dip towards the ground. Before they could comprehend what was happening, Sergio and Omar were hurtled over the front of the ibis's handlebars onto the ground in a deep drainage ditch on the side of the road.

It took Sergio a moment to get up, his ears ringing so loudly, so sharply, that he temporarily struggled to hear the loud sounds of the battle around him. In a daze, he took off his camo jacket and looked down at his injuries.

A few scrapes and cuts, but I'm okay.

He put the jacket back on and turned to look at Omar. He saw similar scrapes on Omar's legs and head, but Sergio didn't see anything that immediately signaled grievous bodily harm. However, Omar had been knocked unconscious and would not respond to Sergio's prodding.

Sergio then heard Quang's voice come through the communicator.

"Omar, Sergio. Where are you guys? We've slowed them down and my team is closing its pincer movement around Moretti, but we've ruptured so many pipes that we're losing sufficient pressure to blow up any more. We won't be able to deter them for much longer."

"Quang, we've been shot down!" Sergio shouted, carefully peeking his head over the drainage ditch's edge in the direction of the soldier who had destroyed the bike. The soldier was a hundred feet away, but slowly walking in their direction. "We're okay, but Omar is unconscious."

"You've got to get him awake, Sergio," Quang replied quickly. "Are you near the bike still? There's a med-kit on every ibis."

Sergio looked around, and saw the ibis was smoldering on the ground forty feet behind him. To get to it, he'd have to run into the open road.

"I can't reach it, Quang. We're pinned down by a Casus Belli soldier."

"Keep trying to wake Omar up. My squadron is pinned down at the moment, but I will try to send someone to help out as soon as I can. Stay covered," Quang said.

Sergio's heart raced faster than it had all morning. From their position, he knew they would have no cover if the soldier made his way to the edge of the drainage ditch. He couldn't find Omar's pistol, but after frantically searching around, Sergio was able to locate the Taser device Omar had given him. *It might not be enough*, he thought. The only luck they had was that the Casus Belli soldier didn't seem to know exactly where in the long ditch Sergio and Omar had landed.

Come on, Sergio, think!

The soldier inched closer, scanning the edge of the road, carefully looking for the best position from which to attack.

Sergio was desperate, remembering every war game he and Charlie had ever played, trying to devise some strategy to keep himself and Omar alive. But strangely, Sergio's mind turned to the Saturday morning cartoons he used to watch with his dad. He shook his head.

This is too stupid to work, but maybe that's exactly why it will...

He tore off his jacket, then, finding a stick on the ground near him, army-crawled along the ditch farther away from where Omar lay unconscious. When he had gone a few yards, he propped the jacket up on the stick and raised it slowly above the edge of the ditch, moving it side to side. As expected, Sergio heard a slew of shots fired in his direction. The soldier had taken the bait.

Sergio planted the stick into the ground, allowing only the smallest piece of jacket to show above the edge of the ditch. He hurried back towards Omar, then peeked over the edge. The soldier was moving at a rapid clip towards the jacket, periodically firing shots in its direction to give himself cover. Importantly, and just as Sergio had hoped, the soldier was walking at an angle towards the drainage ditch that left his back mostly turned away from Sergio and Omar's position.

As the soldier got within a few yards of the jacket, Sergio picked up the Taser and triple-checked that he was holding it in the right direction. Then he climbed to the edge of the drainage ditch, waiting for the right moment.

Mom is really not going to be pleased with me if she finds out about this.

Taking a deep breath to calm his nerves, he threw himself over the edge and charged down the road as if he were running to home plate in one of his baseball games.

The Casus Belli soldier was staring over the edge of the ditch, but realizing he had been deceived, he turned his body to look down the rest of the drainage ditch towards Omar. He swung his rifle up to take another shot, but before his finger could reach the trigger, Sergio activated the Taser and watched as purple electric sparks shot from the end of the device. The soldier collapsed to the ground as his muscles contracted from the electricity. He made a weak attempt at grabbing Sergio's hands before passing out a few moments later.

Sergio took the rifle out of the soldier's hand and sprinted towards his downed ibis. After digging through the back of the bike, he found the med-kit Quang had mentioned would be there and rushed it back to Omar. Having played in his father's medical bag many times as a child, Sergio recognized the majority of its contents. He grabbed the small packet of smelling salts, ripped it open, and shoved it under Omar's nose. At first Omar was nonresponsive, but as his nose began to wriggle, he slowly opened his eyes.

Relieved, Sergio touched his communicator.

"Quang, Omar's awake now! Our ibis is completely destroyed and I don't see any others around us, so we're gonna have to make it on foot. We're coming back to you as fast as we can."

Sergio waited for a response, but not hearing one, he turned his attention back to Omar.

"You okay?" he asked.

Still groggy, Omar grabbed the bottle of water from the med-kit and took a sip. "Thanks for waking me up. My head is a little sore, but otherwise I think I'm good to move in a second. If we skirt around the fighting, I think we can make it to the Council building in a little more than ten minutes."

◇◇◇◇◇

"We're coming back to you as fast as we can!"

Sergio's voice came through the communicator, but Quang was too busy blowing up the remaining water pipes to answer. Since the two of them weren't in immediate danger anymore, Quang would respond to Sergio and Omar shortly. For now, he focused his attention on the pincer movement playing out in front of him.

Even amidst the chaos around him, Quang felt a strange sense of pride. As the *đi qua* had been missing for thirty years, at least half of the current Saolas had not yet received the Gift, and none of the Saolas had seen much action since the last invasion of Núi Giàu. Despite this, Saola forces drilled constantly, giving each training exercise their full energy and attention. This pincer movement Anh had devised was one such drill, and the troops were executing it flawlessly. Quang was incredibly thankful that Anh had tasked him to help her reorganize the Saolas thirty years ago.

He took out his binoculars and scanned the battle in front of him. Though still barricaded behind electro-barriers and a wall of Casus Belli forces, Quang identified Trinh amidst the throng. She was being held by a Casus Belli soldier, and the contrast between their two countenances could not have been greater. Trinh, even amongst the terror around her, looked completely calm. She trusted in her people's ability to rescue her. However, the soldier holding her looked absolutely terrified. Quang pitied him.

Then Quang heard a loud explosion off to the right of the Council building. He put the binoculars down, tapped the device on his wrist, and looked at the map it displayed. As expected, there was a mix of his own troops and Casus Belli forces directly in front of him, but he saw no sign of Casus Belli troops in the direction of the explosion. Confused, he turned to the small squad of soldiers next to him.

"Why did you set off an explosion in that area? The fighting is concentrated in front of us."

"Sir, that wasn't us," the Saola replied.

"What do you mean it wasn't you?" Quang turned his attention back to the map on his wrist. "This is showing me that the pipes in that area are still intact, but that can't be right…"

As he turned back to look at the Saola, a purple whir zoomed past his eyes and into the soldier's chest. The man dropped, and Quang turned to look back in the direction of the shot. Suddenly a torrent of purple lights rushed towards the Council building and the right side of the pincer.

"Take cover!" Quang shouted towards his men, who were being picked off in the firefight. Ducking behind a column, he checked the map again. Out of thin air, Casus Belli troops were appearing on his right flank. "This can't be possible…" he murmured in panic.

But looking up, his worst nightmare was confirmed.

A massive contingency of Casus Belli forces was flooding out of a side street next to the Council building, causing heavy casualties to the Saola troops stationed nearby. He watched as his soldiers turned to engage the new and more pressing threat behind them, loosening up the right half of the pincer movement and allowing Moretti and his men to press closer towards the Council building. Quang couldn't believe it.

A portion of the new Casus Belli soldiers made their way to the Council building steps, taking out the remaining group of Saolas who had been guarding the Council building with Quang.

Disheartened, Quang realized the defense of the Council building now lay entirely on his shoulders.

He fired off as many shots as he could towards the approaching Casus Belli soldiers, but he was hopelessly outnumbered. As his enemy slowly surrounded him, Quang was prepared to fight to his last breath, until, out of nowhere, he felt the butt of a rifle hitting him in the back. Turning to look, it was one of the Council building attendants who had been hiding inside. Quang was utterly confused as he fell to his knees.

The Casus Belli soldiers walked up on a weakened Quang, bound him, and left him facing the battle in front of him. He was helpless as he watched Moretti and his men break through the last line of Saola troops in front of the building.

"How did you make it through?" Quang shouted at one of the Casus Belli soldiers.

The soldier turned and backhanded Quang before speaking. "You'll know soon enough."

His head ringing from the smack, Quang turned towards where the explosion had occurred and saw a figure slowly leading a group of soldiers towards him. The soldier who struck Quang then bent down and yanked Quang to his feet as the man came closer. Quang's weakened legs couldn't barely support his weight, so another soldier came behind him and held him.

"On your feet. Show some respect to your beloved councilman."

The figure stood next to him, and like a veil being lifted, Quang finally knew who he was addressing.

"Councilman Xuan."

"Hello, Quang. How lovely it is to see you here."

Chapter 21

"We're nearly there, Sergio," said an out-of-breath Omar.

Sergio was in relatively good shape, but after their accident and ten-minute sprint, his legs were starting to drag. If he was lucky, he'd be able to get a glass of water and catch his breath inside the Council building.

"Hold on a second!" Omar shouted again as they neared the far side of the Council building. "Duck behind this planter box."

Sergio hurried to join Omar behind the large planter filled with bright Vietnamese flowers, and after peeking over the edge, he saw why Omar had stopped them from going any further.

The Council building steps were overrun with Casus Belli soldiers.

"How could the lines have shifted this much?" Sergio asked. "From what Quang told me, the water pipe explosions were doing a great job slowing down Moretti."

"Something's up," Omar responded, still trying to assess the situation. "You sure he said they had it under control?"

"Definitely. The *đi qua* is secure inside the building, right? Like even if they've gotten inside, it won't matter without someone to show them the way to the vault?"

"That's true, but what worries me is how they could have gotten this far..." Omar scanned the battle. "Hand me the scope in my rucksack. It's in the tall side pocket."

While still crouched, Sergio opened the side pocket of the backpack still on Omar's shoulders and pulled out a rifle scope. Like passing a baton in a relay, Omar took the scope from Sergio without taking his eyes off the scene in front of him. He adjusted some settings on it, then looked toward the Council building steps.

"Oh Quang...what have you gotten yourself into?" Omar muttered.

"What is it?" Sergio replied, unable to hide his rising concern. He'd only known Quang for two days, but the Saola's kind demeanor had already made him feel like an old friend.

"They've got Quang tied up on the steps. He's surrounded by Casus Belli soldiers," Omar replied as Sergio squinted towards the building steps. He could just make out Quang's clothing against the contrast of the uniformed men around him.

Sergio then noticed a hunched figure walking into view from behind one of the columns.

"Moretti is there, too," said Sergio. "There behind the column."

"I see him now," Omar replied.

"Do you see Trinh?"

"...Yes. She's crouched down not too far behind Quang." Omar put the scope down for a second and handed it to Sergio. "Take a look."

Sergio picked it up and scanned the steps. Quang had clearly been beaten, though Trinh still looked relatively unscathed. He handed the scope back to Omar.

"I'm a little confused..." Sergio said. "If Moretti's this close to the vault, why isn't he going inside to get the *đi qua*? He's got

Trinh and Quang right there. Especially if the other Council people and Anh are secured."

"That's what concerns me," Omar said, taking the scope and putting it back to his eye. "I know you haven't known him very long, but believe me when I tell you that Quang would sooner die before giving away any security secrets. And as head of the Council, Trinh would do the same."

Omar touched his communicator. "Anh—Omar and Sergio checking in. Moretti has Trinh and Quang tied up on the Council building steps. The fighting has broken through, and Casus Belli has made it inside."

Sergio heard Anh's voice reply. "They're on the steps? Does he have the *đi qua*?"

"No, I don't think he does. I don't know why he's just sitting there, though," Omar replied. "Hold on, I see someone coming out of the building."

Sergio strained his eyes to see past the shadow obscuring the main door to the Council building. A silhouette was coming out, and though he could see the person had their hands raised, he couldn't make out who it was.

"It can't be..." Omar said.

"What? Who is it?" Sergio quickly replied, and then a gleam above the building's steps caught his attention. It took him a second to understand, but the glint coming off the small disc in the figure's hands was unmistakable.

It was the *đi qua*.

"No!" Sergio shouted.

Omar handed Sergio the scope again, shaking his head. "That traitor! He always fought the Council on everything, and now it's clear why."

Sergio peered through the scope, his vision obscured by the sun's reflection on the *đi qua*, until the figure shifted and he saw that it was Xuan.

"I can see Moretti walking to receive it from Xuan!" Sergio said.

Moretti was standing near Trinh and Quang, posturing himself in front of his enemies.

Omar touched his communicator. "Anh, Xuan betrayed us. He's giving Moretti the *đi qua*. We need a plan, now!"

Through the scope, Sergio saw Quang slowly move his bound hands to his communicator. "Hold on!" Sergio said into his own communicator." I think Quang is trying to tell us something."

"Standing by..." Anh replied.

Suddenly, Sergio heard a frail Quang speaking through his communicator.

"How could you do this, Xuan? You're on the Council! You have a duty to the citizens of this city!"

Sergio heard a woman's voice reply, and without having heard her speak before, he knew it was Trinh.

"Xuan, have we failed you so greatly? That you would willingly give up the sanctity of the Visitor's Gift to those who would use it only for harm?"

"You both have been isolated for far too long," Xuan said, slightly muffled through the communicator. "In your long years, you've lost touch with reality. We've been wrong to deny others the Gift, and to restrain ourselves from revealing our power to the world."

"You were there the day Moretti and his men attacked this city!" Trinh exclaimed. "Are you proud of the bloodshed? Is that your vision for the world?"

"Oh, I remember that day vividly. I heard the sirens…I heard the screams. And like you, I was terrified. But as days turned into weeks following that fateful day, I learned something.

"They're right.

"We've misinterpreted the meaning of our ancestors' story. In the twelve hundred years since our people first received the Gift, we've restrained ourselves, thinking that that restraint would facilitate a more peaceful world. But you know what? We were wrong. Our people have more blood on our hands than any society in history."

"You can't be serious," Quang chimed in.

"Oh, I'm quite serious, Quang," Xuan continued. "All this time, we could have been freedom fighters, toppling tyrants and dictators at the drop of a hat. Casus Belli understand this—they know that the world is corrupt and needs a strong hand to keep it in check. Which is why I guided them here today. Why I led them through our hidden passages and unlocked the doors for them. But now is our time—we have the might, and with Casus Belli under our control and Mr. Moretti's guidance, we'll finally be able to wield the Gift properly. Can't you see? We'll finally be fulfilling our purpose. Once we patch you up, Quang, you'll come to your senses. And Trinh, you'll still keep your position, though maybe as more of an emeritus role."

Sergio saw Xuan turn to Moretti, extending his hands holding the *đi qua*.

"Mr. Moretti, it is my honor to initiate you to our Council and begin your journey towards building a brighter world," Xuan said, slightly genuflecting as he spoke.

"It's not too late, Xuan," Trinh said. "You don't have to do this."

But Xuan ignored her plea.

"Put a gag on her already!" Moretti shouted over his shoulder to his men before turning back to Xuan.

"Thank you for your service and your gracious words, Xuan," Moretti said. "You have been a faithful friend of our organization for almost thirty years, and I am grateful for your service."

"You are most welcome," said Xuan, bowing again.

Moretti grinned warmly. "Unfortunately, I have no further need for your partnership."

From a holster hidden on the small of his back, Moretti pulled out a small scuffed pistol and, with surprising accuracy, put three rounds straight into Xuan's chest.

Xuan silently fell to the floor, confusion in his dying eyes at the betrayal.

"Of course, Xuan is right." Moretti paused, checking his shoe for blood as he stepped over Xuan's drooping body. "We will make the world a better place when we are through. The lives lost will be remembered fondly as sacrifices towards a greater good. But this city needs completely new management, and we'll sort that out soon enough."

Moretti walked towards Quang.

"Is this how you treat your friends?" Quang said.

"Would you choose to befriend a man that actively sold out his own people for thirty years?" Moretti replied. "No, Xuan isn't a friend. His treachery against this city was useful as a means for us to stand here today, but I can't abide insubordination within my ranks. What if he changed his mind and decided to sell me out the same way he did you? As a military man—and don't kid yourself, that's exactly what you are, despite whatever 'peaceful' persona you put on—you understand the necessity of weeding out the weak links."

Sergio couldn't believe the exchange he was hearing through Quang's communicator.

"And *I* understand that you want to prevent Trinh from making her appointment with me in the Temple. Is that correct?" Moretti continued, waving his pistol casually in the air.

"You will not receive the Gift today, nor on any other," Quang replied sternly.

"I'm so sorry to hear you say that," Moretti replied, now pointing the pistol at Quang's chest, "because from what Trinh tells me, you're quite the loyal servant. We could have used you."

"You definitely could use more loyal servants...or at least, more intelligent ones," Quang replied, digging one of his hands into his pocket. Sergio saw a small metal cylinder in Quang's hands. "Your men forgot to search me before they tied me up."

"Get back!" Moretti shouted as he hurried backwards, dragging Trinh with him.

Sergio watched as Quang rolled the cylinder towards the group of Casus Belli soldiers nearest to him, and heard the electric buzz of the grenade going off. Sergio had to turn his head away due to the brightness of the flash.

"Quang! No!" Omar shouted in shock.

When Sergio put the scope back to his eye, he saw several of the Casus Belli troops lying on the ground. Scanning to the side of the blast site, he saw Moretti pulling himself up with his cane, then pulling Trinh to her feet as well.

"Moretti is still alive, and he's got Trinh!" Sergio shouted.

Omar turned and grabbed Sergio by the shoulder. "I will come back for you."

Before Sergio could reply, Omar rushed around the planter and sprinted towards the Council building, pistol in hand. Sergio heard Omar's voice through the communicator.

"Moretti is unprotected! We can stop him and save Trinh!"

Sergio looked and saw Saola troops, who until this moment been pinned down by enemy fire, abandon their cover and charge recklessly at the Casus Belli soldiers blocking their path to the Council building. The enemy troops fired back, but began to scatter as more Saolas rallied to Omar and the Council building.

Sergio grabbed the rifle scope once more and instinctively turned it towards Moretti and Trinh. They had made their way off the steps of the Council building and were slowly making their way towards a squadron of Casus Belli soldiers now forming a barricade around Moretti and Trinh. However, the Saola troops were wreaking havoc on Casus Belli's chain of command. Where only moments before, there had been clear direction, Casus Belli troops were now scrambling around the city trying to find any bit of cover or means of escape they could manage. The veneer of cohesion was quickly breaking down amongst their ranks.

After a few minutes, the majority of the fighting had been pushed away from the Council building. Saola forces were in hot pursuit of Moretti, taking any stragglers as prisoners. Sergio decided it was safe for him to make his way to the Council building now, and headed towards Omar, who was sitting beside Quang, holding the fallen man's hand.

As Sergio approached, Omar looked at him, his expression grave, then tilted his head towards Quang. Sergio understood—Quang was bleeding profusely from several spots on his body and looked unusually pale. Sergio sat down beside them. He'd never seen death this closely, and his body began trembling from the overstimulation of the experience.

"We're going to get him, Quang," Omar said delicately. "You saw to that when you scattered his troops."

"Wish I was as good at...at throwing grenades as our pal Sergio, though." Quang said, winking in Sergio's direction. Omar gave Sergio a puzzled look.

Sergio smiled, but was still too stunned to speak.

"You've spoken to Anh?" Quang asked Omar, coughing as he spoke.

"Yes, and she's spoken to the surviving Council members. After Xuan's betrayal, they are prepared to do what must be done if the time calls for it."

"Good...good...I believe in you two," Quang said very slowly, his eyes starting to close. "And who knows...maybe we'll meet again someday..."

Sergio watched Quang's grip loosen from Omar's hand, and without having to ask, he knew Quang was gone.

Omar signaled to a Council building attendant who had come out from hiding to check on the wounded, and she brought a large bolt of red cloth to cover Quang's body. Then Omar stood, and Sergio followed him as they walked away from the Council building steps.

"Anh...he's passed now. But Sergio and I were with him in the end." Omar said, touching his communicator.

"...We'll honor Quang by winning," she replied.

"We're making our way to you now, but in case we don't make it in time...we support any decision you have to make," Omar said, taking his hand back off the communicator and turning to Sergio.

"Let's go help our friends end this, once and for all."

Chapter 22

From high on the steps leading to the Temple, Emily had a good view of the entire city. Growing up, she'd watched plenty of old battle footage with Charlie and Aunt Ada, but seeing it play out in front of her was a completely different experience. Sitting on the third of seven landings built on either side of the long stairs up to the Temple, she saw flashes of rifle fire, flying debris, and swarms of troops—those of both Casus Belli and the Saolas— trading ground throughout the city. But since she, her dad, Aunt Ada, and Charlie had made their way towards the Temple, there was an eerie, unnatural calm surrounding them.

She was standing near one of the most sacred places to the Middle Way, and accordingly, the path to the Temple was richly decorated, even more so than the city gardens below. The flowers in bloom gave off a delicate fragrance, and up high, closer to the jungle beyond the city walls, the sounds of animals moving through the trees were easily heard.

But despite the beauty, the fighting was always on her mind, especially as Omar or Sergio gave updates on the ground.

How is it possible that chaos and complete serenity are only a few hundred yards away?

She looked at her hands.

Still shaking a bit...I just need to breathe.

Emily closed her eyes, then slowly inhaled through her nose. She held her breath for a few seconds, then exhaled even more slowly. After repeating this cycle a few times, she could feel herself calming down, even amongst the clamor of Soalas getting into position.

You don't have to do this alone, and you don't have to know all the answers. Just pay attention and try to keep up.

After receiving a quick tutorial on the volt-action's functionality from a tall Saola, Emily watched as her dad and Ada snapped back to their old military habits. They seemed as ready as ever to get back into the fight as they sat down next to her and Charlie. James fidgeted with his rifle next to Emily.

"You two have been in a lot of fights," Emily said. "How do you calm yourself down before a battle? I can't stand the waiting."

"I've always thought the waiting was worse than the actual fight," Ada replied, "because at least once the fighting starts, your training and instincts kick in. No time to think about anything else."

"Agreed," James replied, inspecting the barrel of the volt-action. "One trick my drill sergeant taught me, though, was to focus on your mission objective. What you need to achieve when the fighting starts, how you're going to ensure that you'll do it, etc."

"Sort of like visualizing it before it happens?" Charlie asked.

"Exactly. So, in our case—and I admit, this is up there with the strangest fights I've ever been in—what's our objective? It's to defend this position and keep ourselves safe. We've got something they want, and we know they'll try anything to get it," James replied.

"That makes it a bit easier I suppose, Dad," Emily said. She couldn't believe how much being in Vietnam had shifted her perspective on the unknown. *If only the Emily from a week ago could see me now.*

"Good. Just reflect on that," James said. "And know that we have good cover up here, too."

"James and I won't let anything happen to you two," Ada added. "We may be a bit past our primes, but with these weapons that Anh gave us, we're going to be fine."

Before she could reply, Emily saw Anh walking down the steps of an upper landing in their direction. She had a solemn look on her face, with eyes that appeared as if they'd been crying. As she approached the group, she took a moment to collect herself, then spoke.

"I am not going to sugarcoat this...Quang is dead. Xuan betrayed us, so Quang sacrificed himself to help get Trinh away from Casus Belli and give our Saola troops a way back into the fight. But there's no time to mourn him, or any of those we've lost so far. The fight is on its way to us right now."

Ada and James had seen death countless times during the war, and since they'd barely known Quang, they were relatively unfazed by the news. But for Emily, this was incredibly tough to hear. She glanced at Charlie and knew he felt the same.

"These are the facts: Moretti has the *đi qua*, and Trinh is still in his custody. There is nothing stopping Moretti and his men from entering the Temple now other than us. You can expect cruel and unusual tactics from him and his men, as you've seen already at the gate path."

"Where do you need us to be, Anh?" Emily asked.

"The five of us will be on the top landing," Anh answered, turning and pointing to one of the small buildings sitting on the ledge just below the Temple building itself. "I need to have complete visibility of the stairs to direct the Saola troops, but it'll also afford you all the best possible coverage. James and Ada, as discussed, you need to provide suppressing fire. If we can get Moretti's protection to scatter, my team will get Trinh."

Anh continued, "But just like before," Anh continued, "you two are going to be additional eyes and ears for me. Report anything on your communicators. All told though, as we are the last line of defense here, we may have the responsibility to use this."

As her expression became even more serious, she pulled out a small black metal rectangle that looked remarkably similar to the standard-issue lighter Emily had seen in her dad's office.

"This is the switch to set off the explosives around the Temple. It's important you know how to use it just in case something happens to me. You have to rotate this top bit here to arm them, then open the lid and push down on the lever inside. I've gotten permission from the Council to do anything and everything that is required. We'll be safe from the blast on the top ledge, but if we are on the stairs higher than that or near the Temple itself, we won't have a chance. Hold on—"

Anh stopped speaking and touched her communicator. "Are you sure?" she said. "Alright. Understood."

"What is it?" asked Charlie.

"We need to get into position now." She turned towards the stairs at her side.

Ada, James, Charlie, and Emily ran up the stairs behind Anh, but before they could make it to the top, they heard the distinct sound of gunfire popping the ground just below them.

Without waiting for instruction, James and Ada took cover behind the top landing's wall and started firing off shots in the direction of the Casus Belli troops who had made their way to the base of the stairs and onto the first landing. Charlie and Emily scurried inside one of the buildings on the top landing, positioning themselves near the open window facing the city. Anh stood next to them, firing out the occasional shot as well.

Emily heard Anh through her communicator. "Nguyen, activate the electro-barriers on all levels."

At once, Emily saw the bright lines of purple glowing barriers appear across each landing—seven in total.

However, down below, the Casus Belli soldiers on the first landing immediately planted charges on the nearest barrier nearest. The explosion knocked out the barrier instantly.

We're already down to just six barriers...

Not allowing her doubts to hinder her focus, Emily started repeating the mission objectives in her head while scanning the landings below her. Something in her peripheral vision just past the main concentration of Casus Belli forces caught her attention.

"There! To the right side of the path!" she shouted into her communicator.

"More enemy soldiers coming in, right flank," Anh echoed in the communicator before turning to look back at Emily. "Good catch."

A concentration of purple electric-rifle fire from the lines of Saolas on the ledges poured down on the incoming soldiers, forcing them to take cover near the base of the stairs. Out the window, Emily saw Ada and her dad locked in on the fight. Like young soldiers again, they skillfully took shots from their position of cover, keeping the main column of Casus Belli troops from advancing directly up the stairs. Emily was astounded that their aim was this good. Turning her head in the other direction, she saw Charlie also watching their parents.

"I guess that's why they got the Medal of Honor," he shrugged before stepping inside the building and opening different cabinets.

"What are you doing?" Emily asked.

Charlie did not respond, simply continuing his search. She hadn't seen him act this confidently in a while. After opening a crate near the back wall, he exclaimed, "Aha! I knew I'd find some."

Emily watched as he pulled out two pairs of binoculars from the crate.

"These might help a little," he said, handing Emily a pair.

After adjusting the focus, Emily placed the binoculars up to her eyes and turned her attention to the column of Casus Belli soldiers still flooding up the right flank of the path. The onslaught didn't seem like it would end anytime soon.

Another explosion shook the ground beneath her feet, and panning her head towards the stairs, she saw another electric barrier had been destroyed. Shots from Aunt Ada and her dad were slowing Casus Belli's pace of advancement, but the volume of soldiers pushing up the stairs was too great. More Casus Belli troops took the second landing and began fighting hand-to-hand with the Saola troops positioned there.

With Omar and Sergio on their way, leading a group of reinforcements to the scene, Emily was confused by Casus Belli's plan of attack. They were advancing, sure, but not fast enough to make it to the Temple before they'd be sandwiched between two sections of Saola forces.

"Where's Moretti?" she asked.

"I don't see him yet," Charlie replied. "But he's running out of time."

While Emily agreed, Charlie's answer didn't satisfy her. She immediately thought of Anh's words—Moretti would use cruel and unusual tactics to get into the Temple. She didn't trust that this, at least for the time being, appeared to be an evenly matched battle.

"Third ledge, send some rollers. James and Ada, covering fire down the center," Anh stated through her communicator.

From behind the electro-barrier on both sides of the third landing, Emily watched as two Saolas tossed down handfuls of grenades as James and Ada fired directly down the center of the stairs. The resulting electric crackle from the explosion made Emily's hair stand on end. The grenades had deadly effect on their intended targets.

She once more turned to look at the Casus Belli troops pouring onto the path leading from the Council building to the stairs, and something strange made her pause.

"Hey, it looks like the reinforcements are here!" Charlie said into the communicator.

Emily touched her communicator. "No, hold on..."

"Em, what are you talking about? I see Saola uniforms coming through."

"What, Emily?" Anh asked.

Emily magnified her binoculars' viewfinder to get a closer look, and her worst suspicions were confirmed.

"They're using our people as human shields!" she exclaimed into her communicator. "And I see Moretti and Trinh behind them!"

Anh gave Emily a serious look, then touched her communicator so that all her troops could hear her speak.

"Moretti and Trinh are in the midst of the throng, but they've got some of our own up front as shields. As they approach your ledges, I need you all to switch to nonlethal weapons and tactics.

James and Ada, pick off as many from the back as you can. Thin their numbers, and once we clear enough of our people from the front, I need you to focus your fire on Moretti. Do not, I repeat, *do not* take a shot at him unless you know Trinh is out of range."

"Roger that," James replied.

Emily was inspired by Anh's resolution under duress, especially given the all-out chaos unfolding beneath them. Through Emily's binoculars, she could see it all.

Wave after wave of Casus Belli troops charged up the stairs as Moretti and his squadron inched closer. The Saola forces on the lower levels were giving it their all, bravely attempting to disarm or incapacitate their sworn enemies in order to save the lives of their fellow citizens. However, the conflict was devolving into a mess. As successive electro-barriers were destroyed, uncontrolled fighting broke out on every ledge. Despite the Saola troops rescuing a number of the human shields, Moretti had somehow still advanced to the fifth ledge. And he showed no signs of stopping.

"James and Ada, listen to me carefully," Anh stated in her communicator so that Emily and Charlie could also hear. "When I say so, you two need to retreat into the building with Emily and Charlie. I've got a better vantage point, so you're just going to have to trust me on this. Em and Charlie, do you see the lever next to the door?"

Emily looked around the room until her eyes locked on a smooth metal lever immediately to the right of the doorjamb. "I see it."

"As soon as your parents are inside, pull it. It will activate a form of electro-barrier over the door and windows. They are not as energy-efficient as the models we have in the field, so their batteries will overload if they're left on for too long. The timing is key. You'll be safe behind them and can still report out on the battle over the communicators, but you have to wait until it's absolutely necessary. Okay?"

"We understand," Charlie replied.

"What about you? Should we wait for you, too?" Emily asked.

"No. If the fighting gets this far, they'll need me outside," Anh said resolutely, giving Emily goose bumps. She knew exactly what Anh was prepared to do.

"I see Omar and Sergio now," Charlie told Emily. "They're pretty far back."

Emily once more lifted up her binoculars and found Sergio running beside Omar and a team of Saola troops from the left side of the Temple path towards the stairs. They immediately opened fire on the Casus Belli troops occupying the lowest ledges of the path to the Temple, providing much-needed relief for the entrenched Saolas on the stairs.

"I see them now, too," Emily replied. "I just hope they're not too late."

By now Emily saw Moretti had made it to the sixth ledge, and was so close in fact that she no longer needed to use the binoculars to see him. He was tightly surrounded by tall soldiers, who at this point only held three Saola troopers hostage. Trinh, still bound by her hands, was held right next to Moretti.

"Concentrate your fire on them!" Anh yelled into the communicator, and every Saola in the immediate area volleyed round after round of nonlethal fire at Moretti. The group of Casus Belli forces was thinning when one of them threw a grenade at the last electro-barrier. The explosion knocked James, Ada, and Anh to their feet as Emily watched the barrier's purple light slowly fade away. Moretti and his men were already marching up the stairs.

James and Ada righted themselves behind the ledge wall when Anh, not bothering to use her communicator, shouted at them. "Get inside!"

"I've got a shot, Anh!" James shouted back.

"No, it's too risky!"

"Anh," Ada spoke up, more calmly, "he's got this. Just get ready to help Trinh escape."

Anh shook her head furiously. "You've got one chance...I'm ready."

Charlie grabbed Emily's arm and the two stood in painful anticipation as James repositioned his rifle.

Taking only a moment to steady himself and exhale, James fired off his first two rounds.

Direct hits, straight into the chests of the two soldiers standing in front of Moretti.

The resulting commotion threw Moretti off-balance, forcing him to dive to the side to regain cover behind additional soldiers.

"Trinh! It's time!" Anh shouted before he could get back to his feet, then, in one smooth motion, she removed the knife from her belt and tossed it down to Trinh.

Time seemed to slow as Emily watched Trinh jump to her feet, bodycheck the Casus Belli soldier in front of her, and catch the knife. With her bound hands, she removed the sheath and stabbed Moretti in the leg.

Moretti's bodyguards flocked to their screaming boss, and in the chaos, Trinh ran up the stairs and dove behind the seventh ledge's wall.

Without hesitating, Anh grabbed her and brought her inside the building with Emily and Charlie.

"Emily, cut her free," Anh said, turning to run back out the door as James and Ada ran in.

They fired off their last few shots as the Saolas on the seventh ledge now fired ceaselessly at Moretti. In the confusion that followed, and after forcing more of his troops to take weapons fire in front of him, a bleeding Moretti cleared the landing and quickly limped towards the Temple with a few troopers in tow.

Emily took the ceremonial knife from Trinh's hands and cut her bonds. Trinh said nothing, but gave Emily a warm smile as she walked briskly to a cabinet by the window and pulled out a communicator from inside.

As promised, Charlie ran and pulled the lever for the door as soon as James and Ada made it back inside. Though they could see Anh through the barrier that was now covering the back window facing the Temple, her voice came through their communicators.

"He's almost inside the Temple. Seventy seconds max. Trinh, what's he doing? He can't get in without you." They watched Anh remove her hand from her communicator and direct her gunfire towards Moretti's men.

"He can't, but he can barricade himself inside the outer building," Trinh replied. "With the *đi qua* and enough time, he still has a chance of receiving the Gift. We can't risk it."

Anh looked left inside the building at Trinh, her expression growing more concerned.

"I instituted the Meteor Protocol yesterday," Anh replied.

"I figured you would," Trinh said. "And you did the right thing." She touched her communicator again. "Councilmembers, the day we've feared our entire lives has finally arrived...We have to destroy the Temple."

Emily heard Quy's voice first. "Is there no other way? Surely we can stop Moretti if he enters?"

"No," Binh replied. "After Xuan's treachery, we can't trust that Moretti hasn't already planned for what he'd do with the Gift."

"The risk is far too great," Trinh answered. "The chaos and evil we've largely kept at bay for centuries would become unstoppable. We have a duty to the world, and right now that duty requires us forgoing that which is most precious to us. Forever."

"Twenty seconds! He's almost at the door!" Anh interjected.

"Trinh is right," Lien replied. "I support you."

"Ten seconds!"

"As do we," Binh and Quy responded solemnly.

Wiping a solitary tear from her eye, Trinh touched her communicator.

"Anh—it's time."

Emily saw Moretti limping more and more rapidly towards the Temple with his men close behind, until was within arm's reach when Anh twisted the top of the small metal box in her hand, flicked it open, and pushed the lever inside.

Chapter 23

Emily felt a wave of heat enter through the window as the entire stone Temple complex exploded upwards in a massive ball of purple and orange fire. The flames bloomed outwards, burning brighter and brighter, sending smoldering, acrid chunks of stone raining down around the Temple path.

Then, with a rushing hurricane-force wind, the flames suddenly imploded in on themselves and disappeared.

Where there had been a massive structure only moments before, nothing remained. No sign of Moretti or his men, either.

There was a heaviness in the air of the small building where Emily sat with Charlie, Ada, James, and Trinh. Charlie opened the building's lever to let Anh inside, and she ran to hug Trinh. Nobody spoke for several minutes—a sort of reverent quiet had fallen over the group as they felt the weight of their actions.

Outside, after witnessing the destruction of the Temple, the remaining Casus Belli soldiers who'd begun to flee the city were either killed or captured by Saola troops. Omar and Sergio eventually made their way up the stairs and found everyone inside. As Omar went to embrace Trinh and Anh, Sergio ran over and hugged his friends.

"I'm so happy you all are safe..." he murmured.

With the silence broken, Trinh turned her head and looked across the room. "You five have done a great service to Núi Giàu. The greatest threat the world has never known was defeated today, and it would not have been possible without your bravery and courage."

"Your people have suffered so much. The sacrifices you've made...I...don't have the right words to express my sympathy for your loss," Sergio said.

"You all saved our lives," Charlie added.

"And reunited us with our families!" Emily added too.

"We owe you everything," Sergio said.

Looking at the empty space where the Temple had stood, Anh spoke up for the first time since the explosion.

"The world will begin a new era of peace. Ultimately, that was our people's goal. With the Gift or without it."

"Exactly," Omar joined in, his eyes still red from crying. "No object is permanent. Things must come and go."

"But our knowledge and values remain," Trinh added. "The principles which have guided us for hundreds of years will continue to guide us. We have more to give to the world."

Sergio's eyes began to water. "That was my father's goal, too."

Trinh gave him a sad smile. "Your father was on his way to us when he was captured. He had an idea for how to eradicate a rare disease and wanted to work with our scientists to develop a cure. Casus Belli got to him before we could, and ultimately, they killed him. I am incredibly sorry for your loss."

Sergio quietly gasped for air, and James, Ada, Charlie, and Emily all placed their hands on him for a moment.

"Thank you for telling me," Sergio replied. "It makes me...proud, to know that my dad died trying to help others."

"He certainly was," Trinh said. "And it's a shame. We knew the gist of the problem he wanted to solve, but never received the information he had in his notes."

"Wait! I have his notebook!" Sergio exclaimed. "It's in my bag down in the city!"

Omar smiled. "We'll get it to our people, Sergio. I'm sure they'll be able to develop a cure in no time."

"And we'll able to able to distribute it to where it's most needed," Trinh commented. "Our emissaries are still in the field, and they will need new missions soon enough."

"We might be able to help, too," James said.

"Between the State Department and my agency, we can help get resources to your emissaries to help continue spreading knowledge," Ada explained. "Nobody outside of this room needs to know what's actually happening."

"The world needs Núi Giàu to continue its mission," James added.

The three teenagers nodded in agreement.

"We will find a place for you all yet," Trinh said. "But for now, I think we need to continue this reunion with your families and my Council back down in the city."

◇◇◇◇◇

After resting in the Council building's lodgings for several days, the Americans knew it was time to return home. They had celebrated Núi Giàu's victory over Casus Belli with the entire city and witnessed Anh's ascension to the Council. They had mourned with the citizens who would never receive the Gift and watched as Trinh helped the people make sense of their anger and distress. They were even fortunate enough to see Omar named as the head of the Saolas, whose new primary directive, Omar had passionately proposed, would be to help keep emissaries safe abroad. The three teenagers, now reunited with their families, were honored guests in all the festivities.

With Bill, Delia, and Maria still gathering their things, Charlie, Sergio, and Emily waited on the Council building's steps while James and Ada spoke to Omar.

"How would you prefer us to announce your...let's call it 'resignation,' from the Agency?" Ada asked.

"Right...that's a good question," Omar pondered. "I think we need something similar to what we decided for Molly: in the line of duty, we were all brought down by a group of local bandits who were hell-bent on destroying the American war heroes. Molly, who brought your kids to the resort as a surprise, selflessly joined the rescue efforts upon learning you were in danger but was killed in action. I was injured in the fight and presumed dead. You all made it back after surviving the attack and trekking through the jungle."

"While it's technically the truth, it's a hell of an understatement for what you all did," James said.

"You'll know the truth of it, and that's all that matters. I'm just glad Molly will get her star on the wall at Langley. She deserves that much, at least," Omar noted. "Just like the officers in your detail. I'm sorry they were caught up in our fight. If there's anything we can do to help their families, even discretely, I'm sure the Council will approve. All of us keep bigger secrets than that."

"We certainly will now," Ada added.

"Also, Ada, I hope you know how much Molly was devoted to you. She really loved you all. She even mentioned to me that she would continue to work at the Agency for a few years until she was needed back at Núi Giàu to train new emissaries."

Ada smiled, tears forming in her eyes.

Over Ada's shoulder, Omar saw Trinh approaching the teenagers.

"Emily, Sergio, Charlie?" Trinh said as she walked up, carrying a small box. The teenagers stood up out of respect. "My engineers were assessing the damage around the city, and particularly, up around the Temple steps. They were excited to find this."

She carefully opened the box, and inside, resting on a small pillow, were three fragments of the *đi qua*. They shined in the sunlight.

"We're not sure how they survived the blast, but when the lead engineer showed me how many fragments remained, I knew what I had to do with them. I would like you all to take them with you.

"They are symbols of the peace you helped win, yes, but more importantly, they are reminders of the obligation you three now have: to help the world in whatever ways you can as new emissaries of Núi Giàu."

Emily was shocked, and gingerly reached out to take her fragment from the box. Charlie and Sergio did the same, and speaking for the group, Sergio said, "We won't fail you," as the three teenagers bowed.

"No locking those up in a filing cabinet, okay?" Anh said with a wink, walking up to the group with Binh, Quy, and Lien.

"You must come and visit us again soon," Lien said.

"As often as you like," Binh added, "for as long as you like."

"You are always welcome," Quy stated.

"Thank you all," Charlie replied. "We will."

A large ibis with Delia, Bill, and Maria already inside approached the group from around the Council building. After bowing to the Council members, James and Ada joined their spouses inside the vehicle.

"You three ready?" asked Omar.

The teenagers took one last look around the city, fully taking in its wonders. Then, Sergio once more spoke for the group.

"We're ready."

◇◇◇◇◇

The summer heat bore down on Washington D.C. in late June, and the parents decided they would much rather relax in the comfort of Maria's air-conditioning than melt in the sun and humidity like their teenage children. Through the large kitchen window, Ada saw Charlie splashing Sergio in the pool as Emily strategically moved out of the way.

"I haven't seen James this excited to get on the road in years," Delia said. "He's like a schoolboy going on a field trip."

"Ada's the exact same," Bill added as he took a bite of a slice of pizza.

"The technology we're going to be able to share is incredible!" James grinned. "I know I struggled with emails when they first came out, but Omar assured me that even someone as un-tech-savvy as me would learn quickly."

"Which was very reassuring," Ada chuckled. "And as for me, I'm looking forward to meeting more of Núi Giàu's emissaries. They've got so much to teach us, and if they're anything like Molly, I'm sure they're going to be great."

"What an incredible young woman," Maria said, raising her glass. "To Molly."

"To Molly!" everyone cheered, sipping from their drinks.

Maria continued. "Trinh told me before we left that her chief medical scientists looked at José's notes and were able to understand the portion of the problem he was getting hung up on. She said they're going to have a test treatment in the works for the disease he was studying as early as September."

Ada placed her hand on Maria's wrist. "I'm so proud of him, Maria. His research is going to help so many people. What a fitting legacy for you all."

"And I hear Sergio is now thinking of going pre-med?" James added.

"Oh yes," Maria smiled. "He has no idea what type of specialty he might go into some day, but I've heard the phrase 'Doctors Without Borders' mentioned at least fifteen times since we came home from Vietnam. Whatever he chooses, I know he's going to get out into the field to help the people where they are."

She glanced out the window and saw Sergio laughing and smiling with his friends. He seemed like a happier kid since they'd returned home.

He noticed his mom looking at him, and, making a silly face, he waved back at her.

"Hey Serge, grab the extra pool noodle while you're standing up there. Emily looks entirely too comfortable," Charlie said.

"Sergio would never betray me like that," Emily replied, relaxing in a pool float. "We made a pact at the beginning of the summer that we would only ever splash you."

Sergio chuckled as he jumped back into the pool on top of the pool noodle. "How about we call it a temporary truce for now until I digest the five slices of pizza I just ate?"

"Fair enough," Charlie laughed, casually holding on to the in-pool ladder.

A moment of quiet settled in.

"Am I the only one thinking it," Sergio said, "or does this all feel strange to you two as well? Knowing about secret societies and everything that's gone on."

"Ha! No, you're definitely not the only one," Emily replied. "I have no idea how college is going to top the experience we had this summer."

"Agreed!" Charlie added. "I mean don't get me wrong, I'm excited for classes and everything that goes along with that, but I don't think house parties will be quite as thrilling as saving the world."

Emily and Sergio grinned.

"You know, Chuck, I really don't think they will." Sergio said, laughing again. "But I like what you said about your classes. Everything feels like it has a greater purpose now. I think most people get out of college and feel a bit lost. But I don't think any of us will have that problem."

"Exactly," Emily replied. "We know exactly what's out there and how we can make a meaningful difference for the world."

"That's pretty cool," Charlie noted.

"We've been through a lot together, and I'm excited we'll get to do the rest of our lives together, too. I love you guys," Sergio said.

Emily smiled. "I love you two goofballs, too."

"I'm still deciding," Charlie said with a big smile.

Without looking at one another, Emily and Sergio both splashed Charlie in the face.

Wiping the water out of his eyes, he smiled. "Okay, I love you guys too."

Sergio continued to float for a moment, thinking about how much his life had changed since Charlie and Emily had come over that day earlier in the summer. He felt lighter now, more inspired.

And for the first time since his dad died, his path forward was clear.

About the Author

Photo by Brian Powers

William Ferrand lives in Atlanta, Georgia, having previously lived in Charlotte, North Carolina and London, UK. He has a passion for storytelling, fueled by his love of history and comedy, and prioritizes traveling abroad to learn from other cultures whenever possible. He is also a 2024 University of Georgia "40 Under 40" award winner.

www.ingramcontent.com/pod-product-compliance
Lightning Source LLC
Chambersburg PA
CBHW020130120726
47903CB00007B/2194